BLUURN

A Novel

PETER HELLER

ALFRED A. KNOPF

NEW YORK

2024

THIS IS A BORZOI BOOK
PUBLISHED BY ALFRED A. KNOPF

Copyright © 2024 by Peter Heller

All rights reserved.
Published in the United States by Alfred A. Knopf,
a division of Penguin Random House LLC, New York,
and distributed in Canada by
Penguin Random House Canada Limited, Toronto.

www.aaknopf.com

Knopf, Borzoi Books, and the colophon are registered
trademarks of Penguin Random House LLC.

Library of Congress Cataloging-in-Publication Data
Names: Heller, Peter, [date] author.
Title: Burn : a novel / Peter Heller.
Description: First edition. | New York : Alfred A. Knopf, 2024.
Identifiers: LCCN 2023028064 | ISBN 9780593801628 (hardcover) |
ISBN 9780593801635 (eBook)
Subjects: LCSH: Outdoor life—Maine—Fiction. | Friendship—Fiction. |
Separatist movements—Fiction. | LCGFT: Thrillers (Fiction) | Novels.
Classification: LCC PS3608.E454 B87 2024 | DDC 813/.6—dc23/eng/20230626
LC record available at https://lccn.loc.gov/2023028064

Jacket image: *Boat Building in Maine* (detail) by Paul Dougherty.
Photo © Brandywine River Museum of Art /
Richard M. Scaife Bequest, 2015 / Bridgeman Images
Jacket design by Kelly Blair

Manufactured in the United States of America
First Edition

To my grandmother Rose Backer Heller,
and to my grandfather Harry Ashton Watkins.
With all my love.

BURN

PROLOGUE

He let the fire burn down to embers, let the dark envelop him, and stood.

Jess stepped to the edge of the trees and looked down to the water. It was a big lake and he could see only the bay and the curve of the wooded shore and he could see that the water held there was nearly glass. The black mirror floated countless stars, and the stars barely rocked. He lifted his eyes to where they held fast in the depthless sky and he saw among them a satellite sailing swiftly east to west, and he wondered what it might be witnessing in its silent transit.

If he himself could be a night bird, like some great horned owl on soundless wings, would he fly north over the next town, over the road beyond it? Randall, that was the name on the map, wasn't it? Would he want to see? Probably not.

In the days since they had found the bridge over the river blown and no way south he had dreamed hard every night. Dreams on dreams, with segues like swinging bridges. He had dreamed of their house, his house now, but it stood in the sage of some high western desert unprotected by a single tree, and the rail fences were broken, the horses vanished. In the dream they had more than one horse, but he couldn't remember how many or if he had asked a neighbor to care for them while he was gone. Because he *was* gone. That was the gut weight of the dream, his own absence from anything like home. He dreamed the return again and again, a homecoming only as much as an old negative represented the photographed image, a homecoming that was as much a leaving, and she was never in it. He called for her inside a house he no longer recognized, and again and again in successive nights he walked around the house to the back, to the clothesline stanchions that gestured like empty crosses, and he found a well and he called for her there and dared to look down it and received only cold echo. He woke from that dream with the pillow of his rolled jacket wet. He lay in the wash of his own story and let the sound of a faint broken music trail off, and he let himself cry, and almost as soon as he gave himself permission to sleep he was pulled back into the dark. There was no swimming above it.

He dreamed then that he was in a pasture digging, first with a spade, which he laid down so he could scoop back the finely graveled mud with bare hands, the ditch some kind of drain, and when he stood he saw a former lover walking past the white clapboard house, her glance back seductive the way any vista is seductive just passing out of view. But he didn't know her. He should but he didn't. She had large dark eyes, as Jan had, and his longing was for something familiar, some beauty that rolled in his raw fingers as the prayer stone she had given him rolled now, while he stood with the trees at his back.

She called it a prayer stone. It was the size of a radish and taken from their favorite creek and given to him as a reminder to pay attention: *Love is attention,* she'd said. *That is all you know on earth.*

He had it in his pocket now, and as he stood at the edge of the woods and watched the drifting stars jostle barely on the water like faint semaphores, and smelled the cold sediment of the lake and the cold char of the town, he squeezed the stone in his right palm and wished he could signal her as the sparked reflections on the water seemed to blink to the thrown galaxies arching above: *I am here. Forever rhyming, forever loyal.*

Or maybe it was just an unheard music that time and space could never quiet. A music that turned and turned like a horse in the wheeling dark. And with that thought, and the warming stone chafing his palm, he thrummed with a grief and love so immense he could not contain it. To stand here. To breathe. To witness. He thought wildly in that moment, *They better be enough.*

Chapter One

They had come to the lake and the village that afternoon. They were on foot and it was the first real town they'd seen. Like the general store at Four Corners and the farm two miles north, it was burned to the ground. The houses, mostly wood, had left masonry hearths for monuments, and stone chimneys, and concrete slabs, and blackened stem walls. So close to the water, and the water table so high, few of the houses had basements; those were pits filling with water like abandoned quarries.

Of an entire town, only four dead, blackened bodies curled in the ruins. Where was everyone else?

They had moved up and down what once were streets, and they shouted, as if they might call them in like elk to a bugle. Nothing. Wind. The veering of the swallows who circled very high and silent and flashed violet-green when the sun broke through. Not much sun left: in scudding cloud, it was less than an hour off the ridge.

They came to the western edge of what once was a main street and stood against the dark woods. From there they could survey the mostly leveled ruin spilling downslope toward the lake. It was odd: Every vehicle they'd come across was a burned husk, but the docks of the marina still stood, and the boats tied there. A scattering of day sailer sloops rocked at their moorings. Rocked in an evening wind that brought the smells of lakewater and char. Jess had lifted the strapped binoculars to his eyes. Any living soul would be there in one of the boats, wouldn't they? Crouched in some cockpit, huddled below in a V-berth as cramped as a coffin. They would be there with two days' worth of canned food and a lake-full of water to drink, wondering if they were lucky or not to survive.

"What the hell," Storey had said.

Jess shook in his fleece jacket as if he were cold. He lowered the binocs. "It's like some war."

"Jesus, Jess, it *is* a war." Storey was ashen. He held his rifle unslung in his left hand and his cell phone in his right. "I can't reach Lena. No reception. None."

Jess knew. He had thought he might find some news on his phone, but there was nothing. They had had nothing for six days.

"I've gotta get home," Storey said again, mostly to himself. It had become a mantra.

"Yeah, sure." But neither knew how. South wasn't working. Unless they walked and waded. It might come to that.

"We'll hike up to Randall tomorrow. Right?" Jess said. "See if we can rent a car or something. Then maybe try heading straight west to Quebec. Then down." They were in the middle of northern Maine. There were a few small towns and nothing else but lakes, woods, ridges, logging roads. It was maybe 75 miles west to Quebec as the crow flies, and much longer by gravel road. Straight to New Hampshire was about 150 miles southwest, but there was no way to go straight. The coast was just as far.

Storey stared hard at his oldest friend. "Rent a car," he repeated.

"Maybe it's local." As soon as Jess said it he knew it was lame. Local. All summer the entire state had been convulsed with secession mania. It had pitted the populous coast against the sparse inland, the islands against the ports, islands against each other, Down East against Portland. County against county and town against town. And old Mainers against those From Away. What it really did, Jess thought, was stress any old fault lines and stir up simmering resentments. There had been calls for a vote in the state Legislature, a few riots, a shooting in Bath. But no one expected it to come to full-bore civil strife. They had discussed the risk while planning the trip and decided that what was happening in Maine was no worse than the stirrings of revolt in Idaho and the failed secession vote in Texas the year before. These were fringe minorities, vocal and passionate, but not a real threat. Also, they would be deep in the wilds of north-central Maine: the only time they'd see a soul was if they drove into some outpost convenience store for groceries and gas. And he'd needed this—Jess had. They'd been meeting for this hunt in the woods of different states for a dozen years now, and after the toughest year, Jess needed the return with his oldest friend to something known and worn and loved. To smells he knew, and ridges, and brooks; to the rhythms of camp and the hunt in which he could lose himself; to tradition.

So, this afternoon, as they stood above the burned town and surveyed the wreckage, they had not been able to countenance what they saw. Storey had rubbed his eyes with the back of the hand that held the phone. His cheek was wet. He shoved the phone into his pants pocket, shouldered the rifle, and sighted down to the lake.

"We need food," he had said finally. It was true: at midday they had eaten the last of the freeze-dried dinners they'd packed for a week of hunting. "There's gotta be some provisions on those boats."

"Gotta be." Jess lifted the binocs again and scanned the far shore of the bay. Where there must have been houses before, there were clearings, flagpoles, the pillars of other chimneys like gaudy headstones. "Camp here at the edge of the woods and go down tomorrow?" he had said.

"Okay. We should stay in cover. From now on." Storey lowered the rifle. Lately, he liked to scan with the scope. One less step, in case. He looked at the lowering clouds. Probably coming rain. Among the swallows, below them, three nighthawks wheeled and fed. They were larger, just as agile, and they darted and swooped with a blinking of wing bars and a quiet muttering of staggered peeps. Someone was acting as if the world were normal, Storey thought.

They turned and walked into the trees.

Jess had gathered wood, the fallen limbs of spruce and white birch. He did not bother to muffle the sound as he broke the longer branches. They could see where the attack had swept out of the town—ash and mud and what must have been blood like oil stains on the county road that continued on north around the shore. How many, who knew. They were gone. A few warm embers in the ruin, and so probably just hours old.

He and Storey had a better map now, a water-stained gazetteer they had found fluttering outside the burned shell of a Bronco as they approached. No corpse, but the strewn contents of a rucksack littering down the two-lane highway—broken flashlight, a Gore-Tex rain jacket, packet of peppered jerky—as if the driver had been apprehended in flight. The Zippo Jess was using now had been lying in the road. Maybe they took them, survivors or bodies, took them all. The thought occurred to Jess as he crushed two handfuls of desiccated spruce twigs and lit them with the lighter. Why not the boats? It was as if they had had no time. Collect as many inhabitants as possible and move on. No time to row or swim out. But why not the boats along the dock? Bumping against their fenders, untouched? Maybe they had night vision, a thermal scope; maybe they could see no one was out there hiding. If they did have infrared, then camping back in the trees would offer little cover. Probably not. If they'd had night vision, he and Storey would be dead by now. Dead at thirty-seven.

The map showed the next town, Randall, nearly five miles up the lake. Ten-minute drive. Twenty. Given the state of the cooling wreckage and the seeming direction of travel, the attackers were there by now, there and gone. No column of smoke to the north, but that meant nothing. Jess shivered. If tomorrow the two of them decided to go that way, he had an idea of what they'd find.

Jess had set two palms on the duff either side of the scraped dirt and blew gently on the lit nest of twigs and watched the small yellow flame climb into the crumpled lace of dried spruce and find the small sticks above. He watched the flames adhere and propagate and run along the lengths of tinder and flutter orange to blue. He reached behind him and broke larger branches and laid them over and let the fire grow big enough to warm them. Storey could maybe read his mind: Jess heard his steps behind, and Storey said, "I'll go down to the boats on the dock. No risk now."

"Okay."

"I've been cold in the summer bag, and someone will have sleeping bags or blankets. And maybe better dinner than mac and cheese."

Jess said no word but nodded once; he did not turn and he heard Storey move off.

He had poured a two-quart water bottle into a pot and set it to straddle two rocks, and he took a stout stick and scraped embers and flaming wood between them. He built up the rest of the fire, and when he heard Storey's steps behind him again he stood stiffly.

"Hey." Storey's voice ragged. "Hey—" The word cracked. Rustle as he set down two rolled nylon department-store sleeping bags. Jess turned. Storey's face was strange, as in the face of a stranger. "I found someone. In the water."

"Alive?"

Head shake.

"What?"

"I pulled her out of the shallows. She had a rock in her shirt. Tucked into the belly. Water maybe four feet deep."

"So?"

"She could've shaken it loose anytime. She drowned herself."

Jess blinked at his friend. "Maybe—maybe someone threw her in."

"No." That simple. When Storey knew something he knew it.

///////////////////////

Jess had made the mac and cheese. There were two nested stainless-steel pots, and in the smaller he heated water, and he gave Storey a cup of Lipton with brown sugar. Some things had not changed much since their first outing, when they were kids. What had changed was the tempo of the music. They had both slowed, Jess more than Storey. It was less a physical ebbing—the expected scars and injuries and stiffness—less about bones and more about the heart. Jess thought that life's mounting losses had slowed him. The loss of a wife the year before. The dog, Bell, he'd inherited from Jan. Jan Jan Jan. All gone into the dark.

They sat on a log Jess had dragged over and ate the noodles and two cans of Pringles and some chocolate bars Storey had found on the boats. A mouse had already sampled the chocolate, and they broke off the gnawed ends. There would be more food; they'd go down and look tomorrow.

They had strung up a tarp, as they had since their first hunting trip. They did not bother to build up the sides with brush for a windbreak because the breeze off the lake was light and with the extra bags as blankets they would be plenty warm. They let the fire burn down. Jess was the last one up and he did not bother to douse it.

They were woken by rain. Rain drumming the tarp, and rolling thunder, and flashes of distant lightning making brief calligraphy of the interlaced spruce boughs. The tarp was taut and big enough and they were dry.

Jess felt Storey bump against him as he shifted in his bag, and he murmured, "That is lightning, right?"

"Damn if I know," Storey said. "That next town is five miles off and north. The flashes seem to be over the lake. Further off."

"Yeah." Jess rolled onto his back and moved the jacket he used as a pillow up onto the pack behind his head and bolstered himself. "You wanna try that village up the shore? Randall?"

Storey hadn't heard him. He had found his cell phone in the dark, and Jess saw it glow and then extinguish. "Nothing, right?" Jess said.

"No." The rain pattered and sifted on the tarp. He couldn't see his friend's face, and he didn't want to.

"Maybe, when we get up there, there'll be something. Maybe there's a tower."

Storey didn't answer. Well. He had two daughters and a wife back in Vermont. He, Jess, had no one. It was a little over a year since Jan had left, and their dog, Bell, had died two months later. Collapsed on her walk. Only seven and with no known health conditions—Jess figured she'd died from a broken heart. Did dogs do that? Some nights he had willed himself to go the same way; no luck.

This trip was Jess's favorite annual ritual. Together, they often hunted the mountains of Vermont and Colorado, but this year, against great odds, they both drew nonresident moose tags in Maine, and so decided to hunt the earliest season in the big empty wilderness of north-central Maine, south of Mount Katahdin and east of Moosehead Lake. The famed and populous coast was more than a hundred miles away. You could drive a gravel road for hours and never see another soul but maybe the glimpsed face and wave of a truck driver, a log truck passing too fast and throwing stones against your windshield. The country was rolling wooded hills mostly, with spines of steeper ridges, and the valleys whispered with brooks and rivers that spilled into lakes and bogs. A country to get lost in.

They had hunted at the first camp for five days. They'd crossed sign—tracks, beds, scat—but not as much as in years past, and they'd come upon moose—cows with calves—but not as many. Neither even saw a bull. So they'd decided to shift the hunt to a boggier watershed to the south. They drove. When they found the bridge over the little river severed, they had parked in the shade and stood on the broken abutment. They blinked in the brightness and the heat—a sultry, humid, late-September afternoon. Storey had hopped out on a twisted girder and crouched. He placed one hand on the sunwarmed steel and ran his fingers over it. He looked up at Jess.

"Blown," he said.

"What?"

"The bridge was blown. Like blown up." Storey would know: he had been a dedicated rock climber in college, and in the summers he had worked on a road crew, blasting loose rock off of highway cliffs.

"Like dynamite?"

"Or C-4. Boom. Remember *The Bridge on the River Kwai*?"

"Who would do that?"

Storey shrugged. "Maybe it was condemned and they didn't wanna risk anyone using it."

"That's crazy."

They had turned the SUV around. They had planned to gas up in Branch and they were low on fuel. But they had no choice, and they backtracked to the next Forest Service road to the west and turned south again. It was a forty-mile detour. The woods were starting to turn, and the low sun came through them and lit them to amber. It was like driving through honey. Again they had come to a river—this one larger—and again the bridge was out. Not out, but deliberately destroyed. There was no cell service. They had topos of only the districts they would hunt and they had the gazetteer and a gas-station road map. They opened the map on the hood of the 4Runner. The closest town was back to the north, on the west side of the big lake. Fifty-seven miles, give or take. What might be a hamlet with a gas pump was about forty miles away on the same road. They had gotten about halfway when the engine revved and died. Out of gas. So they locked the Toyota and shouldered their hunting packs and took up their rifles and walked. They only had an hour and a half of daylight on that first day of hiking. On the afternoon of the second, they wondered aloud why they hadn't seen another logging truck, or the vehicles of other hunters. Jess began to carry a stone in his gut he recognized as dread. On the morning of the third, they passed a green sign that said "Four Corners, Population 9." His first thought was: *How often do they change that sign? Doesn't anyone go away to college or retire to Arizona?* But then they smelled a black stench like the inside of a woodstove and they came around the forested bend to the burned remains of seven buildings. Four Corners, Population 0.

///////////////////////

They had walked on the verge of the roads then, where they could duck into the woods if they needed to. They walked with a round chambered in their rifles, which they usually never did. They kept their cell phones on airplane mode to conserve battery, but when they stopped to take a drink in the shade of some brook, one or the other turned his phone's receiver on and scanned for a cell signal. Nothing. Out here they didn't expect any, but it cost nothing to try. They both had water-filter straws and the hills were threaded everywhere with streams, so thirst was never an issue. Once, at midday, they trotted down to the bank of a black-water pond and stripped and swam. The water was ice cold, but neither whooped. They clambered out through horsetail and dried in the breeze and let the sun smooth the goose bumps on their arms, and on any other day they would have hooted and grinned.

On the afternoon of the third day of walking, they came to a meadow maybe two miles wide. The road went right through the middle. Jess set his pack down and walked away to scout the edge along the treeline.

When he came back he said, "Ton of blowdown. And blackberry bramble. Tough walking. Very."

"Okay. I guess we'll take the road."

Neither felt good about being in the open for half an hour. They both unslung their rifles and they opened the breeches and checked again for the rounds there. Storey had a Model 70 Winchester .30-06, bolt action; Jess his father's .308 lever-action Savage 99. Both were scoped and both men were very good shots. Jess had always made clean kills; he could not remember when he had wounded an animal. Neither spoke, and they crossed the meadow without incident.

That night, they had pushed through the dense alders at the edge of a swamp and made a small fire and cooked one of the two remaining backpack meals. "*Gallo Pinto,* Costa Rican Rice and Beans," it said on the pouch. Jess said the name seemed pompous. "What makes it Costa Rican?" he said.

Storey shrugged.

"And as if that was somehow better? Or more hip? Where does this stuff come from, anyway?" He tilted the packet in the slant light. "Figures."

"Where?" Storey turned. Jess thought he looked for a second a little less like a zombie. He had noticed that every time Storey had checked his phone and found no news or way to connect with his family his eyes seemed a little duller.

"Golden, Colorado."

"No kidding?" Storey's eyes actually sparked. "That's your back-yard, isn't it? Coors and *gallo pinto*." Storey knew it was his back-yard; he had visited Jess in Denver at least a dozen times. The last time they'd hunted elk over in Paonia, they'd celebrated the end of the week at the Silver Dollar Hotel, in Golden.

"Yep."

"So you'd probably call rice and beans *gallo pinto,* too, if you could get away with it."

"I do it all the time."

Storey's smile fluttered and stuck. Jess felt such relief to see it. And they ate the second-to-last supper with gusto. While they were eating, Jess said:

"Do you think this is some militia thing?"

"You mean about the stupid secession?"

"Some people clearly don't think it's so stupid."

"What would they be doing way up here? Don't they have better bridges to take out?"

Storey added a couple of sticks to the fire. Jess refilled the pot with water and nestled it into the coals for tea. "It's weird. Do they want to keep moose from moving south—the moose and the loggers? And what's the point of burning down some crossroads general store? Except to keep you and me from getting gas?"

No point. But neither slept well, and the next day they walked into the town by the lake. What was once a town.

Chapter Two

So that's how they got to the lake and the ruined town. The town, according to the map, was named Green Hill. They had never been through it before, or to the shores of this lake. There was no green sign on the road this time; it had been blasted or burned. As if whoever had come through the day before had wanted to wipe it off the face of the earth. Was that just yesterday?

That morning, camping in the woods above the wreckage, they lay in the predawn dark and listened to the rain patter and sweep across the tarp with the rhythm of the winds, and neither was willing to move from the warmth of their sleeping bags. Jess thought that if he could just focus on the nested heat and sound of the rain and the smells of the wet woods he might lie there in relative peace for the rest of his days.

He said, "What do you think they want?"

"We don't even know who *they* are."

"Yeah."

"Secessionists, I guess. I don't know." Storey reached back with both hands and bunched the pillow of his jacket tighter under the back of his head. He said, "If we knew, maybe we'd have a better idea what the hell's going on."

"I was thinking about that woman down there."

"The one I found?"

"Yes. You think she held on to that rock?"

"No. That's why she tucked it in her shirt. She was smart. Also . . ."

"What?" Jess said.

Storey coughed. "I wasn't going to . . ."

". . . tell me?"

"Yeah."

"Kinda too late for that."

"I know."

Another flash, silent, and for a moment they saw the rain as a luminous scrim, and the dark lacing of the boughs, and then the far-off thunder boomed and rolled off the edge of the night like distant artillery. Maybe it was.

"She was pregnant," Storey said. "Like full-term."

"Oh."

And they were silent, and Jess felt grateful for the drum and rush of the rain, which muted even his wildest imaginings. Because he didn't have it in him. To keep guessing at why any of this was happening.

///////////////////////

By first light, the rain had calmed to a gentle sift on the cloth roof, and it was a mere mist when they zipped into Gore-Tex rain gear and stepped out into the gray dawn. Cold, nearly frost. They walked to the edge of the woods and pissed and could not see the lake for the fog that lay over it and shredded in the tops of the trees on the far shore.

"I'll go down," Jess said. "Maybe I can find us something for breakfast."

"You will. After the . . . I didn't have it in me to scavenge."

Jess picked up the .308 and slung the rifle and walked. He stopped, turned. "Did you leave her there? In the water? I don't want to . . ." He trailed off.

Storey shook his head. "I carried her up to what must have been the marina shack and buried her in cinders."

"Okay."

Jess walked. Down the corridor of a paved street blown with drifting ash. The street dropped straight into the fog, and he descended into cloud. As he walked, the skeletal masonwork on either side faded to shapes spectral and half formed in the moving shroud and he made himself keep on. Where were the vehicles? Burned husks, every one. He felt it before he saw it: the lakewater warmer than the night air. And smelled an almost sea-like rank, maybe old algae on the rocks of the shore, or discarded fish, and he thought how fathers and daughters or sons might have been fishing here off the double docks just yesterday afternoon. Not possible. Years had passed since then.

He skirted the wet ash-and-cinder heap of what must have been the marina office and found the flagstone pavers that brought him to the docks and the boats tied there. The main stems of the docks extended eastward into the lake; they branched to either side with the shorter, planked decks of the berths. There were two docks, and he chose the one to the south, on his right hand. J-boats, day sailers, cats, and outboard skiffs. These were small sloops with cockpits and windowed cabins, and Jess knew they would have chests and latching cupboards with some provisions.

The first he came to had beautiful salmon-colored sails reefed and tied along the boom. No cover had been snapped over them, which meant probably that she was regularly used. What day of the week was it? He didn't know. Maybe yesterday was Saturday and the owners hadn't buttoned the cover on the sails because they knew they'd be back to sail today. What we take for granted—that another day would come. Everyone had to know in their bones that every life hung by a thread. That the world did. But if we couldn't pretend to count on a morning of sailing, or fishing, or a visit with someone we loved the next day, we'd go nuts, right? Right. So pretend away.

The boat was called *Isabella*. That simple. No pretense to sophistication like the catamaran beside it called *Aphrodite*. No crude pun like the fishing cruiser in the next berth with downriggers and twin Mercs called *Fish n Chicks*. Jess hopped over the cable rail of the sloop and into the cockpit with its stainless-steel wheel.

He faced a locked hatch that battened the entry and what he knew were steps down to the cabin. The hatch was stout teak, beaded with rain, secured at the top with a padlock. He climbed back onto the dock and up to the ruin of the marina shack and past it. He did not want to dig around in the wreckage and find the woman. He went on between what once were houses and, in what had to be a backyard with a single standing apple tree, he found the small foundation of what yesterday was probably a toolshed. Beside a toppled rolling toolbox he found a blackened fireman's ax. It was solid steel and had heft and balance but was not heavy; the head was larger than that of an ax made for splitting wood, and he swung it like a batter warming up, and though the rubber grip had burned away and the metal was wet, it felt good in his hands. Maybe he'd keep it. He walked with it back down to the *Isabella* and again climbed aboard, and he was about to take a full cathartic swing against the planks of the hatch when it occurred to him that they could sail this very boat up to Randall. The winds by late morning were westerly, and they could follow the shoreline generally north on a single tack and be there faster and with much less effort than walking. And the sails were the ruddy, uneven, washed color of red dirt, and he liked the name. So he set down the ax and jumped onto the dock again and went back to his ruined shed and dug around in ash so fine and wet it turned to paste where he stirred it. Against the far stem wall, in cinders burned hard like clinker coal, he found the bolt cutters. The rubber grips had melted off this, too, but the handles and the blades, though seared, were usable.

He cut the padlock off the boat and went down into the cabin, which was lit by a skylight and rows of high windows. In the tiny galley was a single cupboard with a half-eaten box of Oreos in a Ziploc and three cans of Dinty Moore beef stew. Good enough. He'd kill for some coffee. He was about to search for chest storage under one of the benches in the saloon when he saw on the cushion a paperback book titled *The Outermost House* with a bookmark partway through, and next to it a teddy bear and a plastic superhero. A wave of nausea shuddered, and he grabbed up the book and went up the four steep steps into the open and gasped for fresh air and did not vomit.

They didn't make a fire this time. They opened the cans with their folding clip knives and ate the beef stew with plastic campspoons. Just as good cold, once they scraped away the white layer of clotted fat at the top. They were both impatient to get moving, though had anyone asked they wouldn't have known why. Because they were in the wake of a rolling catastrophe, moving behind some malign harvest whose shape and intention they could only guess, and neither could have articulated why that was so. They could just as easily have fled south. If another bridge was blown they could have tried to swim or wade, couldn't they? But they were not fleeing, they were following. They were both hunters. Were they hunting? No. They were trying to find a working vehicle they could take home. Home for Storey: Burlington, Vermont, where Storey was a professor at the university; it would be a long day's drive from anywhere up here. It was southwest, but the roads in the big woods were so sparse and so harried by lakes and swamps, the fastest route was always due south to Bangor and across. Not an option, it seemed.

So they would walk up along the lakeshore. Now they sat on the log beside the water-soaked ashes in last night's fire ring and scraped the last of the stew out of the cans. Storey said, "It's strange: The buildings are all burned to the ground. Every single one."

"I was thinking that, too."

"In a wildfire, say, that overruns a town, there will be half-burned houses, whole buildings still standing that were jumped and spared. Here everything is gone."

Jess scooped the thick brown sauce from the bottom of the tin and he sucked on the spoon. He could have eaten two more cans. "I got half a pack of Oreos, too," he said.

Storey nodded.

"There's a lot that's strange." Jess looked into the empty can with real sadness. "Do you want me to go down and look for more food?" He didn't tell Storey about the doll and the teddy bear and how he had dreaded boarding more boats and had returned. Storey already knew, and shook his head. "Randall is a shore town, too. Bigger. On the map there's a marina. Should be plenty more boats. We can get lunch there. And more."

Get lunch. Like a plan to visit some eatery. Words it seemed now from another era.

"Do you think they're dead? All of them? We saw so few bodies. Maybe they took everyone out before they burned it."

"Maybe. I think they hit it from the air first."

Scorched earth. Indiscriminate. Easier from the air. Neither said it.

"So I was thinking we could sail," Jess said. "The food came off a twenty-four-foot sloop. The sails are on the halyards and reefed. The wind is picking up and we could be there in an hour."

"No."

"Because we'd be so visible?"

"Yes."

"This thing, whatever it is, is not looking back. Doesn't seem to be."

"We don't know where it's looking. So far it . . . they . . . keep moving. But—"

Storey stopped midstream, as if he could not carry the weight of everything he did not know. He set the can on the damp duff and rubbed his eyes with the back of his hand. Storey had a wife and two daughters, eight and fourteen. These were three of the things he did not know about, and every once in a while they overtook him. Jess thought that it made him more cautious, because—to be blunt—he had more to live for. Jess asked himself if he, Jess, was cavalier with his own life, and if so, was it because he had no children and no longer had a wife. He didn't think so. On all their hunting and canoe trips and travels in the past, he, Jess, was the one more willing to take risks. If he wanted to sail it was because there was a calculus of energy conservation and he figured that the energy they'd save on the boat might be energy that later on would save their lives. But was that it, or was he just lazier than Storey?

Storey collected himself and dropped his hand from his face. "It'd be like breaking cover and shouting, 'Hey, over here! Look!' You know that, right?"

"Yes."

"We can walk."

"Yeah."

Jess saw Storey dig for the phone in the pocket of his pants again, tap the airplane-mode icon off, and check. A gesture now almost reflexive.

Jess said gently, "Store."

"Yeah."

"Maybe we shouldn't check so often—"

Storey lifted his eyes. They were flat and bleak.

Jess said, "To save battery. And we should turn one off. For later. For emergencies. I've got one portable charger. I'll . . . I'll turn off mine."

"For emergencies?"

Jess blinked. He turned and let his eyes travel down the hill, over the charred townsite. "Yeah." He swallowed. "I know."

One thing he did know was that Storey was worried sick not only about the safety of his family during a civil convulsion, but also about what Lena and the girls would be going through in their panic to reach him. If this was secession or something like it, Lena would have heard by now. She was also a professor at UVM, political science, well connected both in Vermont's contingent to Washington and in the state Legislature, and she would be using those connections and lighting up dozens of phones in a frenzy to find her husband. And she would not be able to insulate her daughters. Andrea, the older sister, was a star cross-country runner and also suffered a form of anorexia and was super-sensitive. She was at serious risk, and upsets and trauma revved up her disorder. When their cat, Coco, had been hit by a car last year, Andrea had lost so much weight the doctor told Storey and Lena that even with extreme intervention she might die.

Jess also knew that the home screen on Storey's phone was a photo of Lena and the girls on a bright, windy day, pressed all together against the rail of a ferry deck and smiling wildly. There was the gray-blue of Lake Champlain behind them, and the distant blue ridges of the Adirondacks beyond. They were going backpacking for the weekend. Lena's ponytail was pulled through the band of her hat, but Andrea, who at fourteen was nearly as tall, wore her tracksuit jacket and her long hair loose, and it blew across her mother's face. Little Geneva tucked up into her mother's armpit like a fledgling and grinned uncertainly, and held her hands out as if to beseech the unbridled beauty of the day to calm down a little. Jess knew that Storey probably lit his phone as much to take solace in the picture as to check for a signal.

"Okay," Storey said finally. "I'll go easy with the phone and you keep yours off. Good idea."

Nobody had to suggest they break down the shelter. They devoured the two stacks of Oreos and stood in unison and went to the olive nylon tarp and unstaked it and unslung the parachute cord from between the trees and folded the sheet and coiled the line. They packed up and shucked the rain gear and hefted the packs and rifles and walked out to the edge of the trees.

For some reason Jess held on to the firefighter's ax. He snugged it through the ice-ax loop on his pack and strapped it tight. The fog was thinning now and spuming over the water in spectral tatters that merged and moved past each other. The two men descended the aisle of an ash-blown street, and when they intersected the larger thoroughfare that became the highway they turned left and walked out of town. On the two-lane county road the remains of burned foundations spaced wider and wider apart, and they followed the detritus of the violently displaced—the single shoes, wallets, upturned strollers, and shattered picture frames—until that, too, petered out on a ribbon of water-stained tarmac drying out, then steaming in late-September heat. Farm fields now, untouched, and woods. The lake through trees on their right. A small sign at the head of a driveway that said "C Bar C, Registered Quarter Horses, Hay, Boarding." No barn or stable visible at the top of the hill. Jess wondered what had happened to the horses. Better not to know.

As he walked he repeated the name of the boat, *Isabella*, over and over like a mantra. It was the name he and Jan had discussed for the girl they did not have.

\\\\\\\\\\\\\\\\\\\\\\\\\\\

The liminal spaces are the ones I love the most and where I feel the most uncomfortable. And the most sad. Do you know what I mean? Jan had nudged him, her face blurred with whimsy.

I think so.

Like my dreams. Between the waking, living world and the sleep of the dead. Mostly in my dreams I grieve. Mostly, they are about loss.

Me, too.

Or I am anxious. Stressed. I am on the wrong train, I watch the platform receding, the one where I am supposed to be. Nobody is speaking a language I can understand. There is usually some menace I should be running from but can't. Rarely do I make love in my dreams or even have sex, or fly, or come over some ridge into Shangri-la.

Same.

But I love them just the same. My life without them would be a hollow shell.

A hollow shell.

He repeated it and thought how there is also a liminal space in an empty shell, one that you can hold to your ear and which will give you, out of its own emptiness, the sounds of surf and wind. A benison from one who holds nothing. And he thought of that conversation many times after she left, and how emptiness was a place he was learning to appreciate if not love, as she had learned to love the in-betweens. He had to acknowledge something. Bow to it, if slightly.

///////////////////////////

The day warmed and whatever mist clung to the ridges faded and vanished. They stopped in the road and stripped off their jackets. The road hugged the shoreline loosely, straying around wooded hills and what looked like large holdings at water's edge. Hard to tell, because where there might have been mansions there were now only blackened ruins and docks. And, again, the boats. Whatever boats, cleated to the docks or rocking on their moorings, had been left untouched. So they walked the edge of the road and skirted the lake, sometimes close, sometimes as much as a half-mile above. They tried twice to shortcut across fields and lost time crossing fences and ditches and scratched their arms in the brambles. Lost time. Did they have time to lose, or gain? Jess wondered. Since they had started walking it almost seemed time was suspended. Or the normal accounting of it. Because time worked best when there was a movement toward or away. Toward desire, away from death. Away from the Big Bang, toward an infinite expansion that might or might not be God. Toward quitting time, beer-thirty, a quinceañera, a vacation, a wedding, a funeral. Toward the sense of a poem, or love, or away from the chaos of a dream. But now they did not know, truly, what they were headed into or out of. Or what flashed on the horizon.

And so Storey, who still believed he had a bearing, which was his family, was more eager to try the shortcuts, and Jess had to remind him that they had cost.

And then what once were houses along the shoreline became more frequent, houses with docks and ski boats tied, and little Friendship sloops on moorings—probably a race class up here. There were flagpoles on the lawns that sloped to the water where American flags still hung and lifted in the pulsing breeze. And Jess knew they were getting close to the town and he wondered if whatever militia had blazed through was unionist and punishing a secessionist county. Could you use that term in the third millennium? Unionist? Was any of this really happening? Or was he now in some long, involved anxious dream, in which his grief at the loss of his wife bubbled to the surface and frothed? And from which he would wake, pillow damp, into a hunting trip with Storey . . . wake into a darkness before daybreak that held the same scents of spruce and fir and lakewater that he smelled now? How many dreams within dreams could a person wake from? In grade school everyone said that if you sneezed more than eight times you would die; was it like that?

And if this grim procession or juggernaut of harvest that they were following now—if it *was* anti-secessionist, why would they burn the places that flew the Stars and Stripes? Wouldn't they leapfrog around them? And why would a rabidly secessionist town—rabid enough to become a target—let anyone fly an American flag? It made no sense.

Maybe they, whoever they were, knew that flying the flag was a shallow attempt to save one's skin. Maybe they knew that the town knew they were coming—maybe they knew that, as they attacked, they could not shut down cell service fast enough, not before a few desperate calls got out, warning other folks along the lake, or farther afield. And those people, the townspeople here, armed with the knowledge that the storm was bearing down, maybe in one last act of apostasy, or its inverse, they ran the flags up the poles and prayed.

It was too confusing. They had no idea who was on whose side, or what, really, the sides were about. Jess stopped in the road and shook his head as if trying to clear it.

"What?" Storey said.

"The flags." Jess pointed.

"So?"

"Didn't we say that this might be some eruption over secession?"

"So?" Storey blinked down to the landscaped shoreline.

"So what do the flags mean?"

"Hell if I know."

"I mean, whose side is who on? I'm thinking destruction on this scale has gotta be full-on military. U.S. of A. So these towns must be rebel or whatever. Right?"

Storey stood looking east and blinked in the autumn sun, a pale, early-morning sun that was barely an hour clear of the ridges. He stood as if smelling the still-cool breeze that stirred in the long grass at the edge of the road.

"I wonder if it matters," he said.

"What?"

"I wonder if it matters whose side anyone is on."

Jess winced at his friend. "What does *that* mean?"

Storey turned. He tucked his thumbs under the pack straps and shrugged the weight up off his shoulders. "I don't know," he said. "All this . . ." He trailed off. Jess waited. "It seems vicious and random."

"Random?"

"Not random, I guess. Indiscriminate. They're burning everything. Except the boats."

"So . . . what, then?"

Storey looked back down to the lake. To the boats there, the flagpoles. "I dunno, Jess. It's like the heat of the destruction, the savagery . . . It's like it's about something deeper than any issue like secession."

Jess watched his oldest friend. Whose week-old beard had flecks of gray. He knew, watching him, that Storey was thinking about the fierce and pervasive violence and that he was praying that it not spill over into New Hampshire and Vermont and touch his children and his wife. In suggesting that the violence felt deeper than secession he was voicing his own dread that it might not have boundaries.

Jess spat into the road, hitched up his own pack. "It's probably just some crazy central-Maine shit. Right? Something like this was bound to happen somewhere."

Storey was more than worried; he was grieving. Already. Jess could see it on his face. But Storey smiled, sad. He appreciated Jess's effort.

Storey said, "The town would have sent out distress signals. One kind or another."

"Right."

"They would have warned everyone else. You know that the attacks, news of them, are zinging all over the news and the internet right now."

"Right."

"Why doesn't it feel that way?"

///////////////////////////

In half a mile they came to a sign, green, that said "Randall, Population 2,732." So they had let the sign stand. That did seem random, or at least scattershot, since Green Hill's, on both sides of town, were gone.

But, as in Green Hill, not much else had been spared. The county road dropped down a gentle hill and into what must have been a pretty Main Street not high above the water. And so the town center was mostly flat, with streets branching down to the shore and a lovely wharf, still intact. On the far side of the wharf, with its walkway and benches and shade trees of oak and pine and maple, was another marina, this one at least twice the size of the one in Green Hill. The trees still stood; the benches invited respite. The boats swung gently on their moorings, as before. The black reek of burned houses watered their eyes.

Again, as they walked the sooted aisles of the narrow streets, they passed only the silent blackened monuments of chimney, hearth, foundation wall. Some still smoked, and when they stirred a heap of cinders with a length of rebar they pushed up glowing embers. They passed what must have been the stone arch entryway to a modest church; nothing else of it stood. Again they called out. Again they knew, without knowing why, that the typhoon of the reapers had passed and gone. Again they found few bodies. There was what must have been a child curled behind a stack of chimney stones, sheltered in what once must have been a hidden cubby or closet. The body was small and blackened and lipless with bared teeth, and Storey lurched from the sight and Jess heard him heave. There was what must have been a couple embraced beneath what must have been a pickup in what must have been a garage. There was a badly burned body sprawled inside a grove of seven poplars whose unsinged leaves spun and clattered in the easy wind. How did that happen? On the north end of the wharf and behind it, at what once had been an intersection, a street sign still stood— bronzed letters embossed on dark steel: "Water Street."

It seemed to Jess almost like a taunt; he wasn't sure why. He didn't want to look anymore. He walked to the edge of the wharf, which was decked with heavy, weather-grayed planks. They soothed him somehow. As did the prospect of open water, far shore, moored sailboats.

On the closest dock was a classic blue Boston Whaler skiff with a 150 Merc, clean and cleated, ready to travel. Why couldn't they climb in and cast off? Gun the motor and aim for the distant shoreline? Land at some unburned camp and warn the family, make the calls, get a lift?

Because, Jess suspected, there were no families now. No cedar-shingled cottages with Adirondack chairs on a wide porch, with nursery-bought geraniums hanging from baskets under the eaves, and some yellow Lab barking good-naturedly as he and Storey coasted in. Some barefoot child running after the dog and yelling, "Opey, no! Opey! Bad dog!" Jess throwing a single hitch over the piling and clambering out, the dog now bumping legs and whining, Jess pounding the top of his mallet head with an open palm, the child yelling "Opey, *no!*" though there was nothing anymore to redress, the child scrambling out to the end of the dock and grabbing his dog by the collar, dragging him back, explaining seriously, "He's nice, he doesn't bite!" The mother stepping off the porch, the father from the garden beside the cottage, wiping hands on thighs of blue jeans as in a choreography, as in a movie, as in a Norman Rockwell painting titled *The Greeting* in which the Sunday-morning boaters are not traumatized strangers but old friends from across the lake who bring jars of honey from their own bees and a Superman comic for Willum, and everyone sticks to their lines. Jess felt a lurch in his chest. Why couldn't anyone stick to their lines, ever? Life might accede to being idealized for a single freeze-frame picture but the characters always cracked. Or went away. And he knew that if that family ever did in fact exist, and did in fact share moments of joy and days of peace, they existed on this day no longer. He and Storey could get in the boat and power across the lake and run up along the shore and he knew what they'd find. And then what? Somehow they intuited that they were safer in the wake of the holocaust, the way veteran wildland fire-fighters will "run back into the black," run for safety into the zone that has just been burned. But you could not follow the devastation forever. Because by the time you were discovered and killed your spirit would be already dead.

"No rental car, huh?" It was Storey on the wharf behind him.

"No."

"You're still thinking about a boat. Maybe running across and trying the other side."

"Yes."

"I don't think running east would help us. Roadwise."

"No."

"It'd be a long walk through the woods and mountains."

"Yes."

"Also food. We haven't seen a single deer. Why not?"

"I don't know." Jess turned his head. If he had been looking with longing over the water, he could see in Storey's grimace that his friend had no desire to go there. Well, Storey wanted to get to his family most of all, and Lena and the girls were to the west, behind them as they stood.

Jess said, "No signal, huh?"

"No."

"I was looking at the road map. The county highway we've been following turns west, away from the lake. But there's one more town up the shore. Not a town, a hamlet. Beryl. The road up there is dirt."

"Okay."

"Do you think we should go?"

"I think we should scavenge as much food out of these boats as we can find. Probably we should have done it before, back in Green Hill."

"Yeah."

"I guess we were in shock."

"Is that what it was?" Is this what shock felt like? Jess didn't know. He didn't think so. He could move, reason. His gyroscope was working; he knew where his body was in space and in the landscape. He just didn't know much else. Like what they were doing here or where they should go. "I was eyeing that Boston Whaler," he confessed.

"I knew you were."

"I figure we can use it to get out to all the moored boats. The ones worth a visit."

"Okay. You wanna hit the docks first?"

"Yep."

Two weeks after Labor Day and no one, it seemed, was in a hurry to trailer their boats off this lake. In other years, the years of their first hunts, most of the summer people would be gone by now, their houses closed up for winter and their vessels towed away. But now, with dependably warmer falls and with new iterations of the virus sweeping the country in seasonal waves, more people were working remotely and staying put in summer camps and homes through Thanksgiving at least. Many stayed all year. And on the warm days, the days of Indian summer that stretched into October and returned sporadically in November, the folks From Away still fished and wakeboarded, water-skied, and sailed. To Jess it seemed decadent. Vacations should have boundaries, shouldn't they? He was surprised at his own puritanical impulse. He couldn't help thinking that if these recreationalists had returned home earlier they all might be drinking coffee now in their home kitchens and not be mixing with rain-slurried ash. God. Nobody deserved this.

"Hey." Storey touched his shoulder.

"Oh. Yeah?"

"Let's find something to eat. Maybe we're getting hangry."

///////////////////

They left their packs on one of the benches and moved fast. The marina contained three floating docks with perpendicular spurs long enough to berth three twenty-six-footers end to end. And they were nearly full. But most of the vessels were either open motorboats built for day fishing or pulling a wakeboard, or little open sailboats, cats and sloops. Jess had noticed a cohort of probably nineteen-foot Friendship sloops on their way up the lake, and there were many more here. Something about the loyalty to an old working design stirred now a sense of admiration or kinship with all these boat owners; but he stifled it. Because right now they were scavenging their bones.

The little sloops had cabins big enough to shelter a lone sailor in a sudden squall—two in a pinch. Probably no food in those, and they didn't think it worth the pain to break the teak hatches. Jess knew that it was because the boats were so graceful—say it: so beautiful—that they could not bring themselves to break them for a tube of Pringles or an old bottle of Coke.

Jess took up his new fire-burnished ax and they trotted along the docks, and when they came to a larger cabin cruiser or weekend sailer they jumped aboard and Jess swung his bladed truncheon and the light lock usually busted and the door swung in or the hatch cracked beneath the broken hasp. And they crouched and took narrow steps into dim cabins lit by skylights and pillaged the cabinets and underseat chests.

On one thirty-five-foot fishing cruiser with a flying bridge, Storey found at the nav station a new pair of Ray-Ban aviator sunglasses and tried them on. He couldn't see anything in the darkened space, so he propped them on his baseball cap. In a chart drawer of the same boat he found a lightweight Leatherman with a corkscrew. On another boat, a sleek Peterson 34 stripped of sails, Jess found four bottles of two-year-old Saint Cosme Côtes du Rhône. There was food also, and by the time they'd pillaged eight likely yachts they had more canned food and bags of rice and boxes of oatmeal than they could pack. The marina had evidently supplied handcarts—a little like the old red wagons but stoutly built—for their patrons to use in shuttling supplies and parts out along the docks, and Jess found one upturned at the end of a spur and they loaded it with far more than they could ever carry and he towed it back. It bumped rhythmically over the gaps in the planks behind him and for one forgetful moment he thought of freight cars trundling over the tracks at the crossing on Box Elder in the little Vermont town they grew up in and he felt for a second what might be happiness. In strong sun he rolled the cart to the wrought-iron bench on the wharf, and whatever that emotion was that was not dread vanished when he saw their leaning packs and remembered where they were. He dropped the handle and a cloud shadow passed over fast, towing its own chill, and then he was in sun again but the moment of peace was gone. Storey was hefting two stuffed heavy-duty trash bags filled with provisions and he set them down and said, "I guess we don't need to go out to the moorings after all. I know you wanted to pilot that Whaler."

Jess waved it off.

"I was thinking about it," Storey said. "Why do you think the cart was overturned? They didn't savage the docks. Again."

Jess shrugged. "Maybe whoever used it saw their kid on the wharf and in their hurry to get to them turned it over. Maybe it's better not to think about it."

Storey grimaced. "Right."

They looked at their haul. "This might be the only easy food we get for a while," Storey said.

"We can't take all of it. Unless we pull the wagon. But, like I said, the road is dirt from here on up, and in about six miles it looks like that ends, too."

"Okay, well . . . we can pull it that far. The wheels are pretty stout."

"Or we can take that Whaler."

Storey smiled at his friend's tenacity. Jess said, "We can pile it with all of this and see what we find in . . . in . . ." He reached for the folded road map in his back pocket and flipped it open. He had carefully folded it all back so that the section they needed opened like a book. "In Beryl."

Storey looked grimly north, up the shore.

"Or not," Jess said. "We can drag the cart. The road is probably good and packed."

"Thing is . . ." Storey wouldn't form the words.

"What if they're there?"

Storey nodded. He looked around them at what was once probably a charming and pretty town. "This place is still smoking," he said. "They can't be very far."

"Could be over a day."

"We don't know. At least if we come up on the road . . . we can backtrack, get into the woods. In that boat, with the sound of the motor, on open water . . ." Storey rubbed his eyes.

"We don't have to go up there," Jess said gently. "We could keep following the highway. It turns away west now."

"Whew, I feel like we need to go see this village, see if it survived. Six miles isn't far. We can come back to this road after."

"Okay," Jess said. "We'll pull the wagon. Maybe we should make a big meal here and then head up."

They did. Jess fashioned a tumpline with a long webbing strap from one of the boats, and he ran it through the handle of the wagon and looped it across his waist and pulled the cart easily without having to strain one arm back. The streets were rough with debris but the cart had large pneumatic tires that bounced along. They retreated into the trees at the south edge of town. They made a fire. The breeze was northerly, but even had it been running south to north they wouldn't have worried much, because, again, why would they—whoever they were—be alerted by the smell of smoke coming from a recently burned-out town behind them?

So they built a nice fire and watched through a scrim of trees the cloud shadows run over the lake and across the ruins of the town. Storey dug through the black garbage bags and pulled out four cans of Campbell's clam chowder. He opened them with the can opener on his new Leatherman and he slid a plastic spoon carefully up the inside and pulled out the contents with a suck of air and the plop of a mostly intact cylinder of stew. They were both starving and figured that two cans apiece would work as an appetizer. Jess added a little water from his filter bottle and set the pot on a wire grill from a hibachi they'd lifted from the deck of one of the sailboats. He stirred and Storey shook in Cholula hot sauce from a fresh bottle and dug around and began emptying stewed tomatoes, kippered herring, canned mushrooms, artichoke hearts, "Escargots!"—he held up the can on a flat palm, as in an ad—and sliced Italian hard sausage all into the larger pot.

"This is gonna be jumble-aya, spelled like 'jumble,' " he said.

"Yum."

"I've got boxes of couscous. When you're done with the chowder we'll cook it up."

"Delish."

It was. To them. They dug into the clam chowder with groans of pleasure. Each shook more Cholula out of the glass bottle as if the burn of the salsa might distract them from other things. Storey opened the first wine bottle with his Leatherman and raised it in a toast—"Skål!"—and chugged half like water and passed it to Jess. While Jess drank he opened a second bottle.

"Good stuff," Storey said. "I'd get it again. Will you remember the vintage?"

"No."

"Me, neither." Jess watched as Storey took out his phone and used some precious wattage from the battery to snap a picture of the cream-colored label with its sketch of a stone farmhouse on a French hill. Jess didn't comment. Storey opened the second bottle and held it at arm's length and addressed it. "Thanks for coming," he said. "What the fuck." And he drank. He held it out to Jess and their eyes met. Storey's were bleary and uncertain, and Jess watched as they watered and welled and leaked from the corners. Storey held out the bottle, refusing to acknowledge the tears tracking his cheeks.

Jess took the bottle, and as their fingers touched he said, "Store."

Storey blinked and nodded.

"The girls? Andrea?"

Storey looked away. He wiped his face on the sleeve of his jacket. "You heard about when her cat, Coco, died."

"Yeah, you told me."

"That was a year ago, April. The anorexia kicked in so badly Andrea almost died. She got better over late summer. I made her a milkshake every day, cooked for her every night."

"I remember. She would only eat certain foods if you cooked them."

Storey nodded. Jess held out the bottle and Storey now shook his head. He said, "I thought she was out of the woods."

"And?"

"And then came the state cross-country running championship meet, and she won."

"Won? I . . . I'm not sure if you told me. That's awesome." Jess lifted the wine in salute.

Storey shook his head. "Not awesome."

"No?" Jess set the bottle on a bed of dead pine needles, leaned it against a fallen limb. "No? Why?"

"Because it freaked her out. Like now maybe she would get scouted by some fancy boarding school and have to leave home and then she'd get recruited by a Division One college and she would become a robot and never see us again."

"She stopped eating."

Storey nodded. Jess saw the tremor in his chest and watched as he shook it off. His stoic best friend. Jess did not know what to say, so he said nothing; finally, he murmured, "Lena is there. She'll know what to do."

"She'll be making a thousand calls. Geneva will be tugging at her, demanding answers—that's what she does. Andrea will clam up and drift. And drift. Hand me the bottle."

They finished it. They took a vote and decided to save the other two bottles for some unforeseen celebration. They added the dregs of the wine to the larger pot and heated up the jumble-aya and poured it over a bed of couscous and devoured it all. It didn't take long. The sun was high in the trees now, and the day was warm but not hot, and without a word they leaned back against their packs and fell asleep.

Chapter Three

Jess dreamed of water. He and Jan were swimming in a green bay. It was not night but their limbs sketched streaks of light as they swam, as of a bioluminescence so strong it was heedless of morning. Their fingers ignited heatless flames and they left two trails of phosphorescence behind them. He knew this because he was at once stroking through warm water and also gyring above, as an osprey gyres, and following the lovers. Lovers. He felt again what that means. She was breaststroking beside him and he did not need to look to feel her joy, her insoluble closeness, her mercy. They would swim together to some other continent if that's what love demanded. He wheeled and banked hard against the wind and soared upward and the world revolved and when he swooped over and down and regained his patrol the swimmers were gone. The wake of green light was there in the water like two contrails, but they lay on the surface inert. He let out a scream. It was an osprey cry meant to pierce the belly of heaven. It could not reconstitute the lovers or rouse the gods—

It was a scream that woke him. Storey was already sitting up and squinting toward the water. "Hey. Hey, *look*."

Jess looked. Someone was in a rowboat, a dinghy with short oars, casting off from a larger sloop moored farther out. It was a girl or young woman. She pushed off and seized the oars and stroked madly for the docks.

The two Black Hawks came over the treeline of the far shore and straight over the water. They came fast and low—Jess thought they couldn't be more than a hundred feet off the lake—and their rotors churned a white wake as they came and drummed, then thudded off the thin skin of the afternoon. They came in tight formation, dark and unmarked, one to the side and just behind the other, and the helicopters banked once, hard, over the fleet of moored boats. The girl rowed, frantic. The whitewater frothed around her and then the choppers leveled and flew north. Jess thought they were departing. But a mile out they banked hard again and came straight at them, at the remains of the town, at the docks. In reflex, Jess and Storey rolled off their packs and bellied down and watched. A few hundred meters out, flames belched from the forward chopper and tore the water in a vicious line, and the girl flew out of the boat with half a shredded oar, and the dinghy disintegrated, and Jess thought he saw a halo of blood spray downwind on the breeze and fly apart under the storm of the whomping blades. The helicopters came on, did not miss a beat, came straight at them and right over the tops of their trees.

They had both squinched down their eyes and covered their heads with their arms, but the Black Hawks were gone, leaving shaken leaves and a tumping, fading pulse on the cooling air.

Jess noticed, when he lifted his head again, that the sun was low over the near ridge.

"What the hell," Storey said.

Jess couldn't speak. Not for a minute. Finally, he croaked, "So much for being safe on the water."

"*Man.*"

The faint throb of the choppers died out. The natural wind off the lake resumed its irregular passes through the canopy.

"Who do you think she was?" Storey said.

"Storey?" Jess said.

"Yeah."

"I could've sworn she screamed. Before they came."

Storey sat up. He brushed some crumbs of dirt and dried leaves off his cheek. "What do you mean?"

"I mean her scream woke me up."

"What?"

"I don't know. I was asleep. I guess we both were. And I dreamed of an osprey flying, I was the osprey, and I screamed, and I woke up. And then the girl was in the boat, but I think it was *her* scream."

"Okaay . . ."

"And then the choppers came over the trees, way over on that side."

Storey scratched his chin and throat, his days-old beard. "So . . . what?"

"It was all out of order is what."

Storey snugged his cap back on his head.

Jess pressed on. "How could she know the choppers were coming? She was casting off. In a panic. She screamed as if she knew. And then they were there, breaking over the horizon, which is the shoreline, those trees on the far shore." Jess shook his head, tried to align the images, the succession.

"Maybe she didn't scream. Maybe you screamed like an eagle and woke yourself up."

"Well, still. She *was* in the dinghy. Like fleeing, like in flight. She was panicked."

Storey stared. "I think we've got bigger fish to worry about," he said finally. "Like who the fuck *were* those guys?"

"Yeah, no shit. They had zero markings." Jess rolled up onto his knees and took up the two pots, the spoons. "You have enough water in your bottle to wash these?"

Storey shook his head.

"Seems fucked up. To wash them in the lake now."

Storey shut his eyes. "It's a big lake. She's pretty far out."

"Okay. Okay, I'll go down. Better to have everything clean before we go."

<hr>

Go where? Jess thought as he carried the dishes down to the dock. *To the hamlet up the shore, to witness all this again?* He scanned the water around the moored boats but could no longer see the dinghy or the girl. It must have sunk, the rowboat. She—whatever was left of her—must be floating just at the surface or beneath and not visible in the evening chop.

He knelt between two outboard skiffs and scooped up water in the larger pot. The skiffs were two nondescript aluminum motorboats with bench seats; rentals, probably. For tourists From Away. The town was clearly a destination spot, designed to attract and charm visitors. It was evident even from the smoking ruins: the quaint black-and-bronze street sign with its Roman letters, the wrought-iron benches on the wharf, the grove of poplars there, protecting the bronze statue of a little boy and girl walking with fishing rods over their shoulders and holding hands. Quaint. The quaintness of the town had somehow survived its immolation.

His head hurt. A bottle of wine didn't help. He squirted bio-degradable soap from a small plastic bottle into the pot and took the piece of plastic scrubby they used for backpacking and scrubbed. He felt the lowering sun on the back of his neck, smelled the exhalation of woods about to drop their leaves, a certain sweetness, of relinquishment maybe to the turning wheel of the seasons, the coming ice. Maybe he should learn from the trees, he thought. Ha! How to gracefully handle loss. How to literally let go.

For an instant he saw himself dressed up like Puck in *A Midsummer Night's Dream,* adorned with leaves and prancing in a dappled wood. And then saw the leaves turn yellow and fall behind him in a fluttering train. *That's me.* Who could not keep a wife, or a dog. Who could not take a simple hunting trip with his oldest friend, whose world now wobbled off its axis. He pressed his fingers harder into the scrubby to get off a blackened burn patch and heard the waves kicked up by the evening wind slosh against the dock and slap the metal hulls of the motorboats. And he thought of the girl floating just off there, probably in several pieces, and thought, *Snap out of it. You are alive, dude, and you have all your limbs, and your best friend is sitting up there, just inside those trees.*

He didn't snap out of it. He could not banish the image of the girl frantically rowing, or the little *Isabella* with her maroon sails uncovered, bouncing against the intact dock, waiting for her family to come and board her. Or the small burned body inside the living poplar grove, just over there. He wanted most of all to call Jan, to tell her everything he'd seen, to hear her sympathetic *Oh, oh God,* her *I'm hugging you now, a big, big hug,* to tell her he was sorry for everything he should be sorry for, and then he could not erase the image of her Forester pulling out and driving slowly up the shallow hill of their street—slowly, so that she would not hit and hurt the dog who ran beside her, desperately barking. The gradual acceleration up toward 23rd Street, Bell finally gone mute, feeling the end of something, standing in the middle of the street looking after the car, ears up and forward, both of them, Jess and the dog, watching it turn the corner and disappear. Both of them because she had said before leaving, in what he wasn't sure was an act of generosity or aggression: "You keep Bell. You're gonna need her more than me." His shoulders shuddered. Was it narcissism to join his own personal loss to the wreckage smoldering around him? Probably.

Still, the quiver in his chest was a grief for all the sundered. All who believed in the next hour and day.

He looked down at his hand in the soapy water of the saucepan. *Here we are. Hand pressing scrubby.* What did the student ask the Zen master? "I have gained enlightenment, what do I do now?" And Roshi had answered: "Wash your bowl." *I have lost everything, what do I do now? Wash the pot, ha. Maybe enlightenment and total loss are the same thing. That is something to chew on.*

He tossed the sudsy water and dipped the pot again and rinsed it. The lake was cold—a hard, serious autumn cold that would not be friendly to a swimmer. These past nights of frost. He looked across again to the far shore, lit now by the sun sinking behind him. What caught his eye was not the woods gone to tender greens, yellows, ambers, but the sharp blacks and grays of the ledge rock at water's edge. The slabs of granite sloping to the lake, the short bands of bedrock that might have made jumping rocks. They somehow reflected the woods above them and were hued with green; they must have been flecked with pyrite and veined with quartz and so sheened like dull mirrors. They were—some of them—exactly the color of the two military helicopters whose thudding still seemed to sound over the horizon westward. Who the hell were they?

They were unmarked. U.S. military or some sleeper militia with powerful connections to the military or their contractors. Or foreign? Why couldn't they be Canadian? Everything they had encountered was so crazy—the upheaval and politics. Had to be beyond the pale. Canadians. The border was not that far away. Fifty, sixty miles at the closest. Maybe this wasn't about Maine seceding at all. What an idiot idea. Maybe some eruption over hydropower at the Quebec border, or oil pipelines from tar sands in Alberta, or mineral rights beneath the melting polar ice . . . or tourists bringing in garlic! To repel mosquitoes! Remember that, Jan? How we laughed and laughed in Thunder Bay when the customs official stared and said, "Good luck with that." Some geopolitical straw that finally broke at last the brittle civility between the North American neighbors. Siblings that fall out hurl the worst vitriol.

But the choppers had not come for just the girl. Right? Right. They came over the trees straight and fast, evidently on their way somewhere. And they had spotted her rowing. And they had circled, whatthehell. Those maybe the words over the headsets: *What the hell.* And: *Engaging target.* They needed target practice, they were psychopaths. They had orders to shoot anyone who moved. They had orders to eliminate completely the towns on the lake. There could be no survivors, no witnesses. Jess's head spun.

It didn't matter. What mattered was that she was alive one second—heart pounding, crying out, lungs heaving, muscles engaged—and torn to pieces the next. And so, if Storey and Jess had any notion that all of this was not their fight, well . . . they moved, they breathed, they were walking bull's-eyes. That frightened him, of course. But what frightened him even more was the nagging sense that the chronology was off—that she screamed and fled and *then* came the choppers. Unless she had much better hearing than either of them. Hearing like a wolf or an owl.

They packed up. Storey seemed groggy. The wine had anesthetized them both for a couple of hours; now the cost. Neither felt like cooking again, and the sun was only an hour off the ridgetop, and so they ate a bag of mixed dried apricots and cherries, a pack of Chips Ahoy! cookies, and three Slim Jims apiece. Ugh. Not the best fuel at any time of day, but especially lousy on top of too much wine. They packed the rest of the food tightly in the wagon and tied down the load with a bolt of sailcloth and a length of rigging line Jess had purloined from a day sailer. He had used the word "purloin" with Storey, who had grunted amusement. "Anachronistic and elegant," he'd said. "I think when everybody is dead you're stuck with 'scavenge.' We are scavengers."

"Point taken." Jess didn't like the tone, but he figured Storey was irritable with hangover. He said, "But don't forget we are hunters, too."

Storey's head swung up from where he was cinching closed the top of his pack. He didn't respond.

Dusk overtook them on the dirt road north. The darkness filled the woods like a tide. The lake was too far below this road for them to see through trees, but they could feel the chill off the water flowing upslope with the first press of night. Maybe they should camp. Neither wanted to see another smoking burn today, another small body curled, another clutch of boats bobbing incongruously at their moorings.

They were walking north slowly, a graded track of smooth dirt scattered with the first fallen leaves, basswood and swamp maple. The woods grew over the ditches on either side and over the road, too, the limbs tangling overhead so that much of the time they were walking through a tunnel of hardwoods. Darkness came early. They had no problem following the road: the sandy hardpack seemed to emit its own glow, and there was nothing to trip over, as the flotsam of flight and wrecked households was weirdly absent.

"I guess we should call it," Storey said as they came over a rise into a stirring of warmer air and a small clearing. "No water here, but my two-quart bottle's full. You?"

"Same."

"You hungry?"

"No."

"Me, neither."

They unslung the rifles and dropped the packs. Jess pulled the wagon off the road into the short broom grass. Out of habit. No vehicle would pass this way tonight. He could smell the thin anise of goldenrod and the round pungence of Queen Anne's lace. So often had he smelled the two together in early fall that he could almost close his eyes and imagine that this was any other year and this any other meadow.

Jess pulled his water bottle from its sleeve on the side of his pack and drank. He said, "Do you think they came this way?"

Storey shrugged up his shoulders and stretched his arms high. In the near dark his outline was huge. He windmilled his arms and dropped his hands. "I don't know. There were fresh tire tracks, a bunch of fresh footprints. But that might make sense anytime. Runners from Randall taking a nice six-mile out-and-back on good dirt; fishermen maybe heading up to secret spots away from the bigger town. Dunno. You?"

"No. There'd be more sign. It's probably less than a mile to Beryl. What did the gazetteer show? A long decline, right? Probably right down at the bottom of this long hill. We could leave our packs and the wagon and walk down and look. Want to?"

"No."

"Yeah." Jess got it. Three deathscapes in one day was more than anyone ought to bear. "So we'll camp," he said.

"If that's what you want to call it."

The sudden turn to bitterness surprised Jess. Second time today. It stung. It wasn't like Storey, not in any circumstance. Well, he was worried about his girls, his wife. Worried to distraction, and he kept it buttoned up most of the time. Storey forgot their agreement and still grimly checked his phone at every stop and then put it away and seemed to put away his panic, too. But that would be too much to ask. Jess couldn't see his friend's face in the dark. He coughed once, spat. "I'd kill for some chew," he said. "Maybe bad choice of words."

"Yeah, chew." Storey sounded chastened. He said, "Might be too much to ask to find a general store in Beryl still standing, with fully stocked shelves and a rack of worm dirt."

"You're beside yourself about the girls, huh? And Lena."

Silence. Crickets chirped in the grass of the clearing. Peepers sang from some seep or spring down below. Jess listened for the threshing of a brook but heard only the vespers of the first night wind.

"I . . ." Storey's voice was husky when he finally spoke. He said, "The helicopters suggest to me it's not just a Maine thing."

///////////////////////

Tonight they did not string a tarp. The stars sharpened over the clearing, and there was no smell of rain. The temperature dropped fast. They unrolled their sleeping pads and shook their down bags out and folded their jackets for pillows. They lay on their backs, side by side, and Jess felt the day sift down through his exhaustion, down into his chest and limbs. For a time without measure he let his attention move into the deepening stars and he imagined himself soaring there, not this time as some pelagic osprey but as a great beast that beat the dark slowly and with great power, and glided past the furnaces of stars on long extended wings. In this silent world only the hiss of incineration and the whisper of his primaries kept company with his traveling mind. And it did travel: far ahead into interstitial gloom where there were no screams and no choppers, and no blue Foresters driving away up a hill. No collapsed dogs. No apoplectic politicians, no states, no borders, no countries.

Storey moved his hands up under his head and knocked Jess's arm with his elbow, and Jess snapped back into his own body on the ground.

"If it's not just Maine, what do you think it could be?" Storey said. "And why were those choppers unmarked?"

Jess felt for his wool hat beside him and snugged it on. "Who knows. It probably is just Maine. Or Republicans versus Democrats. Or the Evangelical South versus the Heathen and Decadent Northeast. Sons of Silence versus Hells Angels. Seems like all we can do anymore is pick a fight."

Storey grunted. "I checked out the gazetteer and the road map when you were asleep."

"Yeah?"

"Burlington on foot is like three hundred miles. Pretty much southwest. Last few days we've been sucked north, first for gas, then along the lake hoping for a car. But the best road route is back south to Bangor, then across. If we counted on picking up some kind of vehicle on the way."

"All burned," Jess said.

"Yeah, but what kind of conflict destroys *all* the cars?"

"This one, maybe. Don't you think it's strange that there's not even a bicycle intact?"

Storey ran the last days over in his mind. The vehicles in Four Corners were all incinerated. He didn't remember any bikes. No scooters, no motorcycles. There had been a couple of motorbikes in Randall, but they had been only half-melted frames and engine blocks. Same in Green Hill. "Strange," Storey repeated.

"We need to talk to someone," Jess said. "Why we're detouring up to this village. What goes for cars goes for people. No war kills *everyone*. Ever. So: The girl. And the other woman. In the lake. With the rock. Someone will know."

As if on cue, an almost human scream rose out of the woods below them. A single strangled screech, frayed at the edges. They both tensed hard, then relaxed.

"Barn owl," Storey said.

"Whew." Jess let his heartbeat settle. "So I guess we should be searching all the boats. Seems like everyone who isn't cremated is on the water."

"Everyone." The scalding bitterness again.

"Well."

"If we board every boat. And break in," Storey said. "If someone's left, they'll be waiting down there, crouched with a shotgun. A Winchester Marine. And won't ask questions."

"Hadn't thought of that."

"Right."

"I was kind of thinking that anyone would be so relieved."

The grunt again.

Jess let that sift, too. That *they*, he and Storey, were interlopers. "I was thinking . . ."

"Oh, no."

Phew. A shred of Storey's old self asserted.

"It bothers me about the deer."

"*That's* what you're bothered about?"

Chapter Four

She had made it clear—*I love you, I love you always*—and *Don't call me. We will never get back together again.* Quick tear of the Band-Aid. Because she knew that he would harbor—hope, some vision of redemption, a future together in which the rough seas of their early years had smoothed into a green bay, in which they were stronger for the trials and heartbreaks. He had broken her heart. He had been recruited as faculty at a midsummer furniture-design symposium in Vermont. He would not have accepted except that the money was decent, the food reputed to be four-star, and the campus an hour from Storey, and Storey had insisted on a July fishing excursion through Vermont and New Hampshire. "I guarantee tiny brookies, anemic rainbows, and stultified browns. And warm water! Way too warm!" How could Jess refuse?

One of his students was a twenty-three-year-old Italian heiress who had just graduated from Middlebury, had been half hippi-fied by four years of overalls and Jim Harrison novels, and had minored in furniture making. She had an overwrought accent that slayed him. It was as if every English syllable took a great effort of her plush mouth, while her golden eyes held a steady, playful, Ligurian calm. Personal design reviews ensued, and he came home with chlamydia.

That he had lost his magnificent wife over a dalliance was devastating enough. That he had done it in such a clichéd, timeworn fashion increased his self-loathing. But he knew: It was not just the affair; *that* she might have weathered. It was that he hunted or fished for ten days in September with Storey. That they both returned to the home of their upbringing in southern Vermont for two weeks of deer season in November; that he went alone in October to his favorite village on Colorado's Western Slope to fish his favorite mountain stream for a couple of weeks, a stretch of creek whose location he told to no one; that summers were not immune from fishing excursions, or winters. That she was left alone with a steady job at the museum, wondering on what balance sheet marriage made sense. And *then* to betray her. Too much: *None of the love I have given you I take back,* she had said. *I just don't want to be married to you anymore.*

He got it. *Now* he did, far too late. Why hadn't he listened to her before? Because he was having his fish and eating it, too. And yet he still felt they were soulmates. *Knew* that neither one would ever find anyone else who understood the language and laughter of the stars or the waves or the birds the way they did together. He still held the love-is-attention stone she had given him to remind himself. It applied to everything, to washing a pot and to hunting.

When Storey heard she had left, he called and said, "You should have married someone who loved you less and was aggravated by you more."

"Gee, thanks."

"The only reason Lena tolerates all my absences is because she is relieved to have time alone."

"You should be a marriage counselor."

"You wanna come out and go for salmon on the Kennebec?"

"Thanks. I gotta stay with Bell. She's pretty blue. Also work."

"Okay."

That was more than a year ago. Still fresh. Still trying to make sense of the seasons without her.

Tonight he lay in his bag in the meadow and wished more than anything that she would drive back down their street. And then he thought how there were never any do-overs. What felt like do-overs never were, because scar tissue is not elastic and it has many fewer nerve endings to feel with, or it may be numb and not feel at all. One can tell oneself that some post-catastrophe peace or measure of contentment has more value than euphoria; that arriving at some balance, some equanimity after storm, is deeper than flitting flushes of joy, because the peace is so well earned; but none of that is true. To honor a love is the only way to keep it alive. To honor anything.

///////////////////////////

He woke once in the night, unzipped, reluctantly, out of the warmth of the bag. Frost on the grass. At first he thought it was the pale cast of moonlight, but there was no moon, only the uneven circle of stars over the meadow. No wind. One cricket managed a freeze-thickened chirp. Storey's regular snore. Out of habit he walked to the edge of the trees to pee. The grass was stiff and furred with frozen dew; his bare feet somehow delighted. Miraculously, no thorns, no wild-rose ground cover or thistle. He was mid-piss when he saw the flash. A double flare as of flickering lightning, a beat, then another, solitary and bright. For a moment they blotted the stars. Out of habit, again, he counted. One one thousand, two one thousand, three one thousand, four one thou—and the boom, deep, rolling out of the north. Five count is a mile, this flash a little less. Lightning or explosion. He didn't think lightning. The sky was clear, and it wouldn't be heat lightning on this night of high pressure and cold. If truly to the north, the explosion was right about where they thought the village to be.

He shook himself and zipped up his fly and stood very still. They slept fully dressed now, in case of a need for rapid deployment. Jess listened. A full mile is not far for sound to carry, especially on the wind. Was there wind? There was always a breeze, no matter how subtle. He wet an index finger in his mouth and held it up. He'd seen the trick in old Western movies and used it all his life. It worked. He felt how the left side of his finger got colder first. He craned his head back and found the ladle of the Big Dipper canted over the trees and followed the back side to the North Star. The wind was ten points east. Yep, the road was heading down the hill and generally north, and the breeze was north-northeast. He held his breath and listened hard.

Leaves ticked and rattled. Oak and poplar, probably; maple, beech. All the birches—white, black, yellow, each with a strong and distinct fragrance when you put your nose to the peeling bark. Black like wintergreen; white like clear water if it could be turned to powdery talc; yellow subtle, sweet and sour together. Soon they, the leaves on these trees, would be turning to color with enthusiasm, and loosing in the gusts and covering their tracks. His and Storey's and whoever traveled before them. He couldn't imagine. And the choppers—were they for or against? Why on earth circle back and kill a young woman rowing alone in a boat? What harm could she possibly do? Why spend the bullets or the fuel? Except that she bore witness, as had he and Storey.

He was still craning back, following the Dipper to Polaris, Polaris to the upside-down "W" of Cassiopeia, when through the soft clamor of the leaves he heard a more percussive rattle. They were arrhythmic pops that rode the breeze, single notes, then a riff that ran together like beads on a string. Automatic-weapons fire. A firefight? In Beryl? Now? Before he could parse the source—how many?—the shooting stopped. If that's what it was. Ceased without echo, overtaken by the forest's rustlings.

Whatever that was, was a fifteen-minute walk down the hill. For all he knew, they were in range right now. You go to hunt a moose who has no weapon but flailing hooves and a span of antlers and you start dodging bullets. Karma, maybe. His toes were going numb. He padded back to the bags and thought to wake Storey and tell him, but what good would it do? He was snoring heavily, sighing on the exhales like a man traveling, a man in a train window watching a strange country unfurl, and missing his family. Jess felt a moment of tenderness for his friend, his vulnerability now—no way to pretend that he was tough or that his spirit could carry any of this. He let him sleep. They weren't going anywhere tonight, and in the morning they would have to decide if they would keep on or turn back in their first flight from the violence.

Do you believe in soulmates?

No, Jan said.

Me, neither. . . . Uh, why not?

Awww, did that ouch? He heard the smile in Jan's sleepy voice and, sure enough, her arm came around him and she was pulling herself to him and spooning his back.

I just wonder why you don't.

Jan nuzzled her nose in his neck, murmured, *Well, I think love is all about the subject, not the object.*

What do you mean?

I mean love is about how you engage the world. I keep trying to drum that into you, but you're so slow. You're like a quarter horse.

Hey, quarter horses aren't slow.

How would you know?

Silence.

I think love is all about our own capacity. So, if I am really good at love, at paying attention, at appreciation, at acceptance, then I can fully love anyone. How deep I love is about the depth of my ability and not the other person. And whom I choose is really happenstance.

Hey! Ouch. Happenstance? Anyone?

Do you think that if I were born in, say, Tonga I couldn't find someone to love as deeply as I love you? That tiny island kingdom in the middle of the South Pacific?

Well.

Look, some folks are pretty hard to love. The mean and cruel ones. But I mean we can love anyone who really interests us.

What about pheromones and stuff? And, like, smelling someone's genetic immune status and discovering it's a perfect match to complement your own. All the stuff they're discovering.

So?

So maybe there is a soulmate. Maybe it has to do with finding someone whose interests and values jibe, and who you are attracted to for a million reasons, half chemical, and who has a variation on Gene Eight Thousand and Forty-Two that fits like a jigsaw puzzle with yours. That's not anyone. Or happenstance.

I don't think that's how genes are named. And: You should have been a lawyer. And, you big dumdum, I love you more than anything on earth.

She squeezed him tight then, and, despite all the dumb theorizing, he believed her.

//////////////////////

Why was he thinking about that now? Back in his warm sleeping bag on a night of frost with Storey wheezing beside him?
In the middle of—apparently—a civil war. His rain shell was
folded next to his head, and he reached up and found the prayer
stone in the pocket, the one she had given him. It came not
from any known religion but from her own practice of deliber-
ate love. *Love is kind attention, dummy,* she once told him. *Which
is why you cannot hunt with Storey four months a year. I need attention, too.* And she tugged his beard. But she meant it with the
force of an openhearted belief, and she tried to give as serious
an attention to the rocks in the river and to the leaning spruce
as she did to Jess or the dog Bell. As much to the act of washing dishes as to the slow dance of making love to her husband.
Love, to Jan, was only that: paying attention. Not a word or gesture, a romance or a vow.

Now he curled his fingers around the stone and tucked his fist
under his chin and drifted. He thought he would never love anyone again. Not the way he loved her. That's what his intuition
told him. And it might be because, simply, he would not survive
the next week.

Dawn. First light moved on the meadow like fog. Dense and
shadowless. Revealing a clearing paled by frost. Jess heard an
owl mourning the dregs of night, a dirge in single, then double
hollow notes, unanswered.

They had found coffee on the boats, but now they didn't make
it. Jess wanted a cup almost more than he wanted to know that
the next few hours would be okay. But. They didn't make a fire.

They were too close to whatever had occurred at the village, so they each ate a can of Boston baked beans and two convenience-store mini–apple pies, stale and glazed with sugar. They tied down the wagonload under sail canvas, and Storey lifted the handle of the cart and snugged the loop of webbing over his forehead and leaned like a beast of burden.

"I can take it today," Storey said.

"I got it. You're a better shot."

Much unspoken. Meaning: *If we come under fire in the next twenty minutes, you better be able to move fast.* It was good dirt road now, falling downhill; they would be there in less time.

They were in cover, in thick woods, down a sandy road that made a long "S," and then they could smell the lakewater through the trees, and then they broke out into open ground, hayfield that dropped to the cluster of houses—houses!—and a quaint miniature lighthouse standing sentinel over a town dock. Not miniature, scaled down: a painted clapboard tower, blazoned white in the long light of the early sun. It was maybe thirty feet high, an octagon with no windows until the top, where a gallery of glass encircled. It drew the eye. Jess saw that the windows had no glazing. Crouching at the edge of the trees, he unslung the Savage and sighted through the scope at the tower. He could see shards remaining, shattered window frames. Bullet holes peppering the siding. He slid the scope down and across, into the village proper. The town, it seemed, had been built or recast as a Maine fishing village. Saltbox houses beside the dock had been painted Penobscot red and hung with lobster buoys. Lobster buoys! This was a lake, and so of course there were no lobsters. Crawdads, maybe. One of these houses had disgorged its insides through a blackened hole on its inland side. Scorched armchair, twisted vinyl table, what looked to be a body thrown. Clearly, it was a real town, if gussied up: people had lived in the houses. Other signs: snowmobiles on trailers in the back-yards, swing sets and hanging laundry. Behind and beside the bombed cottage were other houses clothed in coastal cedar shingle, with stacks of old-school wood-slat lobster pots in the yards. The stacks, Jess saw, were still neatly standing, but the houses betrayed mortal wounds on roofs, in blasted doorways.

"What the hell," Storey said. His growing refrain. He, too, was bent to his rifle.

Jess groaned in answer. Said, "They're standing, mostly. The houses. At least there's that."

"Fuckin' A."

"Fuckin' A."

Jess said, "I guess we leave the wagon and go in."

Storey didn't answer. He was moving the scope house to house. Up the one street they could see. He was counting under his breath. Bodies, Jess thought. He could see them, too, twisted and thrown. Some charred, as in Green Hill and Randall, others unburned. Storey slid the scope over the sign that said "General Store," over the wooden Iroquois on its long porch, the carved and painted black bear on the other side of a front door that was blown off its hinges.

"Last night I heard a firefight," Jess murmured. "I forgot to tell you. And I saw flashes, big explosions."

No answer. Storey thumbed up the safety on the Winchester.

"You see something?"

"Not sure." Storey speaking to the rifle now, moving it in increments. As if around a door frame, a window.

"You're not gonna shoot."

"No."

Okay, Jess thought. But he was ready. "Do you think we should go in?"

Storey was breathing the way a hunter—or a marksman—does when he is steadying his shot. "Store?"

"Yuh."

"Do you think we should go in?" Jess said again.

Storey finally lifted off the eyepiece, glanced over. Jess thought he looked in a trance. Or coming out of one. "Hey, hey," Jess said. "Store. We're not shooting anyone. Right? *Right?*"

Storey licked his dry lips. "Yeah," he said. "I was just looking."

"Okay. Good. We don't know who anybody is. For or against. What against what. Jesus. I don't get any of this. Why is the town still pretty much standing?"

Storey blinked, stretched his mouth as against some retainer left in too long. Seemed back to himself. They were talking softly, as much not to startle crows or doves or a covey of exploding partridges. The morning was new, the chill barely above last night's freeze, but Storey wiped the sweat from his eyes with the back of his sleeve. He said, "We've got to go in. See if anyone is still alive. See what they know, see what the hell is going on."

"Okay. Agreed." Jess swallowed hard. The prospect of crossing this wide field with no cover was not appealing.

"We can't cross here. I mean, it would be stupid."

"Right." Relief.

"I don't know if I saw anything or not. Probably just the light."

"Yeah."

"And nobody wants to shoot at us, anyway. If anything . . . if anyone is still alive they would want help."

"Yeah."

"We are unaffiliated."

Jess didn't answer. *Are we?* he thought. *Right now I am on the side of the girl and against the helicopters. And I don't know who any of them are.*

They slipped back into the dark of the woods. Now they didn't speak; they didn't need to. They had been hunting together since they were boys. Jess shucked his pack and put out a palm against the wagon, motioned that they would leave the stuff just off the road, and Storey didn't need to nod. They slipped into the trees on the west, the inland, side of the track. They moved fast through the sparse understory, making little noise. How many times had they moved this way? In tandem, crossing a drainage, moving up on a bull or a buck? But never in pursuit of humans. Were they in pursuit? No. They were just being careful.

They stayed in trees and circled to the west end of the town. Not hard to do. There might have been sixty houses altogether. The streets were not running parallel to the water, but they all ended at the gully of what must be a large brook in springtime. The creek was low now, showing its bones—gravel bars, and blowdown propped on smooth boulders—and it ran through a little rock canyon. It must circle the village and run into the lake on the far side. A footbridge suspended on steel cables crossed the gorge. The little ravine was surprisingly deep, and the cliffs on either side were sheer. Without the little bridge it would have been very tough to cross. On the other side of the bridge a cobble street began. Cobbles. How cute. Clapboard and stone houses lined it on either side. The buildings were not widely spaced, but they were well built and quaint, with wide porches and flowerpots hanging over the railings and gracing the front steps; and the wood-sided cottages were painted white and yellow and brick red. Again, lobster traps in the front yards, colorful lobster buoys tacked to the sides of toolsheds. Jess rocked with vertigo. Lobsters were ocean; last time he checked, the water down there was a lake. He shifted ten feet to his left so he could get a clear view down the middle of the bridge and the street, down to the dock and the water. Nothing moved. Except, almost imperceptibly, the boats at their moorings. He blinked, as if trying to clear his sight. A few of the boats were clearly lobster boats. Not full-sized, but scaled down like the lighthouse. Half-sized replicas of classic Down Easters with open sterns and winch arms over the starboard rails. Jesus. He had never heard of such a thing. If a pint-sized Penobscot ferry rounded the point and steamed into the cove with a double blast of its horn he would not have been more surprised. They had been coming to these woods for fifteen years; he would have thought that a contrived half-shrunk seaside village in the middle of the big woods would be a famous tourist attraction, like the gingerbread cottages at Oak Bluffs.

"You see the boats?" Jess whispered.

"Yeah. This is screwed up. I mean, it's kinda cool."

"Any other day it would be cool. Let's go. I gotta see this place." Jess stepped to the bridge before Storey could stop him.

They moved slowly down the right side of the street, house to house, rifles unslung and across their chests. To the side of one house and cautiously around the front to the side of the next. No dog barked, no cat watched them from the shade of a porch rail. There were few vehicles, but they were not completely absent. On this street Jess counted six: four pickups, an old Bronco, a rusted Subaru. Two of the trucks carried blue plastic barrels in the beds, the kind lobstermen used for bait. Carrying it a little too far, Jess thought. He wanted to call out as they had in Randall and Green Hill, but the silence of a mostly unscathed town prevented him. The fourth house was fieldstone. Two stories with a wooden porch. They crouched in its shadow.

"I'm kinda creeped out," Jess whispered.

"No shit."

"Doesn't seem like they left anyone alive. Neither animal nor human."

"I know."

"We might search the houses."

"Not yet."

"Okay."

"Let's get to the dock and check the lighthouse. Somebody put up a fight from up there. Then we can double back."

"Okay."

Storey stepped around the corner of the porch, and the shot cracked, and Storey was thrown back and sprawled. Hard sting in Jess's cheek. Oh Christ. He, too, stumbled back, hand to cheek wet with blood. Storey was on the ground, sitting like a kid who had fallen off a swing in the schoolyard. Jess guttered a *"Store, Store!"*—expected to see a gut pile in his lap. But Storey turned his head and gaped, soundless, then heaved and caught his breath.

"You all right?" Storey gasped.

Jess nodded. *"You?"*

"You're all bloody."

Jess held a hand to the stinging cheek, felt the protruding wood. "Splinter." He pinched and yanked and it pulled free. "I thought you were shot."

"Breath knocked out when I hit the ground. Fuckers."

Jess breathed. He could barely hear Storey for the pounding in his ears. His own heart. "Where do you think it came from?" he said.

"I dunno. Sounded high. Maybe the lighthouse. Fuck." Storey bent forward, reached for his rifle in the mown grass, tugged it to him. "We need to talk to these guys. Tell 'em we come in peace. Hold on." Storey grasped the sling of the gun and stood, huffed a breath, gathered himself. Took a step as if to test his status: okay, he worked. He trotted to the back of the house, where they could see a clothesline and laundry pinned. He was not in view of other houses or, presumably, the line of fire, but he did not dally. He ripped a stained white T-shirt from the line and hustled back. On the way he picked up a rake leaning against the fieldstone wall. Jess nodded. Storey scooped a loop of orange baling twine out of the grass and knotted the sleeves of the shirt to the rake handle to make a flag. He crouched and slipped to the corner of the porch, kept his head below the deck.

"Hey!" he screamed. "You fucker! We come in peace!"

Jess said, "Jesus, Store, be more diplomatic!"

"'Kay." Then: "Hey! Motherfucker! No harm, no foul! We know you're scared! It's *scary*! We just wanna talk! We are unaffiliated! Can you hear that? *UN-AFF-IL-I-ATED!*"

Silence.

"We've got no beef with anybody!"

Storey stuck out the flag, well clear of the porch. He shook it. "Okay, great!" he yelled. And the next shot cracked and bit off a corner of the porch deck, a chunk that smacked and ricocheted off the clapboard of the next house back.

"Damn!" Jess exclaimed.

Storey crouched low. "Let's get out of here," he breathed. "Go back to the woods and think about it. We're clearly not welcome."

"Shit, yeah. Okay."

And just then the pressure wave hit. The explosion shook the ground. It was a charge from back up the hill, and they both hit the dirt, covered their heads. The thunder echoed across the lake below them like a skipping stone and rolled away.

"That was the bridge," Storey said from under his arms.

///////////////////////

The bridge. No way out now but across the open field or on open water. Neither a good option. Jess lifted his face, spat out grass. "Why in hell would they do that?" he said. "Trap us in?"

"Same reason they blasted a young girl into chum."

"No witnesses."

"Must be."

"We don't even know what the hell we're witnessing. Except some creepy tourist trap."

"Let's tell that to the dude in the tower. Or wherever." Storey reached out from where he lay and grabbed the rake, shoved the handle and shirt out beyond the porch again. Sharp report, immediate. His head was lifted off the grass, half cocked; he was using both ears, the way he would listen to an approaching elk. He was echolocating. "The lighthouse," he said. "Sonofabitch. I'm taking him out."

Jess said no word. They stood and he followed Storey behind the house, past the hanging laundry, behind a one-car garage with vinyl siding. They moved down a sort of alley now, a grassy dirt track between staggered backyards and sheds, heading for the water. A steel Jon boat on a trailer, patched with welds, stuck halfway into the right-of-way, perforated with a spray of neat holes. Jess made the mistake of looking over the gunwale. A man lay in the bottom, a big man in coveralls with part of his skull in a baseball cap that lay beside one ear. Congealed blood pooled in the scupper and under the bench seat. Storey didn't stop. He said over his shoulder, "Someone thought they'd head up the road with this boat, had second thoughts, and unhitched. Left their buddy."

"Maybe it was his dad. Or son."

"Likely." Storey's tone was edged with a cold steel of contempt, or hatred. Jess had never heard it before.

They passed a doghouse nailed together from slabwood, a stake and chain, a Catahoula hound at one end of it lying on his side, his short cream-colored hair constellated with the dark flecks of his breed, and blood. His tongue lay on the dirt, and he did not stir as they walked by.

The last house in the line was a gray Victorian trimmed in black, with gables and a wraparound porch, all too small, like most things in town. Beyond it, the sidewalk T'd into Water Street and the dock, except the street was not so much an avenue as a cobbled plaza, forty yards across at least, lined with archaic streetlights whose lamps hung from wrought-iron hooks. Of course. Directly across was a red shack, not much bigger than a tollbooth, which must have sold berths to the dock, or held the boat keys. Beside it was another bronze statue, same style as in Randall, probably the same artist, this time a fisherman in slicker hat beside an overturned dinghy, repairing, of course, a net. They peered around a corner of the Victorian. One eye. There was the lighthouse, its broken windows beneath the block glass bubble of the light. Jess thought it looked like a very skinny coffee percolator with a small hat. He turned to confer and—

The shots clapped, one on top of the next. One tore gravel into their legs, the other punched a hole in the clapboard of the house. They dropped. As fast as a shot deer, but they were not hit, they hugged their rifles close and rolled underneath the deep porch and scrambled back into the dark.

"Whoa," Storey huffed. "That was two. Two more. Those guys were behind us."

"Makes three."

"Three at least now. Now I'm really pissed. Let's go."

"Where?" Jess said.

"We sure as shit can't hang out here. They are probably moving right now. We need clear lines of sight and we need cover."

"I'm glad you can think right now."

"Listen, Jess, can you see the red shack by the dock?"

"Uh, yeah. Jesus, Store, they are really, really trying to kill us."

"Jess, listen. *Listen.* See the life-sized sculpture beside it?"

"Yes."

"It's like God put that there just for us."

"God?"

"It's like a damn duck blind. Clear view probably of the targets, and cover. You ready?"

Jess groaned. "Yes, ready." He started to crawl for the light. Felt Storey's hands on his pant leg tugging him back.

"No! No!" Storey hissed. "That's where they expect us. To bolt from under the porch. You can bet all three rifles are trained on that spot. Stick one finger out there and— *Look*."

"What?"

"This thing wraps. Look, past that support post. We can get by it, squeeze between the concrete and the post. I can see light where the front porch meets the front steps. We're going out the front."

"The front?"

"*Yes*. We can stay back in the dark and get a bead on the tower. From there it should be line-of-sight. We'll fire off two rounds into what once were windows and sprint. The dude up in the lighthouse will be taking cover, the others will be trained on the side porch. They're gonna have to be very good to swing over and catch us running."

Jess tried to picture it. He was having trouble stringing together the sequence, as he had with the helicopters and the girl. It was as if this lake, or maybe all the smoke, or the trauma of what they'd witnessed was scrambling his sense of time. Or timing.

"Wait," Jess almost pleaded. "Again: We don't go out. Not here. We crawl up front. We shoot at the lighthouse, then sprint for the statue. Take cover."

"Simple."

"Simple," Jess repeated. As if repeating it would make it so.

//////////////////////////////

Are you scared? she had said. They were camped at the end of a twelve-mile washboard road in southern Baja. They were alone. Until now. From the screen window of their VW bus they could see only the shadow arms of the tall Cardón cactus gesturing against the faint luminosity of the bay. The luminescent rip of waves. And flares, shooting over the beach from the top of a high dune. And they listened to the growing growl of outboard motors and the voices of men. Nothing happened in the middle of the night out here, in the middle of nowhere, but drug drops. They had heard recently of one American couple who had been camping and surfing, as they were now, and who had accidentally witnessed a drug delivery and had been buried alive.

You scared? she repeated.

Yes, he said. You?

Oh, yeah.

What should we do? he said.

Count our blessings, she said.

They barely breathed. They listened. Out of the chorus of sounds half muted by distance they heard snatches of "gringos" and "camper." Jess's heart thudded against the thin foam mattress. Later he thought it must be how a buck feels, frozen in a field, when he whiffs the close human scent and hears the crackling of footfall.

Now he and Storey were side by side in the shadow under the porch, in prone firing position, aiming at the windows at the top of the tower. There was only a two-foot gap off the ground, and hard to get the angle to shoot that high, but they had it. Lucky the lighthouse wasn't full-sized. Each steadied his breathing. Jess watched the crosshairs skip with the beating of his heart. Okay, the jump in the scope was tiny, moving at that distance from maybe the heart of a buck to the lungs. Breathe. Beyond the frame of the window was an interior brick wall painted white. What it looked like. That's what he had a bead on. Half pressure on the trigger. *Jesus, calm—calm down.* And an olive flash. Like a just-glimpsed bird. What he saw, and without thinking he squeezed the trigger home and the kick went through his shoulder and Storey yelled *Now!* And he was squirming out of the gap under the porch into bright sun, too bright, and levering the Savage and he was running. He was lighter, faster than Storey and he overtook him on uneven cobbles as the shots rang from their right, more than one or two, a fusillade crashing into the bright after-echoes of their own reports and zinging electric whine off stones at their feet, the swept cobbles a sun-shimmered expanse impossibly wide, a territory of ingots paved, heavenly killing floor of gold, and in the yellow morning he sprinted as through molasses and heard the subaquatic shouts bending, maybe Storey yelling *"GoGoGoGo!"*

Jess dove. How he remembered it: headlong over the bronze of the overturned boat, and he crashed onto his right shoulder and rolled and shoved his whole self into a belly slide up into the lee of the sculpture skiff and shook. His face was against Storey's back, shoulder blade through the jacket jumping as Storey shifted to his side, said, "You okay? Jess? *Okay?* Fuck fuck that was close!"

Silence now. Storey shifted over, got an eye past the fisherman's bronze low-boots and up to the windows of the tower. Nothing. Shifted back.

"Did you see that? Dude up there, had to be. I think you shot him." Faces turned to each other now, a foot apart.

Jess's blink. Felt an ant crawling on his cheek. A tear.

"Yeah," Storey said in sympathy. "Not what we bargained for, is it? God." Shoved a hand down into his jacket pocket. "You got ammo? Too bad we don't use the same." Came up with three brass-jacketed 180-grain shells in an open palm.

Storey snapped into sharp focus. Jess fixed on his face and nodded. Felt himself reaching for his own cargo pocket on pants leg, feeling to the bottom for the loose shells there. Watched Storey thumb the brass into the open breech of his Winchester, shove down once into the magazine, load another into the chamber, and shove the bolt home. "Damn," he said. "How'd I fire two? Could've sworn I only fired once."

Now Jess. Levered the Savage and replaced the single shell that had been chambered there. The shot that had struck the tower. The flash of green, there then gone. He banished the image, felt no elation, felt nothing. Nothing?

Storey said, "Nobody up there. Not now." He pried off his sweat-stained baseball cap. It was forest green and embroidered with a rainbow trout. Above the band in back were sewn words that read "Silver Gate, Montana." Where they fished last September, after Jan had left, after Storey had called Jess and said, "We're going up to Yellowstone and fish the Lamar." He didn't ask about the separation, just booked Jess's ticket and picked him up at the airport in Bozeman in a rented Escalade. "Thought you'd get a kick out of going fishing in a Caddy," he said. "You know the beast is surprisingly solid. Got XM Radio. Here." And Storey turned the dial to the Merle Haggard station and they listened to *Mama Tried* and Red Sovine singing "Phantom 309" as they drove toward Livingston, and the cold breath of the Yellowstone River poured through the open windows and for the first time in weeks Jess felt that he was alive and that living might be an option.

Now Storey winced a smile and said, "Hate to do this," and, pinching the brim, he flapped the crown of the cap up over the keel of their bronze boat redoubt and the shots cracked instantly, one striking and whining off the solid hull, the other shredding an inch-long tear in the side of the cap. *"Wha!"* one or the other shouted as they both flinched.

"Damn, these guys are good." Storey propped himself to elbows, ran the cap through his fingers with a grimace. "Sorry, buddy." Huffed. Reached across, tugged Jess's ten-day beard, said gently, "You okay?"

Jess's nod.

"Dude was trying to kill us. Kill your best buddy. Right?" Storey's smile meant to reassure, but looked sad, the way Jess felt. "Right?"

Jess's nod.

"So thanks. I mean it. You did good." Heavy breath, reconstituting, tightening the straps, whatever cords held himself together.

"Those guys, those guys that are left . . . definitely two dudes. Or women, whatever. The way the one ricochet sounded, it skipped. Shallow angle. They are way left, our left." Storey motioned with the blade of his right hand, motioned past Jess's head toward the final buildings and sheds at the bottom of the town, the ones closest to water. He shifted onto his side, winced.

"What?" Jess said.

"Nothing. Just stiff."

"What do you wanna do?"

Storey snugged his newly vented trout cap back onto his head, brim backward. "They are really frigging good. We can't do anything."

Jess blinked. "What do you mean?"

"I mean we move one inch from this thing, we die. There's no end-around like before."

"Okay."

"So we wait. We've gotta wait 'em out. For all we know, they think they hit one of us on that run and just hit the other in the head. If we wait long enough they'll come to check."

"What if night falls?"

"I know. We've gotta stay alert."

"Crap."

"I know. Maybe patience isn't their number-one virtue."

"They're fishermen, right?"

"They're fake fishermen, seems like."

Jess grunted. "I could really use a chew," he said. "Look." Jess pointed the barrel of his rifle to a metal sign that dangled by one corner from a post behind the statue of the fisherman. It spun slowly in the light breeze and read in stamped letters, "Lobsterville, Beryl, Maine. Thanks to a generous grant from Maine Tourism and the Cabot Foundation."

Storey grunted. "Weird."

"I thought the Cabot family made cheese," Jess said.

"Cheese and dreams," Storey said, and closed his eyes.

////////////////////////

Sun rose at their backs and the morning warmed. Jess shucked his jacket where he lay and turned his collar up to cover his neck. Good light ahead on the bottom houses. Houses gussied to look like fishing shacks on the coast, red clapboard and colorful lobster buoys striped with blues and yellows and greens. Mesh traps in the yard, stacked haphazardly, as if just unloaded from a day's lobstering. All like a postcard in the long light. Or the picture on a thousand-piece jigsaw puzzle, the kind he and Jan used to do on rare rainy evenings, quietly murmuring, *I found the corner, here . . . Here's the next . . . I need a red and black, black stripe . . . Dude, don't force it! . . .* Patter of a life proceeding on smooth waters. The scene here so disorienting Jess seemed to smell salt water, drying kelp. Actual laugh of a lake seagull didn't help, the herring gulls here veering among the masts of moored sailboats, chattering and crying. As surreal, he thought, as everything else in the past week.

No sound, footfall or gunmetal. Jess crawled to the stern of the bronze skiff and put his eye to a pencil-thin crack between bronze transom and bronze rudder. Have to hand it to the sculptor, he was literal. There were screwheads on the rudder post. Good thing—the gap provided a prospect, however narrow, and Jess was certain the crack was so thin they would not detect the movement. Blank windows, blank doorways, empty porches. No one at the corner of a shed. Whoever was shooting at them *was* patient. Because they were somewhere up there—at least two—kneeling or prone or benched, maybe leaned into a rifle propped on a sandbag, maybe behind one of those lace-curtained windows. Unwilling to give away position, willing to wait it out. Maybe they even had a spotter standing behind them, calling the shots.

He slithered to Storey, rolled on his back, closed his eyes against the sun. Just a second here, he thought; a second of repose. Storey made no comment. They both knew that now was not the time to take a nap. Knew each other well enough to know that the other would not fail and sleep. That if one closed his eyes now it was only for a needed moment.

Jess's eyelids seemed crimson in the full bore of sunlight. If any color at all. Veined as if a map of rivers viewed from very high, a satellite view. A blood country, rivers and mountains washed in it. He felt his mouth twitch. If he had killed a man. Was the man afraid of *him*? He couldn't imagine, but that was clear. Was the man in the tower defending his own family, who were hidden somewhere in the town unmoving, as he and Storey were huddled now? Was he a restaurant owner? A busboy? They had seen the sign: "The Black Pearl, Chowder House and Spirits." Too cute. Anything too cute always seemed to be hiding something, maybe nothing more menacing than the daily pain of normal life.

Whenever he had killed before—an animal—he had thanked it. Elk, grouse, deer, trout. Thanked it for surrendering a life so that he might eat. It never felt contrived. He recognized every being's right to exist, knew that everyone—ant, mushroom, mouse, owl—was just trying to make a living, and so the thanking always seemed a transaction steeped in rightness, and it seemed the least he could do. But this. The person in the tower had clearly died. He had clearly done it. It had happened lightning fast, but the dude was the first to shoot and the green swatch had vanished as his own shot rang. He felt himself drifting. Untethered. In his torso a rising nausea. He rolled onto his side, away from Storey and out of the full sun, and forced his thoughts away. Gratitude. Return to something like appreciation—it always grounded him.

I am grateful for Storey. I am grateful for this dumb sculpture of a saltwater fisherman and his boat a hundred miles from any coast.

How did that happen, anyway? He found himself wondering about the life-sized bronze that shielded them. And what about its maker? Odd to think of that now. Did the man or woman grow up admiring the sculpted works of Remington and turn to replicas for the public commission? Because this was a replica, nearly. He wondered if the maker put a real skiff through a CAD duplicator. She could not have put the fisherman in his gear through the machine, or maybe now, with digital tracing, she could have. The hands of the fisherman probably had fingerprints, it was that realistic, and Jess noticed somehow, in his panic and relief at not getting shot, that the ring finger on the hand holding the net sported a wedding band. Jess had an image of an artist from maybe outside New York City, maybe holed up in Tarrytown on the Hudson in a spacious studio in a repurposed barn, the artist who wore a light patterned scarf always, like the French, coaxing an old-salt Mainer she had picked up from Rockland or Damariscotta, the man in full anachronistic oilskins confused as she cajoled him to lie down inside a machine that looked like an MRI so that he could be faithfully copied . . .

"Hey!" Storey's urgent whisper, Storey's hand on his shoulder shaking him, roughly. "Hey, wake up! Check your safety!"

"Wha—?" Jess's eyes flew open. For a split second he did not know where he was, thought for a moment he was on his own couch at home in Denver, woken suddenly from a nap. It *was* a nap. With something like horror he saw that the sun was sinking into the tops of trees, on a ridgeline he could see above the burnished skiff, above the town. He had passed out cold and slept. Fuck. Storey had let him sleep.

Jess rolled fast to his knees, scooped up the rifle, levered the action back—a shell was chambered, good.

"What?" he said again, almost a gasp.

"They're moving. I heard it." Storey was whispering fast. "Clicks, a latch, boot scuff. They probably think by now we're dead or passed out." He didn't say: We almost were. *You* were.

"Okay," Jess said. Was it? Okay? He was trying to clear his head, fully wake up. Also steady himself. Killing another human, it was . . . not something he was getting used to. The air off the lake was chilly and he sucked it in gratefully.

"Get ready," Storey said. "Listen," he whispered and put a finger to his lips. Jess watched his oldest friend notch the bolt of his rifle back to check for chambered brass, then shove it home. He watched him thumb the safety off and suck in a long, steadying breath. Watched him stare sightlessly at the cobbles beneath his knees and tune his hearing to the plaza beyond their blind and intone something to himself only he could hear. Suddenly, sharply, his hazel eyes bored into Jess. "Get *ready*," he mouthed.

Oh. Yeah. Fuck. Jess rechecked his own rifle, shoved the slide of his own safety forward with his right thumb, and tried to focus. *Focus!* He heard a click of stone and a low voice—was it?—and in an instant the grog of sleep cleared like fog in a gust and his ear was on the new sounds, his eyes on Storey. Who nodded, whispered: *Now!*

They came over the bronze keel together, a single tandem motion, and they were firing. They both shot scoped rifles, both eyes open, and as soon as he came up Jess found the figure, the sight picture, and led the man like a running deer, big and tan and flying right to left, and he led center mass, and fired and levered the Savage as fast as he could. Fired and fired and swung on the second as the first fell. The blasting of the ought-six to his right was like a clash of overhead thunder, the kind that sends you flat and obliterates all thought but *Live! Fuck, yeah, I'm gonna live!* And the second figure, following, was smaller, small, some blur of green and black and slower, and

Jess swung and fired with instinct and levered and fired, and he and Storey must have hit together, because the man flew off, feet into air, seemed like flight, and arced into near dusk and thudded to ground. Flat echo rolled away over lakewater. Jess's ears rang. He rubbed his right eye with the back of his trigger hand, spat past his left shoulder, turned. Storey's face was blank and taut. He looked past Jess at the lake, or beyond it, and breathed. The crow's-feet at his eyes were threads of white that quivered minutely. Storey blinked hard and let his eyes find Jess. Held up a palm, cocked an ear. Meaning: *Don't frigging lift your head yet.* Jess dropped his chin: *Okay.*

They listened hard and heard it, a groaning, guttural and choked. "Oh shit," Storey whispered. "Wait." Storey belly-crawled to the fisherman side of the boat and peered around it. Two beats in which the encroaching evening stopped stock-still. "Goddamnit," he said, full-voice. And Jess watched him stand, as reluctantly as he had ever seen Storey do anything.

The boy—it was a boy, maybe twelve or thirteen—lay on the clean granite cobbles. Head back, blue-black eyes open to sky. He wore camo that was torn in three places and blood-soaked. Left thigh, right torso, right chest. His breath gurgled in his throat and his mouth gushed blood, and he arched once and heaved, and Storey stepped forward and shot him in the head. Jess doubled over himself and crouched, spread a hand flat on cold stone as if the heedless earth might steady him.

The other lay sprawled twelve feet closer to the water, beside the boy's rifle, which had been somehow thrown. He was a big, heavy-shouldered man in sand-colored coveralls, frayed at cuffs and hems and stained by oil and what Jess recognized as blood. Ginger beard and green eyes open to the dusk. The eyes stared, startled. Why wouldn't they be? His own rifle, a scoped Remington Sportsman, lay touching his knee, and his baseball cap rested over the action as if neatly placed.

Storey tugged the back of Jess's jacket and pulled him to his feet.

"Hey," he said gently.

"I'm all right," Jess said. "I just—"

"Yeah." Storey motioned him to the boy. "Look at this." Storey touched the boy's shoulder with the barrel of his Winchester. On the arm of the camo coat was an embroidered patch, red and white, with the number "49." "And here," he said. He walked to the man and touched the same patch on the breast of the man's Carhartt coveralls. "What do you think that means?"

Jess looked. Mostly, he saw what was probably a father and son seeping blood and splayed to the coming nightfall. Whatever ritual they were used to enacting at end of day would forevermore be reduced to vespers of silence. Jess imagined them seated at a kitchen table in low conversation, scooping up sliced potatoes in cream. He was a good father, must have been to teach his son the discipline needed to shoot so well and to follow him so blindly. Where was the mother? She was not in the scene he envisioned. Maybe it was just the two of them. He got that sense, he wasn't sure why. They lay now on the stones more than a man's length apart, more than two. Why did that trouble him? As if the spirit of the man would extend an arm and try to touch his son. There was no reaching across now, no matter the distance.

"Dunno what it means," Jess muttered. He shrugged. Did *he* do this?

"Jess."

"Yuh."

"They were trying to kill us. They would have."

"Yes."

Storey said, "I may have shot them both."

"Sure." Jess knew it wasn't true. He knew his first shot was perfect, the way you know a free throw is going in before it leaves your hands. He also knew that at least one of the holes in the boy's camo came from the Savage, because Storey could not have gotten three shots off that fast. So.

Clear bowl of sky, the high blue nearly dark and deep enough for the first stars. Probably frost tonight. If there was an answer there, or any solace, Jess could not see it. He turned to his friend. "You don't have to say stuff like that."

"Okay."

"We're in it now. We're in it. Sure as fuck didn't ask for it, but we're in it." He put the barrel of his own rifle on the man's breast patch. "It means forty-nine states. Fifty minus Maine. Secession. Hold on." On the man's other breast was a zip pocket, which bulged slightly with what looked like a hockey puck. Jess crouched and unzipped it, pulled out a tin of Copenhagen Wintergreen. He shut his eyes tight for a moment, as if asking for forgiveness, and tapped the lid hard with two fingers. He twisted it off, held it out to Storey. A fresh can, almost full. Jess was not surprised to see that Storey's eyes were wet. "I feel grateful to the sonofabitch now," Storey said. "For the chew. Weird, huh?"

"No."

"What do we do now?" Storey said. He pressed a wad of chew into his upper lip.

"I was gonna ask you."

But Storey didn't have a chance to answer. The thrub and growl of a marine diesel engine startled the gulls on the dock, and they flew up like blown rags as the two men hit the cobbles. Half crawl, half crouch and run. To where? Neither knew from what direction they were most exposed. The percussive motor revved into a thrum, and it came off the water. One of the moored boats—it was leaving fast. They fell against the town side of the sculpture now.

"Holy shit."

"We were—"

"Yeah, wide open. We were ducks."

"Why didn't they—? The folks on the water, why didn't they engage us?"

"Too busy with the boat. Maybe thought we were more than two."

Storey lifted his head, elbowed Jess. "Look."

"Jesus."

The lake shimmered with a luminous blue at the edges that deepened toward the center. Cutting across it, pushing up a frill of bow wave and leaving behind it a silver gash, was one of the replica lobster boats. White, trimmed with teal along the rails and around the wheelhouse. It was not far off, they could read the name in cursive on the stern—"*Newsboy*, Beryl Harbor." Whoever was at the helm was gunning it now, and the bow rose higher in the water. They could not see the captain, but they could make out two men and a child on the open stern.

"Let's go," Storey said.

"Go?"

"Yeah. Let's go after them."

"Them? Why? It's the wrong direction."

"They'll know." Storey was up, tugging on the shoulder of Jess's jacket. "C'mon. They'll *know*, then we'll know. And then maybe we'll know how to get out of this."

Jess uttered a groan that was not quite acquiescence, but he stood. "C'mon," Storey urged. "They should have keys for all the boats in the shack."

Chapter Five

In the scattering of boats at their moorings, one inboard was larger than the rest. It was a Rhode Island Marine Design forty-footer, two-thirds scale of the lobster boats he had worked out of Newport when he was eighteen. The bigger boats went offshore for three or four days at a time and dropped strings of lobster traps a mile long at the edge of the Continental Shelf. He had been a rail man, swinging the traps up onto the gunwale as they rose out of water to the winch. He flipped open the wire door to the pot, tossed whatever lobster back onto the banding table, rebaited the trap, and slid it down to the stern man. He loved the work maybe more than he had loved any job since. It was high-pressure speed work, paced by the relentless turning of the winch, which rarely paused—the next trap would breach the surface, shedding water, and spin on its leash just as he slid the one on the rail away—and the days often stretched late into night, the repetitive dance colder under the acid lights, the seas often rougher, and he loved it with a wildness of heart he never found again. Maybe he did—in the first months of love with Jan, when the possibility of sharing a life with a partner so game and beautiful dawned on him like the prospect of a strange sea seen from a trackless height.

As much as the strenuous work in big swells, in wind, in rain, he loved the nights cruising between sets. If there was a four-hour night watch, he took it. Because there was nothing better than chugging ten knots on a clear autumn night when the stars turned all together like vast schools of minnows and the biolu-minescence left a glowing green wake a mile long. He'd set the wheel on autopilot and walk back to the open stern and steady himself and pee a stream that sparkled when it hit, and he'd imagine what it would be like to lose balance and tip overboard. They were in the Gulf Stream and the water was pretty warm, and he could probably tread water for hours as he watched the running lights slip away and blink out over the curve of earth. His skipper, Dave, told him that 80 percent of the bodies they found floating at sea had their flies unzipped.

What the open-stern vessel was doing here, turning slowly against its mooring buoy, he wouldn't know. The lake was big, sure—twenty miles at least in length, and here maybe four miles across. Big. But. No lobster and no commercial fishery, he was certain. And it would be an odd boat for tours, unless you wanted to hold a dance on the stern deck. Maybe they did.

Storey was already in the doorway of the marina shack, which had been riddled like the lighthouse. Jess read the name on the stern of the big boat and called out: "Hey! Find the keys to *Claw-dette*. Should be fast."

"Got it!" Storey was already running to the dock. They'd start one of the outboards to get out to the mooring.

"Hey!" Jess called. Storey did not break stride. "Hey, Store, stop!"

Storey nearly skidded on the planks. Pulled himself up, impatient.

"What about the packs?" Jess said. "We can trot right up the road now, right across the field, retrieve it all. Nothing stopping us."

"Fuck 'em," Storey said. He turned away.

"Wait! *No!*"

Storey never got pissed at Jess, but now he did. Jess could tell, because Storey waited a beat before turning back around. He spat, crossed his arms.

"We could starve on the other side," Jess said. "We don't know. It'll take us half an hour, tops, to get the packs and the wagon. We can catch up. This boat is bigger, faster."

"In half an hour it'll be close to full dark and they will be on the far shore and gone. We can come back for the food."

"No."

Storey closed his eyes. "Jess, fuck! They're getting away. We catch 'em, make them tell us what the heck is going on, and come back. Okay?"

"No. They can't move easily in the dark, either. We can track them."

"I'm going. Suit yourself." Storey showed Jess his back and trotted on.

"Fuck you, too," Jess murmured, and trotted after him.

〰〰〰〰〰〰

But he jumped into the first outboard, squeezed the bulb on the gas line, primed the motor, and yanked the cord. He had more experience than Storey with boats. Storey tossed the lines and jumped in and Jess throttled hard so that Storey missed his seat and had to grab the gunwale with both hands. "Damn!" Storey yelled.

"Sorry!" Jess called over the motor.

"No you're not!"

"No!"

Jess turned to starboard sharply and water sprayed back over the bow into Storey's face, and when Storey whipped around they caught each other's eye. If there was a shred of laughter in the look, no one uttered a sound. Jess throttled back just as abruptly and Storey lurched forward and they bumped the hull of *Clawdette*. "You should never make a guy skip his afternoon snack," Jess said and cut the engine.

They just shoved the skiff off, let it drift, and Jess slipped into the wheelhouse with the keys and started the big diesel, and Storey cast off the mooring, and they gunned out of the shallow bay.

Chapter Six

At the helm, he could pretend. For a few seconds at a time. That he was eighteen and on his watch in the wheelhouse somewhere off Nantucket; that he was beholden to no one and not broken-hearted and that the lake, tilting in stillness and luminous with last light, was not a lake at all but the deeps just west of Georges Bank; that he might sing "Barbara Allen" to himself and to the loud thrum of the diesel, sing it the way his father sang it to him when he was a boy, and feel the pathos of the lovers as a fable, a sweet abstraction, and not something personal; that the stars, when they floated out of the dark, would kindle a kinship with the infinite and a longing for adventure.

That's what it felt like then: that the sea and the stars cradled him like something woven in which he swung in the dark, swung to a beat that was his own and yet belonged also to the ocean and the constellated night. Now, in the middle of his life, as often as not, when he looked to the heavens they answered with a presentiment of death and a cold and distant solace.

How did he get here? To the sense or suspicion that somewhere along the way he had been derailed?

Now he aimed *Clawdette* toward a point on the far shore and edged the throttle back just enough not to blow the engine, and remembered. Not so much remembered as let himself be buoyed and transported in time. The throaty sounds of the motor and the wash of the bow wave, the feel of the wheel and throttle under his hands, the rhythmic press of the water against the hull, and the frame of silver-blue through the thick window . . . they transported him. If only for a moment he felt again, in muscle and bone, what it was to stand snug and capable in his own skin, and to wonder at the ramifying vastness of everything beyond it and the possibilities there. How his heart had opened.

He thought, as he scanned the lake for movement, that the value of a life reckoned by the one living it was always determined in relation to the landscape of spirit through which that person moves. How that changes over time. So, if he was in a dark wood now, a spiritual nadir, he might be apt to believe he had wasted his life.

Well. He had just killed probably three people: *Buck up! It's a rough patch!*

The bow thudded as if in exclamation. Probably a chunk of driftwood. The hull thunked twice more and shed whatever it was, and Jess startled and prodded himself to pay attention. *Don't maunder,* he thought. *Keep your shit together. You are not a starry-eyed teenager, thank God. You are thirty-seven, and a whole bunch of folks, it seems, are trying to kill you.*

Would that matter? he thought. *Whom would it matter to?*

He had never envisioned himself alone at this stage in his life. Childless and wifeless. Dogless. He and Storey had grown up in a small town in southern Vermont where family was perhaps the highest value. Few people, even among the most wealthy, had fancy cars, which was a good sign as far as Jess was concerned. When he was old enough to be aware of such things, he thought that wherever Audis and Range Rovers proliferated, such as in the ski resort towns like Stowe or Jackson Hole, the real-estate gods were kings and the inhabitants were warped by envy and status seeking. He knew he had a tendency to oversimplify, but the observation seemed true.

In Putney, the energy seemed to flow toward league soccer, meals and picnics with extended family, and cooperative efforts between families like the maple-sugaring co-op, the Storrs Pond Hockey Association—beginners welcome—and the boathouse and town landing on the Connecticut River where veteran oarsmen and kayakers gave clinics and offered boat storage to locals. It was not a Currier & Ives holiday card. There was alcoholism, incidents of domestic violence, and drugs—siphoning up the interstate from Hartford and Boston and claiming the lives of young people every year. There was plenty of gossip, and there were real fights over the allocation of funds toward the Historical Society, the Cemetery Committee, paving or not paving the Saxtons River Road. But in the context of a wider nation spiraling into an epidemic of polarized communities and fractured families and personal loneliness, it seemed to Jess a haven. When he looked back it did, after he had moved away. When he lived there as a kid he was just swimming in it, just a fish who could never know what water was.

His father was an architect who drove down to Amherst twice a week to teach a design class. His mother had been a math teacher who started, when Jess was about ten, a second career as a surveyor. They lived in a simple, rambling one-story house with Japanese lines—shallow rooflines and wide eaves and small square rafters. Jess's father, Jay, had crafted shoji screens to fit over the glass of the double front doors, and the doors had facing flat half-moon handles. Jay had spent a year in Japan, in the hills above Osaka, doing an apprenticeship in Japanese landscape design. He never pursued it as a profession, but the aesthetic sensibility made a deep impression on him, and many motifs and proportions made it into his designs, unfiltered through what he thought of as the blunt and clumsy interpretations of the Craftsman movement.

The house was on a hill above a hayfield with a view across the Connecticut River Valley to the wooded ridges of New Hampshire. Storey lived very close by, a mile down the twisting dirt road; he lived with his parents, five horses, and two younger sisters. He was three months younger than Jess and they had shared classes from kindergarten through high school, played soccer together in the fall, hunted deer together in November, skied cross-country in the winter, and often gotten the same summer jobs painting houses, mowing lawns at the hospital in Brattleboro, or cutting firewood for a business they started when they were sixteen.

To Jess, Storey's place was an irresistible draw. At his own house in the evening it was quiet and peaceful. His father read poetry and novels, mostly, and his mother devoured books on history, evolution, anthropology. Later Jess thought that his father, in all his pursuits, was focused on the present-future and his mother on the present-past. Architecture was all about envisioning and planning an environment to be; surveying was all about reconstructing the strictures and relationships that came before. In their reading they were both transported, but the places they went were often separated by decades or millennia. Maybe, Jess thought, it was how they got along. They nested like yin and yang, or like boots in a shoe box. If they could not see eye to eye sometimes, it never felt like schism but more like they were looking past each other.

Not at Storey's house.

Storey's house was boisterous, buzzing with activity until the lights were out and beyond. The parents were voluble in love and war, and the yard, the barn, the kitchen rang with frequent laughter and the yells of heated disagreements. One sister, who was just a year younger than Storey, had a wicked sense of humor, knew just where all his buttons were, and was famously stubborn. Cecily was born with cerebral palsy, which required the use of a quad cane; she walked slowly over rough ground, and though her left hand was strong, her right was curled and could only pinch and lightly hold. She was exceptionally pretty, with large soft brown eyes, and she had an IQ of probably 140. Jess had had a crush on her through middle school and she never had to flatly reject him because, over the years, whenever she caught him looking at her she carped, "Forget it, Less-of-Jess, you're too skinny!" He always flushed, his neck got blotchy, and he said something stupid, like "*Nice*. The only thing that rhymes with 'Cecily' is 'messy'! I mean, 'messily' . . ." The younger sister, Annie, was five years behind Storey and so implicitly under his protection. She was fey, featherweight, had cornsilk hair like no one else in the family—all the others were one tone or another of chestnut, like the horses in the meadow—and Jess thought of her as accompanied by a cloud of whimsy, the way Pig-Pen moved within a cloud of dust. In early mornings she swore she saw a green fairy with dragonfly wings and a sunhat who hovered about the window like a hummingbird. When she was seven she read an entire deck of cards flipped by her mother in another room, the calls of "And this one, Sweetie?" getting more and more incredulous and perhaps panicked with each correct answer. Annie was touched, with spirits. She also never got enough attention at home, having parents that—let's face it—drank heavily, and siblings so much older—one a superstar big brother and the other a sister with special needs—and so she was often left to her own devices, which meant roaming fields and woods, collecting bugs, fishing in the brook, talking to and jumping on the horses, and acquiring a certain melancholy or sadness that she carried with her for the rest of her life.

"You see them?" Storey called over the gunning motor.

Jess jigged the lake back into focus. Across the water, in shining blue, he could see a faint rip of silver beneath the far shore, and he knew that within a couple of minutes the *Clawdette* would bump against the dock of a burned estate and their quarry would be hoofing it up some logging road to who knew where. They probably had no idea where they were going, either.

"I've got them," he said over the motor. "One o'clock. This side of the dark patch. Probably a pine wood."

"Yep, I'm on 'em." Storey had unhooked the heavy marine binoculars hanging over the chart table and he was scanning the terrain on the other side.

Jess eased the throttle back, and Storey lowered the binocs, glanced over sharply.

Jess said, "Have you thought about what we're going to do when we catch up to them?" With the engine on easy cruise, he didn't have to shout. "We're not gonna go in full-bore and start shooting. Right?"

Storey stared at him.

"I mean, that would kill the point, right?" Jess spat out the sliding side window and looked back at his friend. "You wanted to talk to them, didn't you?"

"You should shove that throttle forward," Storey said. His voice was neutral. "We didn't hustle our asses to lose them now."

"Yeah, but I'm asking you: what's your plan when you get there? I'd kinda like to know."

Storey shook his head as if trying to clear it of the disloyalty that was presenting itself.

"We don't know jack," Storey said. "We haven't known jack since we came onto that first bridge. It's all been nine hundred percent insane. I don't have a plan for total insanity. Sorry."

"Okay. You have an idea? Like a vague idea? Like what we'll do when we're charging in and fifty yards from whoever the fuck they are? And they are heavily armed and not happy and about to start shooting?"

"No. Yes. I'm gonna hail them and tell them we have zero beef with anyone and we just want to know what the heck is going on."

"That didn't work so well with the dude in the lighthouse."

"No."

Jess's right hand was on the throttle. He eased it forward, one inch of concession. As he turned back to their heading he noticed the pigtail cord and the mic clipped overhead. Duh! He reached up and clicked on the VHF radio mounted there. The digital channel window lit to 16. He unclipped the mic and offered it. "You wanna hail them?" he said. "They'll have marine band, too. All these little replicas have to have radios. Authenticity is their thing."

"Go ahead."

Jess shrugged, keyed the mic. "*Newsboy Newsboy*, this is *Clawdette*. We are"—he squinted at the shore—"two miles west. *Newsboy.*"

Static. It waxed and waned like gusty wind.

"*Newsboy Newsboy.* This is *Clawdette,* to your west. We mean no harm. Repeat, we come in peace. We shoot only when shot at. We want to talk. Only talk. We want to know what the hell is going on."

Snow. Snow in pines, in wind, a whine like wolfcall if a wolf could hold a single thin note . . . Then a fracture like thin ice breaking, a voice: "Congratulations. What is going on is you are dead men. Nice work." And the blip, powering off.

They frowned at each other. Jess kept them at half-speed. Still they came on. And when they were a quarter-mile from the shore they heard the choppers stuttering over the trees.

///////////////////////

They dove in. Not one word spoken, but they hitched the slung rifles square across their backs and dove. Both swam hard for the bottom and they were both jolted sideways and rolled by the pressure waves of the double explosion and Jess panicked and flailed upward, toward the soft lambence of evening sky seen through water, and curled on himself again when the flaming debris pattered over the surface like a flock of hell ducks landing above, and then his own lungs exploded and he breached up, choking, into stinking air and a slick of flotsam on fire. He gasped in acrid lungfuls and choked on his own coughing and yelled and yelled.

///////////////////////

His heart stopped when he felt the squeeze on his shoulder. Flailed around and there was Storey, treading, his face blackened and striped with burns. And shouts came out of him, Jess, screams or laughs or sobs, and he heaved more air and more; his arms grabbed at Storey and he hugged him tight, gripping shoulder, back, head, hearing words, discernible, "Don't fucking drown me! Jess!" and the whispering and hiss of wood and composites burning on water, and the distinct Dopplered throb of helicopters receding.

///////////////////////

That part was not over. There were sinuous channels through burning debris, snakes of black water in the settling dusk, and as they breaststroked through them they heard the pop of rifles— hunting rifles, surely, because they came singly, came as fast as a person could jack the bolt. They came in staggered series, in two distinct percussive voices, like a duet, Storey thought, one clearly firing a larger round. But it was twilight now, and the smoldering fragments of a fake fishing boat cast uneven flutterings on dark water that shifted like an inconstant mirror, and so the shooters, who were clearly hunters and not soldiers, never got a bead.

They swam into a tumbling of granite boulders backed by sloping ledge rock, and if they shook with cold or shock neither noticed. Storey tapped the top of his head with a flat palm—the universal query, "All okay?"—and Jess repeated the motion, "Yes, okay." Neither spoke. Whoever was now trying to kill them was in the woods just yards above. Hemlock woods and pines, they could smell them, and the dried needles floated in a wind-pressed band against the rocky shore. They crouched with feet still in water and shook the guns and checked the slides. Storey buried his hands in his jacket pockets and came up with a palm-full of extra shells, his only reserve. Nodded to Jess, who found three in his cargo pants. Not much.

So much for asking directions, for being polite.

Where was the others' boat, the *Newsboy*? Storey leaned in until his mouth was against Jess's ear, barely whispered, "Boat has to be tied or anchored somewhere close. Such a still night they might've just tied it to a tree, let the keel scrape." Storey craned back over his shoulder. The shoreline to their right, the south, was dim but visible for more than two hundred yards. Nothing there. Storey shook his head, chopped air with a flat palm to their left, north, toward an outcrop of granite. Jess nodded. They half waded, stayed low. The footing was sharp stone and slab and they crabbed slowly, in and out of water. When they got to the jutting point, an eight-foot-high bulwark of stone, they sank to their chests and swam around it. Whoever was above them did not have the angle to shoot down so close to shore.

The *Newsboy* floated there, in a depression of shoreline. She was hastily tied with a single line, and she rocked barely in the half-light, gently grating a boulder at her bow. So close against the shore the choppers had not seen her. Above the rocks fireweed bloomed, the pinks faded in dusk, and above the flowers stood a wall of dense alders, then pines. Whoever had been on the boat had scrambled to high ground to get a clear vantage. They had heard the radio call, they knew what it would summon, and they were not too worried anymore about pursuit: they wanted only to get high and into good cover, and have clear shots should any on *Clawdette* survive an aerial assault. Best-laid plans.

Storey motioned Jess to the boat and pantomimed himself untying the bow rope, and Jess nodded once and waded on and pulled himself over the rail. He went straight into the standing shelter over the wheel, not a true wheelhouse but just an open-air roof over the controls and nav station with a windscreen forward. Just enough light to see the lobster-buoy key chain dangling from the ignition switch. Whoever they were had been in a hurry. Probably knew they'd be in a bigger hurry if they had to disembark tonight, and so they left the keys in. Jess felt the bow swing as Storey jumped aboard, and he turned the key and pushed the starter.

///////////////////////

It took a minute for the firing to begin again. A full sixty seconds, maybe more. The shooters were on high ground with a good vantage westward but not down into the tiny cove, and they'd probably had to reposition. Jess stayed close to shore—it would be tough to shoot straight down through trees and over rock outcrops—and he slammed the throttle full and worked north. But he didn't want to be too close to land and rip open the hull on some outlying rock, and so when he'd gone about half a mile he peeled hard to port and headed straight for open water. They ran without running lights and night was thickening, and he heard over the roar the last few shots pop and fade. Another two miles, halfway across, he banked her again to port, gently this time, eased the throttle back, and ran straight south.

He felt Storey's stare on the side of his face.

"What?" he said. Storey was just a shadow, backlit by the twilight glow of the lake. Almost twilight no longer, soon they'd be running by feel, by the stars. Jess was loath to switch on even the instrument lights.

"I thought you wanted to go back and get the food," Storey said.

"I do, but . . ."

"But what?"

Jess pulled the throttle back to idle and let *Newsboy* drift. It seemed to slide on the water the way a toboggan slides on ice, and through the low chortle of the diesel he heard a loon cry and another answer. "I should've asked you. I was lost in thought."

"You've been lost in thought a lot since—" Storey stopped himself. Since they killed men and boy. Made sense. He himself had shoved it down, turned away. "Yeah," he said. "I get it. Can I have a dip?"

Jess felt himself smile, pried the dip out of his soaked chest pocket. Lucky he'd buttoned it. The chew would be damp in its cardboard tin, but it would be usable. He handed it across. "You cold?" he said.

"Haven't thought about it."

"Me, neither."

"So why not go back?" Storey said.

"Because . . ."

Storey could guess why.

"Well," Jess said. "There might be others. I mean a bunch of families could have been in hiding, right? They'd have weapons. They'd hear us coming and we could walk right into it."

"Sure. But." Storey leaned out the port side of the shelter and spat, handed back the tin. "Hold on, there's stowage under here, maybe a V-berth. Bet you a steak-and-potato dinner."

Jess groaned and Storey reached for the handle of the square door in the bulkhead behind the wheel.

What was in there was a child.

Chapter Seven

Storey jumped back as if bitten, and she crawled out slowly. Jess pulled the throttle back and risked the binnacle light, and in its glow she stared from one to the other. She was not crying. Her face was tearstained but dry, her mouth compressed. She wore lion pajamas with tail and claw feet and a hoodie with mane and ears.

"Where's Crystal?" is all she said.

"Who's Crystal," Jess said.

"My dog."

"I don't know," Jess said. Her pressed lips quivered. Jess was stricken. He had no idea what to say. Storey crouched so that they were level, eye to eye. She would not look at him.

"Was Crystal with you on the boat? Before?"

She shook her head, wouldn't look at him.

"No?" Storey said gently.

She shook her head. "Crystal was with Mom and Papa." Her mouth quivered.

"Those weren't your parents?" Storey said. "Hey," he said gently. "Was that your mom and dad with you on the boat?"

Now a tear leaked and ran. She shook her mane.

"Where are your mom and dad?" he said.

The tears spilled from both eyes now, her lips pressed again. She refused to sob. "I'm a lion," she said. "A brave, brave lion."

"You certainly are," Storey said. "Hey," he urged gently, "are your parents back in Beryl? Back home? Back in the town with the lighthouse?"

"Crystal," she said again, almost as if calling her. "Crystal is *my* dog."

Storey glanced at Jess. Who had cut the engine back to near idle. He said as softly as he could over the puttering motor, "What's your name?"

She didn't hear him, or wouldn't. "She will come back," she said.

"She's a good dog."

"She's the best. She is just sleeping now. What Mom said." The little girl's face crumpled and she fell against Storey and he put his arms around her and her mane, and she sobbed so hard he thought she might drown.

***

He let her cry and cry and he patted her back and repeated again and again, "She's just sleeping, Crystal is sleeping, she's the best dog . . ." and after a while he stood and held her in one arm and she passed out over his shoulder.

"Now what?" Jess said.

Storey shrugged against the sleeping girl. "She said clearly that the people on the boat weren't her parents. Maybe friends of the family, who knows." He hitched her higher against his chin. "We've gotta go back, don't we?"

"We do?"

"We've gotta search the town for her parents. For anyone."

"Like I said, the last time we tried that it didn't go so well."

"You have a better idea?"

"No."

For the first time that evening a cold breeze pressed over the aft quarter and rocked the boat, and reminded them that it was late September and they were soaking wet. A northeast wind that might bring weather. They'd been lucky the last few days. Or maybe, Jess thought, "lucky" was not the right way of putting it.

"Well," he said. "We've gotta make a fire, find food. So . . . I guess we do. Go back. All of our stuff is sitting right across there, on the hill."

"Right."

"I guess we could search for her people in the morning."

"Okay," Storey said, as if it was Jess's idea.

///////////////////////

They did not run in to the town dock. They had learned their lesson. They got within half a mile of shore and cut the engine way back, until they were barely moving and the motor was a low chortle, and they eased their way into what seemed a coast under blackout. They could see by starlight and the light of a rising, dusky quarter-moon the white-painted lighthouse standing vigil over the harbor. They could see the rough shapes of the clustered houses climbing the hill toward what they knew was the blown bridge, and they could see the pale curve of dirt road ascending the hayfields into the black woods. Jess edged *Newsboy* over to the south and they came into a small clearing a mile from town. Looked to be a dock there, and there was, and a little boathouse still standing. Good. There would be some kind of track or drive that intersected the dirt road they'd walked in on and that they must have missed in their hurry that morning.

Could it have been that morning? Again the dizzying sense of time compressed. Or expanded—Jess didn't know. He knew that, standing at the wheel, wet-through and shivering now, and piloting a miniature of the boat he had worked on as a teenager, and motoring toward a spurious coastline carrying his best friend and a child in a lion suit—he knew he was moving in dream territory. It would not have surprised him to wake with a start and find his pillow wet.

He didn't wake. He cut the engine and let the boat slide into the dock without power and, with just enough headway, he turned the wheel and offered the log piling the starboard rail, and Storey reached into the forward cubby and yanked out a wool blanket and with one hand twisted it and piled it and set the girl down still asleep. Storey hopped to the foredeck and fended the dock off with one boot and jumped across with a line. Jess dropped the starboard bumpers and reached up and cleated the stern line himself. *This time you're coming with me,* he thought, and he grabbed the key on its buoy key chain. He picked up the girl as gently as he could and handed her up, and he climbed after. "Let's go," Jess said. "I'm frigging freezing." And they went through the boathouse and found a good track, recently mowed.

Chapter Eight

Storey's mother loved Jess. He was an only child with pretty serious parents, and the way he sat at their kitchen table and sometimes looked baffled—partly anxious, partly thrilled—and wasn't quite sure what to make of the drama, of whatever noise, whatever raucous storytelling . . . his presence made her aware that life in her house was possibly rich and terrifically entertaining, and certainly never boring.

His sensitivity was a mirror that she came to depend on. Sometimes, when she drank too much, she sat Jess down at the table and made him recite his latest poem. Back then, a poet was all he wanted to be, preferably Chilean or Brazilian. That and an international soccer star. She would badger him until he acquiesced and he would shyly proffer a stanza or a few lines, never the whole thing. It usually terrified him, but he felt, too, a frisson of affirmation and an unburdening. At home he never shared his writing; his parents were too erudite and he feared more than anything a polite smile, a civil encouragement. But Storey's mother, Hannah, was never polite. She could be ebullient, sometimes indulgent, but never simply polite.

And so Jess spent many evenings at the Brandts', and nights, too. There was a small heated room in one corner of the big old barn, off the tack room. There was a bathroom between the two. The room held a sewing-machine table and a bed and a window that looked over a field and treeline and down folded hills to the valley.

The room, like the rest of the barn, smelled of horses, and also of saddle soap and leather and sweated blankets and oats. Hannah made up the bed with worn flannel sheets and a pile of tatted heirloom quilts. Storey's father, Daniel, had gone to Dartmouth College, about an hour up the Connecticut River, and had been a celebrated ski jumper there, and the only decorations in the room were a fanciful Winter Carnival poster featuring snowy hills and ski jumpers with wings, a green cloth college pennant, and a rifle rack holding two rifles and a shotgun. The rifles were a .22, a deer-hunting .270, and a stainless-steel Winchester Marine shotgun. Daniel was a dedicated hunter, and in his youth, before he had met Hannah, he had sea-kayaked up the inside passage for six weeks along the B.C. coast and had brought the shotgun for bear protection and to hunt ducks. Now he was a family doctor with offices in Putney and Brattleboro, and Jess idolized him. He was a short man, maybe five-seven, with a trimmed beard and hazel eyes behind round tortoiseshell glasses that were usually sparking with humor and mischief. A consummate storyteller. A woodsman who had no problem camping with minimal gear for days or weeks at a time. What was not to idolize? But mostly what Jess loved about him was that he seemed to love Jess. Daniel brought him into the fold and treated him like a nephew who could have been a son except for the inconveniences of birth. And he seemed to appreciate Jess's own attempts to spin a yarn and laughed with real delight whenever Jess shared something quirky or some story that featured the fragility of human vanity.

Storey was so close to his father in spirit if not demeanor that he was not jealous of the relationship; he made room for Jess as if he were the brother he'd always wanted. And so the Brandts, who were always jostling, jostled enough to squeeze Jess in. Jess could jog down to their ridge in seven minutes or ride his bike in three, and by middle school it was fair to say he spent two or three nights a week there. And he slept better under the heap of barn-smelling quilts than anywhere else on the planet. Happier. Sometimes at night, looking out the window at the flowing shadow of the treeline under stars blown like grass seed, and listening to the barks of geese drifting down from the high dark, he felt that he might die. Not perish, but simply cease at the apex of his own fullness. There would be a rightness in it. Joy could not be sustained for more than a minute, but what if one was lifted on a wave of happiness and—right on the breaking crest—one's spirit flew off like a windtorn albatross?

What if. As he followed Storey up the freshly maintained track that smelled of shorn grass and trimmed saplings, Jess thought: *I am already dead. A long time ago I died of fullness a hundred times and so now I need not be frightened. But I am. More now than two nights ago. Because, I guess, now we are three.*

///////////////////////////

The track climbed and topped the ridge and broke out onto the smooth dirt road. Easier now to see, as the woods over the road opened to a swath of sky, and the road itself was sand and seemed to give off a faint but integral light. They turned right, north, back toward the town and their gear at the top of this last hill. They walked side by side and Jess could see that the girl slumped over Storey's shoulder and was still fast asleep. Who knew what her own last two days had been like; the village had been half decimated.

At the top, just inside the trees, they found the packs and wagon where they had left them, and they rearranged the provisions to make a central depression, and they made a bed for the girl on the sailcloth with one of the flannel sleeping bags. It was a high load, and Jess pulled the wagon carefully over ruts and bumps. They walked back down the way they had come, to last night's camp in the little clearing a mile back, and they quickly made a small fire and laid the girl in the bag beside it. By headlamp now, they gathered a heap of sticks and limbs and piled these next to the flames and stripped off the wet clothes and hung them there on the tangled stack and broke pieces out of it to feed the fire. They kept their thin wool long underwear on, and it dried quickly in the wavering heat. The girl was curled in the bag with only her mane and ears sticking out, and the mane twitched and she whimpered in her sleep and cried out. Jess noticed that one hand went to her hood and gripped the edge of the mane as if it were a lifeline. He'd had a furry plush skunk when he was little that he'd clutched the same way. They stoked up the fire and then banked it, and they laid their own bags on either side of her and pulled the blue tarp up over them all like a blanket, and Jess slept like someone half dead.

When he woke the sun was already firing the tops of the trees on the west side of the clearing and the blue tarp was white with frost.

Chapter Nine

He had dreamed of Dusty Ridge. That was the name of the road that wound up the east side of Putney Mountain, the road that Storey's place was on, and his own. The road climbed out of the valley and wound through orchards, forest, hayfields. Past one family dairy farm at the top of Tavern Hill. He dreamed that he was on a bicycle with no seat and so he stood as he rode the steep pitches and stood as he rolled down to the next and his legs seared with effort and no rest and the road went on and on, rolling and climbing, past dark-windowed houses and empty farmyards and it never ended. That was it. When he woke, quivering, he thought that it was one version of hell.

They made a fire so that she could have a hot breakfast. The sun broke over the trees and ignited the frost to a crystalline brilliance that for a few minutes blinded them. They turned toward the popping flames and smelled over the fire the yellow leaves releasing and floating to the grass on no wind. The pale wood smoke drifted straight upward out of the meadow. Jess wondered if anyone in town who was still alive would notice the faint plume.

She sat up out of the sleeping bag and rubbed her eyes with her fists and took in the campfire, the clearing, the two men, and her mouth opened and she stuck the knuckles of one paw in it and Jess saw the lion breast heave. "Where's Mommy?" she said around her fist. Her eyes were huge. "Where's Crystal? *Crystal!*" Storey was beside her. He stretched out his arms and lifted her from the bag until her tail and the claws of her feet were clear and he brought her to him and simply hugged her. He held her tight and rocked slightly and said, "I'm Storey, we're going to look for Crystal and your mom after breakfast." He repeated it as the bundle heaved and he let her cry and cry against him, and Jess watched as her arms, which curled tightly between them, reached up finally and one groped for his neck and the other clawed into his beard. She pressed her eyes into him and sobbed until there was nothing left. The frost had melted in the grass and yarrow and goldenrod, and the meadow was wet and glistening, as if after rain. Jess rummaged under the sailcloth of the wagon and found a can of Quaker oats. He dug out the wire grill from the sailboat hibachi and pressed it flat down on the half-burned sticks and dusted embers. He emptied a quart water bottle into the small pot and added oats and stirred it as it boiled and as the girl's breathing steadied.

Storey shifted her and stroked her mane and said softly, "Everything is going to be okay. We're gonna go look for Crystal after breakfast. Okay?" Said it until she pulled her head away from the soaked patch on his jacket and pinched the hem of her mane hood as she had before, as if reminding herself that she was a lion and finding courage there, and said, "Are you a friend of Mommy's?" and he said without hesitation, "Yes. In a way. We've never met but she's my friend." The sincerity in his voice was unmistakable, and the girl pushed back the lion hoodie from her forehead and rubbed at the red line it left and compressed her mouth and nodded at Storey through bleary eyes.

"You like oatmeal?" Storey said. "With lots of honey?"

She nodded.

"How about funny dogs with one ear that can sing when you play the harmonica?"

She thought about it, wiped one eye with a paw. "One ear?" she said.

"Her name is Mickey. She got it bit off by a raccoon."

The girl frowned. She got serious. "Did it get blood?"

Storey realized his mistake. He said quickly, "Not much. We taped it up, she's fine. Wanna see her sing?"

The girl nodded, unsure. "Okay, hold on." Storey shifted again, so that he could reach for the phone in his pocket. Quick glance to Jess: *Dude, I know I'm about to use precious battery, but I think it's worth it.* He lit the screen, and as he brought the phone up she reached for it. "Who's that?" she said. Storey hesitated. Her fist worked out of the claw and she tried to grasp the phone.

"That's Lena, my wife. And those are my two daughters," Storey said.

The girl worked her arm free of his neck and reached for the phone now with both hands. He let her take it. She brought her face close to the screen. "Ohhh," she said, crooning to herself.

"Pretty hair." Then: *"Skinny like a stick, like a bean, like a bean."* It was some song or ditty and Storey felt himself wince. "What's her name?" she said, and Storey was relieved to see that she was pointing at little Geneva.

"Geneva," he said.

Jess covered the pot with its lid and set it on a flat rock beside the fire. Storey played the video for the girl. It began with him playing a crude blues riff on the harmonica and she frowned hard as if tasting something sour, and then Mickey the one-eared dog tilted her head back and began to howl. Not howl, exactly, but yelp and moan, in a sympathetic rhythm. And then the dog lifted her song into a sustained register, something between a woodwind and a ballistic whine that might have broken glass. The girl was transfixed. She twisted her lips, tilted her head, grabbed a hank of her own hair, and then worked her mouth into a credulous unconscious half-smile that was goofy and earnest and seared Storey's heart.

When it was done she said simply, "Mickey." And: "Do it again."

They were in no hurry. They had coffee now from the boats, and two cans of sweetened condensed milk. It was a brilliant fall morning in one of their favorite territories on earth, and the air stirred barely with the particular sweetness of fallen leaves and turning woods, of moss and spicy ferns and wet earth. They had two nested pots and Jess poured most of a two-quart water bottle into the larger one and shook coffee grounds from a bag until they rounded on the surface, and he set the pot on the fire to let it boil and rise. He was hit with the aroma as it heated and he closed his eyes. He thought again that he might pretend— that the world was a vessel of beauty and peace. He didn't have to: The clear cold morning was real. Storey was real—his chosen brother—and he had Jess's back as always. These woods, in their exuberant transition to a dark and frozen winter, were real. The coffee he would soon pour into cups that would warm their hands, the welcome heat off the fire, the quiet wheezes and pops as the flames burned down were all real. One could focus, couldn't one? Mightn't one sit in the full bore of a sun just clearing the trees and drink coffee quietly as the meadow dried and the day warmed? And feel a measure of peace?

The formality of the question suggested the answer: probably not. But one could try.

And again: they were in no hurry. Because when you had no idea which direction to go, and the threats were pervasive but at the moment peripheral, you might as well stir a heavy spoonful of condensed milk into a hot cup of strong coffee and sit for a while longer.

///////////////////////////

They still didn't know her name. They found a can of regular milk and poured it into the oatmeal until it was runny, and Jess stirred in generous spoonfuls of honey, and they gave her a bowl of the gruel. At first she shook her head at the blue plastic bowl, but when she saw Storey take a bite and close his eyes and murmur, "Mm, mm, warm milk and honey, my favorite," she relented and scraped the bowl clean and asked if there was more. She had surely skipped a few meals and was starving.

Jess gave her one of the smaller water bottles and she drank. Storey asked if she needed to go to the bathroom and she nodded. "You know what to do, right? You can use a bunch of old leaves like this for toilet paper, okay?" She nodded and walked into the woods, her tail dragging in the grass and Queen Anne's lace.

Again they packed up. They took their time. The sun was warming their bones and unfreezing the crickets, who chirped with ardor out of the grass. When they were ready, Jess hitched the webbing tumpline around his waist and Storey picked up the girl and they went on up the middle of the road.

At the top, at the edge of the woods, with a clear view down across the hayfields to the village, they stopped. Jess dropped the webbing strap and picked the binoculars off his chest. As he had before. Storey set down the girl, who blinked at the town as if she had never seen it before. Maybe she never had, not from this vantage. Storey slipped the slung rifle from back to front and sighted at the lighthouse and scanned. Now there was no movement at the top of the tower, no movement anywhere. Through the binoculars Jess picked up the two bodies on the bricks of the wharf plaza and winced. Hopping over them was a flurry of birds, the white of seagulls and the black of crows.

The men were in no hurry. They studied every structure, every inch of street they could see. Nothing. Storey said, "I guess we can walk right down."

"We'll be wide open. On a straight road, against the backdrop of a hill."

"We don't have much choice. I mean if we are set on going in again. Right? With the footbridge blown? It's either this or the boat."

"Yeah," Jess said.

Storey reached for the water bottle over his shoulder, in the pocket of his pack, drank.

Jess said, "I was thinking I could go down first. I would draw any fire and . . . well, I could scout. I could wave you in if all is good. Go to the base of the lighthouse, say, and take my cap off and wave. And you don't come down unless I take my hat off."

The girl could not take her eyes off the village. She reached up blindly for Storey's hand and he slung the gun and took it. He looked down at the mane on top of her head, the darker-brown ears, glanced at Jess. "You will have no one to cover you. I can't cover you from up here."

"I know. But. We kinda gotta look for"—he caught himself, mouthed—"her mom."

Storey nodded. "How much ammo do you have?"

Jess shrugged. "None. Just what's in the magazine."

"Take my rifle. I still have half a box." Storey began to unsling his Winchester. Jess held up a hand.

"No. I'd rather have what I'm used to."

"Well, how many? You better check so you know."

Jess dropped his pack. He picked up the Savage and jacked the lever, and the top-loading magazine began ejecting shells. He kept working the action until the gun was empty. Only three shells lay on the road. He picked them up, pushed the brass one by one with his thumb back down into the breech and worked the lever one more time so that a shell was chambered. He felt with his thumb that the safety slide on the tang was snugged back tight. Good. Ready. He nodded at Storey, said, "I'll wave my cap," and walked out of the trees, right down the middle of the smooth dirt road.

When Jess was seventeen, he was helping Storey's sister Cecily mount Lupine, her sweet big-boned mare. She had a set of three steps with handrails to a platform that was just big enough for her and another to stand on. With Lupine's halter tied to a ring, the horse rarely tried to move off or even shift when Cecily got on or off her, and Jess was convinced that the mare loved the girl as the girl loved the horse. Cecily loved her so much that the biggest picture in her room was a photo of the strong brown Lupine standing chest-high in flowering alfalfa and looking in three-quarter profile at something that piqued her interest. Her ears were forward and her shiny dark eyes held a sweet atten-tion, and she looked somehow noble and loyal and brave, but mostly as if she was capable of a simple and unbreakable love. It was a powerful portrait that did not belie the horse's character.

So Jess did not even tie the lead rope, he just ran it through the ring, as he'd done before. The mounting platform was a perfect height, which allowed Cecily to maneuver with her cane and pivot and sit against the top of the saddle, and then, with help, bring her right leg up and over. Once she had straddled Lupine and fit her boots into the cup of the specially made tapaderos that covered the stirrups, she was remarkably stable.

"Thanks," she said to Jess. "I'm good." She felt the top of her head with her good hand. "Shoot, I forgot my helmet. Can you please hand it up?"

"Sure." It was lying on grass worn nearly to dirt, a black, velvet-covered hard hat. He trotted down the steps and jogged around the back of the mare and had crouched to pick it up when the horse suddenly swung her butt around and kicked. It was not an annoyed feint but a full strike that caught Jess in the ribs, left side, and blew him off the ground as a grenade would, and left him with no breath and somehow on his back unable to move. He blinked upward. Fleets of purple clouds sheared low over the treetops, and they were painted by a long August light that freighted them with maybe heavenly significance and he thought he might have died. But through his trance he heard screaming, "Mom! *Mo-o-o-om!*" and blinked to see Lupine's big eyes looking curiously into his and he felt the whiskers of her nose against his cheek and smelled her warm hay-meadow breath as she sniffed him. Apparently, there were no hard feelings.

Somewhere up there was Cecily, because he heard her alternately yelling *"Mo-o-o-o-om!"* and "Jess, Christ, can you *speak*?" The breath had been knocked out of him, which was always scary. Also, it hurt to breathe and he was sure he had bruised, maybe broken, ribs. Hannah ran up from the garden, wiping the dirt off her hands onto her cutoffs, and her face replaced the horse's. She leaned close, and her straw-blond hair—which she could never contain with a chopstick—brushed his nose, and her expression was frightened and concerned. He remarked for the first time that she had a spray of freckles across the bridge of her nose that scattered out like broadcast seed onto her sun-burned cheeks. "Jesus," she said. "Jess. Oh God. Can you move?"

He tried to speak.

"Hold on!" she said. "I think I read not to do that." She must have sat up, because her face was replaced by streaming clouds. "Can you wiggle your toes? Jess!"

He wriggled. He heard, "Phew. How about your hands?"

He felt one of his hands lifted in hers and he was relieved that he could feel the roughness of dried dirt and the warmth. He wriggled his fingers and squeezed. "Good!" she said. He lifted a knee. He breathed. "I'm okay," he croaked.

"No, you're not."

"I just got the wind knocked out." He tried to sit up, and a bolt of pain went through his left side. "Ribs," he said.

"Is your head okay?" Hannah said. Her hands were on his head now, cradling and feeling for blood. Feeling his temples gently and rooting into his hair and surveying his scalp.

"Yes. She kicked me in the side."

"Whewww." Hannah's gust of relief. He wasn't paralyzed or con-cussed. "Can you wait here for a sec? I'm going to get Cecily down and then we're gonna get you some ice, okay?"

"Okay," he murmured. He was actually quite happy to lie back flat on the grass and not move and watch the dense clouds.

Sometime later—he would not have known if it was minutes or hours—Hannah's face came back into view and he felt her hand on the back of his neck and she was kneeling beside him and helping him sit up. He winced and she said, "I know. I've broken ribs before."

"Me, too. Playing soccer." He tried to smile.

"No point in going into Brattleboro," she said. "There's nothing they can do but tell you to take it easy and not do anything that hurts."

"Yep."

"Let's get up out of the barnyard. I'm gonna walk you to your room and get some ice, okay?"

"Okay."

They walked slowly, and there was a certain point in his stride that sent a sear of pain into his chest. He put one arm over her shoulder and he noticed how hard the muscles were in her back, the strength there, and it surprised him. It shouldn't have: she spent most of her time outside, either on horseback or splitting wood or working the garden. They went through the outside door to the left of the tack room and into the hutch with the big window and she eased him down onto the bed. "Does it feel best to be on your back?" He nodded. "I've done this before," he said. "I can tell it's just a bruise." "Still," she said. "Hold on. Ice and ibuprofen." She tried to smile as she went back through the door, but he could see that she was terribly concerned.

He might have fallen asleep in those few minutes. Or passed out. When he opened his eyes again she was gently pushing his shirt up and he heard her whisper, "Ow, oww." And he felt the ice pack go gently against his side. "There." She turned for a glass of water on the bed table and then she thought better of it and whispered, "Let's help you sit up first. You can't drink the water lying down, but I think you better take some Advil."

She leaned toward him. Her left arm went behind his neck and he breathed the warmth on her skin, which smelled like sweet grass. Her stray hair fell against his cheek and her dirt-streaked, white open-necked linen shirt fell loose from her freckled skin and he noticed with a shock she was wearing no bra and her breasts were smooth and much paler than the rest of her and her nipples were small and pink, and the next shock was that he felt himself get instantly hard. He was wearing nylon gym shorts, which offered little resistance. As he tried to help her help him sit up his face came into her collarbone and top of her breast and her right hand reached down between his legs to the bed for support and brushed him. He heard her breath catch. "Here," she said, and her voice was husky, "good. Here, swallow these, good, and drink." He drank. But his whole world at the moment was not the water or the four pills or the pain but her neck and the smell off her work-heated skin, which was grass and summer brook, and the freckles that wandered onto the tops of her very pale breasts inches from his nose, and her hair, which streamed down onto her collarbones. Her right hand had found purchase on the quilt between his thighs and now, as she supported his head with her left and he tilted the glass and he swallowed, he felt her shift as if to help him and her forearm bumped into him where he was hard and then she said huskily, "Good?" and he wasn't sure if she meant swallowing the pills, and he nodded. She took the glass from him gently and set it on the table and then she leaned into him and kissed him. He had kissed girls before, but her lips were soft and plush and unhurried. At some point she shifted forward and his mouth was on her breasts outside her shirt, and at some point she lifted it enough and he was surprised how cool she was, and then she stood briefly and worked off her cutoff shorts and in the flash of the image—her standing in the now stormy light of the window in nothing but her gauzy gardening shirt, reaching back to slide out the chopstick and let her thick hair fall—he thought maybe he was dead, maybe he really had gone to heaven.

He was seventeen and it was his first time. She never said, "We can't tell anyone," but he never did. Not Storey, not anyone. She was not sauced, as she often was by the end of an evening. She was clear-eyed. There was no shame in her eyes, and no desperation, either. He thought about that later. There might have been both, in spades, and it would have been a much different act. She did not condescend, or embarrass him with instruction, or take any high ground at all. She met him right where he was. And since she had prepared him a thousand dinners, and suggested afterward a thousand times that he and Storey help Daniel with the dishes, and had taken him to a thousand soccer games, and cheered wildly when he or his best friend made a brilliant play or scored a goal; and since she had helped him hundreds of times with homework and listened with delight as he shyly recited his poems; and since she had yet somehow kept a respectful distance and let him know in a thousand ways that she was not his mother, that his mother knew him best and had the final call in all things . . . it seemed natural and right that she lead him now into this new territory. There was a hunger in her that pressed and tugged him like a steady current and it was not scary but somehow magnificent and it allowed him to relax and give himself. She seemed to know that it was his first time and that he might trigger easily and she made love to him very very slowly and he let her carry him.

Years later he thought it should have been a confusing, maybe traumatic memory, but it wasn't. When he remembered the afternoon he felt gratitude. The fact that Storey, had he ever found out, might have killed him was another matter. But maybe the strangest thing about the episode was that after she eased off him and smiled—it was kind and grateful and warm and maybe a little sad—and said, "You rest. I'll get you more ice in, like, an hour," and after she dressed and closed the door gently behind her . . . after that they carried on as they had before. He came over for meals, spent nights, went on training runs with Storey, and ended by helping Hannah and Cecily in the barn, or Daniel in the shop. It was not as if it never happened, but that the moment was so sweet and natural it would never interrupt the flow of their lives.

That's how it felt then. But it did change, if subtly, the dynamic between the boys. Because ever after that Jess felt he owed Storey a debt. For simply concealing a great fact in his life. And for having a connection with Storey's mother that felt significant and deep, if brief—a connection that Storey could never have. That part felt a little creepy, and as much as Jess tried to banish it, a tendril of shame and the sense of a deep debt remained.

Which was why, he thought now, as he picked up the rifle and walked out of the trees: *Why I am walking down this straight dirt*

*road across an open hayfield in full view of whatever rifle scope. Why
I am leaving Storey in the woods. Why if I die in the next minute it
will be okay, and just.*

////////////////////////

He did not wish to die. But if he lived long enough, and got
drunk enough, he might tell Storey everything, which would
not be good. Nor could he now think of a good reason to live.
That was the thing about living: there didn't have to be one. You
put one foot in front of the other, as he was doing now. Scuff-
ing the packed dirt overlaid with fine gravel and sand. Whistling softly. Hoping the shot would not come, and wishing it
would . . . so that the heartbreak would be quenched forever,
tandem et in aeternum. He had lost his wife, his dog. Ha! *How
did I get like this? I am like a country song.* Except he really did
need to get through this day and the next—to help Storey get
home. And now the girl. Reasons enough. And a morning like
this morning, with strong coffee and a friend and sunrise in a
meadow.

Nor was making love to Storey's mother a capital crime. Even
as he walked down into bright sun and noticed the first morning wind push through the tall tawny hay grass as if a hand
were passing over . . . he thought that he'd been lucky. It was
not a first screw, it was not two teenagers fumbling and afraid,
he was lucky that his first time had been love. Because he did
love her, as deeply as one can love. *Didn't I? Yes. And she loved
me, too.* And he thought, as he walked and braced himself to
die, that every love is like a fingerprint or the unique timbre of
a voice and that there was no name in any language for the love
he felt for Hannah. It was not incest, it was not a first crush, it
was not the adoration of a revered teacher, or the transference

ignited by a therapist's unconditional acceptance, or the depth-less affection for a lifelong friend. Be honest: it was all of these and so could not be any one. Relief. It was a Long Island Iced Tea of love from which three sips could knock you flat, and so he had been shaken and intoxicated and euphoric. And he'd had a hangover, which passed. And he remembered mostly the sur-prise, like a cliff edge, and the delight of falling, and the pure wonder. And the sense that he had been extinguished, died, and at the same time felt pleasure that could barely be distinguished from prayer or pain. Good enough.

Months later, senior year, he took up with his first girlfriend, a boarding student from Oregon. And the first place he brought her was not home, up on Dusty Ridge, but to Storey's house. Hannah's and Daniel's and Annie's and Cecily's. And they had fêted her as a guest of honor, and honored her as another accom-plished equestrian, and she and Hannah had hopped bareback up onto the two most spirited and difficult horses and galloped into a cross-country run that Gwen would never forget for the rest of her life. She came back soaking wet and told Jess breath-lessly that they had pushed the horses to leap off a three-foot ledge into an ice-cold pond and swum them across a quarry. Who *did* that? And Jess almost cried when the two women came out of the barn after putting the horses up and feeding them, came out arm in arm, damp hair straggled, faces turned toward each other and laughing. How blessed he felt then.

But now he had to admit that something snagged. Something hooked in the gut. Admit that maybe there had been something deeply wrong with all of it.

The boom shattered the thought. The shot exploded, and he dove into the high grass off the right ditch.

////////////////////////

There was only one shot, and as the percussion rolled out over the lake and echoed away, he knew in the roundness of it that the blast was from a shotgun, not a rifle. Which meant a killing range of fifty yards max with double-ought buckshot. And he was now at least 250 yards from the first houses at the south edge of the village. What the hell? Who would waste a shot and alert him at the same time? He was flat in waist-high timothy and the seedheads swayed above him and he crawled around so that he was facing the road. The road was straight and ran down into the south end of the plaza beside the wharf—under the lighthouse—and so there were plenty of windows and porches with a clear view of the track. A shotgun did not have a scope, but there might be another shooter, near the first, who did have a rifle with long range and optics, and he had just learned from Storey that there was a good way to find out. He took off his cap and hung it over the end of his gun barrel and pushed it out across the ditch and into the edge of the road. Nothing. Whoever had fired the shotgun was far enough away not to see this bit of movement unaided. Okay. We are already dead, right? Wasn't that the point of all these musings just now? The samurai creed, the yell of Russell Crowe in *The Gladiator*. He had yelled something like that, hadn't he? To his men before the charge? Jess stood. What a crazy bastard. Who on earth . . . ? Fuck it. He stepped up out of the ditch and began walking again down the road.

////////////////////////

When he got to within about 150 yards he broke left and ran through the grass toward the upper end of the village. Seed-heads whisked against his thighs, and he did not sprint, because he did not have to. He just had to get behind the first row of houses descending down to the water and then make his way past them to wherever he thought the batshit shooter might be, and then all he had to do was take him out. Simple.

Take him out. How a person might change in a few short days. Just yesterday he would have thought to get close enough to hail whoever it was, to yell that all he wanted to do was talk. Get shot at a couple of times and the calculus changed fast. He had become, within hours, a predator and a killer.

That's what he thought as he ran: *This crazy person with a shotgun is going to die. And I will dispatch them. Because, though I cannot come up with a great reason to live, I have no patience for people trying to kill me.*

In the middle of the outer row of houses, climbing the hill, he trotted between a cedar-shingled saltbox with a half-sized lobster boat up on a two-by-four cradle in the backyard and a clapboard cottage with double dormers and a sperm-whale weather vane. *What the hell is up with this place?* he thought again. Why this insistence on make-believe? Was it only for tourism? He realized that he could not recall a single fudge or souvenir shop in their progress through the village. A tourist trap would have that stuff in spades. Or maybe all the voting-eligible residents got together in the Grange hall or wherever they did it up here and passed some strange charter based on the premise "If we build it, they will come." Tourists and lobsters. But no lobsters were coming until they evolved like crawfish to live in fresh water. That could take a while. His father would have said the place was "totally pixilated," meaning sparked with eccentric energy, not normal and maybe not quite of this earth. How he felt now. Death maybe was imminent, but he felt like he was trotting onto a movie set, or into a dream. That sense again. He wondered if all wars felt this way.

The shot, as he came out between the buildings, dashed the hope. He ducked back behind the corner of the cottage, ran behind it, and worked between it and the next house down, a neat Cape with multiple decks. He peered around it. Holy shit. There was an old man on the porch of a cabin three houses down and across the street. He was hatless, and his soft shock of white hair feathered in the breeze. He wore red suspenders and patched jeans, an L.L.Bean flannel shirt, Black Watch plaid; Jess recognized it, he had the very same one hanging in his closet at home. The old dude was right out of Central Casting. He wore battered sheepskin slippers and had a dribble of what was probably oatmeal or breakfast gravy down the front of his shirt. Jess blinked the stinging sweat out of his eyes. The man looked like Robert Frost in his last years. Could have been his brother or a twin. The same lantern jaw, doughy nose, no-nonsense farmer mouth that knew no difference between smile and grimace. He was holding a long over-under shotgun, probably twelve-gauge. If he was using buckshot, and especially if the barrel was choked, then Jess was definitely now in range.

The man hadn't seen him, and Jess ducked back and leaned against the gray shiplap siding of his house. Damn. This was an easy shot. He could play the entire motion in his mind, the step to the end of the wall, the twisting of the left forearm through the strap and lifting of the rifle, one more half-step as he pressed the walnut forearm and barrel of the gun into the corner of the building and sighted and flexed against the leather sling, the whole rig rock-solid as he swung smoothly across on the inhale, both eyes open, and found the man in the scope's reticle, crosshairs settling on the blue and green squares of the man's chest, now exhale, pressure the trigger, smooth and steady: *fire*. He might or might not then see the bloom of blood on the flannel, because it seemed a man could drop out of view as fast as or faster than a shot deer or moose. Drop faster than a bullet could throw him or gravity could pull him—pull him home to earth, to the worn planks of a porch that he might have trod for most of a century.

I've gotta stop thinking so much, Jess thought. *And now I'm thinking about thinking. Too many echoes in the world.* Get your shit together! *My mantra, hah!*

Jess thought that the old coot was standing on his porch with his shotgun just the way the farmer did in Western movies: out in the open, brave and tactically challenged—stupid—and quaint, defending his homestead. Didn't he know this was a war? Nobody cared how you looked. Maybe, like Jess, he was just sick of cowering.

"Hey!" Jess yelled from well back of the corner. "Can you hear me?"

"No!"

"No??"

"What are you, some kind of idiot?" Jesus. The voice was like Robert Frost's, too. The same northern New England flattening, not quite Down East.

"Then you got your hearing aids in, Pops?"

"Fuck you! And your skanky mother, too."

"Hey, I come in peace. I swear. And let's not talk about my mother."

"Whyn't you step out and we'll talk about whatever you want. You big ass."

Jess burst into laughter. He found himself laughing out loud. First time in what seemed like months. *Big ass.* God. Good one.

"Hey!" he yelled and wiped the tears from his eyes. "I can shoot you from here right now. Scoped .308. You're standing on that porch like a Beverly Hillbilly, wide open. What the hell was the old guy's name in that show?"

"Jed."

"Like Jed."

Did Jess hear the old man hawk and spit? Damn. "How old are you?" Jess called.

"How old are you, you stupid donkey? Six? Were you put back in first grade? Sure as shit sounds like it. Come on out, we'll play checkers. Or, if that's too complicated, I bet we can find a crayon somewhere and play tic-tac-toe."

"I will!"

"Okay, then."

"If you tell me what the fuck happened here."

"What happened here, gutter mouth, is that you screwed with my morning."

Jess leaned his head back against the fresh-painted cedar of the house and closed his eyes. *Really?* The man had not killed him before only because he'd been out of range. Now he was in range. Was the old dude demented? Didn't sound like it. Jess worked two fingers into his breast pocket and tugged out the tin of chew. He leaned the rifle against the building and twisted off the lid and took a good, respectable pinch of the long-cut and pressed it under his upper lip. He spat. Closed his eyes again and felt the quickening and instant relaxation as the nicotine hit his bloodstream. The mild sense of well-being. Crazy that it could do all that at once. He rocked himself off the wall.

"Hey!" he shouted.

"Not listening!" the man shouted back.

"Who did this to you?"

"You did!"

"I'm serious! We're just a couple of hunters."

Silence. Jess heard the weather-vane whale on the house next door creak on its bearing.

"There's more of you?" the man said. Jess thought he heard a touch of alarm.

"A couple," Jess said honestly.

"More on the ball than you, eh? The others?"

"Can I ask you something?"

"I don't care what the hell you do."

"Do you want to die?"

Silence.

"I'm only asking cuz I can take care of that right now. And you sincerely tried to kill me. And I'm getting tired of chitchat and I can tell you are, too. Just saying."

Silence. Jess peered around the corner. The man was gone. Then he heard the growl of an engine. The growl got louder and here came an ATV, a one-seater with cargo box, bumping into the main street and turning down it toward the water. Jess noticed that the four-wheeler had a plastic rifle scabbard and that the butt of the shotgun was sticking out of it. The old man was probably going too fast. The engine blared, and Jess saw that he was gripping the steering bar the way a songbird clutches a limb in a big wind and he was getting tossed into air as he hit the potholes from whatever recent attack. Jess marveled as he hit the plaza and turned right onto the county road that crossed the fields. *Crap.* Jess ran to the back of the house and watched the crazy coot run his machine straight up the road, up the hill, right toward Storey.

He braced himself for the sound of the rifle. Easiest shot in the world, and Storey would need only one. Or maybe he would try to disable the machine; he really wanted to question somebody. Jess could imagine the initial conversation and would bet money that it would not go well. But all he heard was the clamor of the machine thinning into a whine, watched the ATV top the hill and enter the trees, heard a sort of stutter and cough and the bleep of a horn, then the pitched rev again, and the engine faded until there was just Jess's muttered cursing and squeak of the weather vane and the hush of a gentle wind. And then he saw the two figures, man and girl. She was riding his back and they came hurrying out of the woods and down the road. Storey was hauling the wagon by the handle, not the tumpline, and his pack was strapped to the top. The whole rig looked like it might topple over with the slightest help.

⁓⁓⁓⁓⁓⁓⁓

They had not waited for him to raise his cap. They had heard the shots, and he guessed that they thought he might have been dumb enough to get himself plugged. So they came. Storey would do that. He might think Jess was lying injured somewhere and needed his help. They came straight down the road, as he had, and now Jess stepped into the yard of the house and waved his hat and yelled. The two stopped for two seconds, came on. Jess picked up his gun and ran to meet them.

They convened on the cobbled plaza and scared up a crowd of crows and ravens and gulls and Jess remembered the bodies of the boy and the man and he pointed away from the wharf and saw Storey's thumbs-up as he steered the girl's sightline up the hill. She was on his back and she had both arms around his throat, and still she craned her head back to stare at the figures lying there.

"What the hell," Storey said as they met on the first block of Main Street.

"Telling me." Jess did not want to laugh but he did. They were in a serious shitstorm, but still. "Take it you met Robert Frost."

"Sonofabitch *did* look like Robert Frost. Fuckin' A, spitting image. I had the same thought."

"What happened?"

"Came right up the road—you saw, I'm sure. Right on up, with his shotgun sticking out of the scabbard like it was any other Saturday and he was going partridge hunting—"

Storey was straining against the girl's grip, which was half choking him. He turned his head. "Wanna get down?" he said.

"No" was all she said. She said it definitively, like she was refusing a forkful of peas.

"Suit yourself." Storey turned back to Jess. "So, anyway, here he comes, and I thought about shooting out the engine but then I thought, *Hey, we could use the damn thing.* I mean, at least until the gas ran out. I guess I wasn't thinking about the cars here in the village. And then I thought, *Well, I'll just step out, raise my hands.* So I did. Bastard screamed, 'Outta my way!' and hit the horn, slammed my leg, veered around, yelled, 'I got *nothing* to say!' and tooled off down the road." Storey's hand came down and he rubbed his left thigh.

"You okay?"

"Yeah, just bruised. Goddamn."

Storey turned his head back to the girl, whose head was at last out of the lion hoodie. Her hair was soft and fine and it stuck out in all directions, as if she'd rubbed a balloon on it. Her pale cheeks were flushed and her eyes were shiny. Stress, Jess thought. Yep, her lips were compressed tight again.

"Did you know that old man?" Storey said.

She nodded.

"Do you know his name?"

Silence. Then she said, "Are the bad men coming back?"

Storey winced. "No, honey," he said.

"Why is Cody lying down there with the birds?"

No answer. Then she started to yell. She yelled, "Crystal! *Crystal! It's me!*" Screaming it over and over.

\\\\\\\\\\\\\\\\\\\\\\\\\\\\\\

It took a while to calm her down. Storey carried her into the shade of the closest porch and set her on a wicker love seat and he sat beside her and put an arm around her, but she threw it off and tried to run. He grabbed her, saying gently, "Hey, hey, let's stay here. We wanna stay here, where it's safe."

She twisted back and bit his arm and screamed for her mother and her dog. Storey could almost not contain her. In his own panic he reached back for a wool throw blanket on the seat and yanked her to him and wrapped her in it, the way you would a clawing cat, and let her squirm and scream. Jess thought that if she had another fit like this when they were trying to stay hidden, they'd all be toast.

He stayed on the sidewalk and watched nervously up and down the street and in the broken-out windows of the houses across the way. He did not think there was anybody left, certainly not any shooters, but one couldn't be sure. There might be people hiding in basements, in attics, scared teenagers with their parents' guns, who knew. The wagon was on the sidewalk beside him, and after a couple of minutes of enduring the girl's screaming, which somehow cut him in two, he unstrapped Storey's pack and slipped the sailcloth off the wagon and rummaged until he found rolls of apricot leather bundled into gallon Ziplocs. He took two out. Storey was now repeating, "Okay, okay, calm down, we'll go look for them in a minute . . ." Jess climbed to the porch's top step and unfurled half a roll and peeled off the sticky skin and began to eat it in thin strips, closing his eyes and muttering, "Yum! Apricot leather. My favorite."

The girl's screaming petered out like a fire quenched with a bucketful of water. She craned her flushed, tearstained face toward Jess. "Roll-ups!" she said.

"Yes, yum."

"Mommy makes that. That's mine."

"It is?"

She nodded emphatically.

"It's delicious. Do you want some?"

She nodded, very dramatic.

"Okay. I got one for you. Maybe we won't give Storey any."

Storey still gripped the blanket and looked like he'd just barely survived eight seconds on a rodeo bull. The girl pursed her lips and thought about it and said, "He can have some."

⁂

Storey put her on his back again. Her chin and one cheek were smeared with sticky fruit leather. Again they left their gear, took only rifles. There were the two long streets climbing the hill and three cross-streets, that was it. Storey said, "Let's go to your house. There?" He pointed up hill. She nodded. "Okay." They went to the grassy alley between the streets and climbed. Jess followed, guarding their backs. Seemed like the right thing to do, but if anyone remained and wanted to kill them they were sitting ducks now. She kept twisting back. Gripping Storey's neck and throat like the harder she clutched the safer she might be. But she was looking behind, past Jess, at something on the lake or who knew where.

"Hey," Storey said gently. "Little lion. Is your house this far? Hey."

She squirmed back around, and her attention swam back up the hill. She seemed confused. Her vagrant eyes swept the alley, the backs of the houses. "This is Cody's house," she said.

"Cody? The boy who—" Storey stopped himself. It was a light-gray Cape with a snowmobile on a trailer parked off the alley.

One of the second-story back windows was curtained with a flag that had a large "49" in the center, red and white, same design and colors as the patches. The window next to it had been blown out, and there were streaks of char up the clapboard and a ragged hole in the roof.

"Is Cody nice?" Storey said.

"He's the best." It's what she'd said about Crystal. "He taught Crystal how to fetch ducks."

"Wow."

"Yeah, and he can whistle."

"Cool."

"We play tic-tac-toe. He taught me how."

Jess thought, *Tic-tac-toe is big in this town.*

They were walking slowly. Storey would be guessing that when she saw her house she would react. Storey said, "Cody's dad is super-nice, too."

She shook her head vigorously, swinging the hooded mane at her back. "He's mean," she said.

"He is?"

"Yep. He told Skye she was too little."

"Too little for what?"

"Cody got his own gun."

"Ahh."

"She cried."

"Like a baby."

"Like a baby," the girl repeated but she trailed off. Her attention was wandering up to the half-burned roof they were just passing, to the German shepherd with the bloody neck stretched out at the end of a chain. She twisted far around as they passed and Jess saw her mouth quiver and her face begin to collapse.

"Is Princess sleeping?" she whispered loudly with her mouth against Storey's ear.

"Yes," he said. "She's taking a nap."

"Taking a nap," she repeated. "Princess is taking a nap."

Storey had sounded so convincing even Jess almost believed it. The beautiful dog, who was the color of wheat on her belly and wet maple bark on her back, would rest awhile, then twitch and wake up. Jess thought how Storey's clan, all of them, were great at pretending. If the current reality is too hard to bear or just, for some reason, unacceptable, invent a new one. Hannah. It was not that they went on as before, exactly, he and Hannah. It wasn't that they pretended nothing had happened, nor was the act so clean and unfettered it created no ripples. There were . . . ripples.

"Pay goo," the girl said. She had sagged on Storey's back and she said it with her head turned toward the houses and her cheek and mouth on the shoulder of his jacket. It muffled the words.

"What?" he said.

"Pay goo."

Storey shrugged her higher and said kindly, "Say it into my ear."

"Play group!"

"Ow."

She pointed toward the back of a house with an elaborate home-made swing set with fort and slide and a sandbox bordered with railroad ties.

"That's where you go?" Storey said.

"We make ice pops."

"You do?"

"Unh-huh. We can eat two."

"Wow. Are we close to your house?" They were almost to the top of the alley, two more houses to go. Storey jiggled her.

"Wanna play horsey?"

"No."

"What's your name?"

"Collie."

"Do you know how to spell it?"

Silence.

"Is your house over there?" Storey pointed north, toward the next street and its opposite row of houses. She nodded against his neck. "Okay, let's go."

<hr />

Again they slipped between buildings and came out onto Main Street and looked down toward the water. Jess thought it looked like any neat, well-cared-for seaside village in New England except that more than half the buildings had bullet holes sprayed across the front, burned porches, projectile holes in the roof. The other half stood in a sort of becalmed idyll, preserved and abandoned. Jess wondered why Beryl had not been burned to the ground like the other towns. Had the residents come out en masse and gathered on the wharf, waving white flags? And so been spared? No, there were bodies. But the village was mostly standing. Made no sense. Especially after they witnessed the way the choppers had responded to the girl in the rowboat, and to them in *Newsboy*. That was it: it seemed like they, whoever they were, wanted no witnesses at all. He shuddered. Maybe the villagers had all surrendered and been taken off to who knew what mass grave.

Her house, it turned out, was on the north end of School Street, the third cross-street up from the water. The house was timbers and stucco, with wide eaves and clean lines along a generous, almost rambling width. Maybe it seemed less boxy because it was not hemmed in by other houses; beyond it were only the pines and hemlocks of the deep woods. Despite the broken front windows along the gallery porch and the pocks in the walls, it preserved a certain calm and grace. Also, it was not pretending to be anything. There was not a lobster trap or buoy in sight. No whaling-ship weather vane. Jess thought this was probably because it was off the two main drags, tucked at the end of this side street. Had the attackers been in such a hurry? Had the girl survived because her parents had hidden her in a cupboard and run out with their hands up? Something about the architecture of the house, the unpretentious elegance, suggested that whoever built it would be capable of such an act.

By the time they got within thirty yards Collie had straightened tall like a rider standing in the stirrups and she was calling for Crystal. Storey walked forward and then veered suddenly.

"Hey!" he said abruptly. "I saw the cutest little deer in the trees! Hold on!" He trotted away from the house and toward the woods as she protested and squirmed backward, and Jess took his cue. When he saw that they were well into the trees he jogged up to the house and dragged the big black mutt fast across the street and behind a boat trailer. The poor dog had been gut-shot and nearly torn in half. Jess ran back to the house and heard Storey saying loudly, "Dang! That was the cutest little doe. All spotted! Okay, we can look later."

He carried Collie out of the trees and exchanged a look with Jess and they stepped onto the porch.

"Mommy!" she called. She struggled and Storey let her slide to the boards.

"Hold on," he said. He crouched down till their faces were level. He held her firmly by both arms and very gently said, "We'll go look for your mom in a second. But first Jess has to go in and make sure it's safe. Make sure there's no one bad in there. Okay?"

She looked from the splintered front door to Storey and back and shrank with a sudden fear and nodded slowly. Jess turned the knob and shoved hard with his shoulder, and the door swung on one hinge.

In the movies, when the bad guys toss a place, the books are pulled to the floor, couch pillows knifed open and thrown, etc. That's how the house looked. Every room. But he was relieved to find no bodies, no more savaged pets. The interior was as gracefully and simply appointed as the exterior, and would have radiated a similar confidence and calm. Lampshades were patterned sparsely with real leaves. Walls were a sanded plaster with exposed timber headers over the windows, probably Douglas fir or red spruce. The curtains, though ripped from their rods, bore an understated twining-vine pattern. Jess could feel, even amid the chaos, the ordered attention to beauty, and even now the return of a pervasive calm.

Below a shelf beneath a large window was a scattering of shattered picture frames. He turned one over: Collie, probably a year or two ago, sitting happily in a pile of leaves with Crystal sprawled against her, head in her tiny lap. Jess slid three more to him, careful not to get glass splinters in his fingers. One showed the four of them, the two parents, late twenties, with Collie on his shoulders and Crystal at their knees. They were on a small dock, the shore of a lake somewhere, maybe this one. The father was broad-shouldered, had a trimmed reddish beard and thick black glasses that enlarged his gray eyes. He wore a navy baseball cap on backward and was smiling hugely, and he had good, very white teeth. Jess felt the charisma from here. Mom was compact and pretty, with black shoulder-length hair in a simple silver Japanese hair clip, which Jess could see because her face was turned gladly up to her husband and daughter. The next photo was in a pewter frame, glass still intact, and showed the dad, hatless now and in a dress shirt, with his arm around a petite older woman with short straight gray hair, unsmiling but not unhappy. She also wore thick glasses, and her eyes were a dark gray—clearly, his mom. They stood in front of a shopwindow lettered with the words "Grantham Gifts." The last picture was smaller, framed in simple walnut, Collie and her dad in an outboard, both holding up fish and grinning. He hefted a two-pound silver lake trout, she a brookie the size of a hot dog, but they beamed with equal measures of pride. Jess collected the four small frames and brushed off the broken glass and carefully set them standing back on the shelf; he didn't know why. As he turned he noticed an envelope under a heap of torn curtain on the floor. He bent again, slipped it out, turned it over. It was a bill from MidLakes Electric, and in the address window above 117 School Street were the names Silas and Suzanne Beckett. He folded it and slipped it into an inside jacket pocket.

He came back out onto the porch and shrugged.

"It's been tossed," he said. "Like in a TV show. Otherwise"—he made a horizontal motion with his hand—"your call."

Collie was wild to go inside now, and Storey understood that unless he let her see what had happened to her home she would be refractory and impossible ever after. He knew this because he had kids. And so he said firmly, "Hold my hand," and she stilled immediately to the command in his voice and reached up and grasped it and they stepped over the threshold.

She could not speak or muster any word at all. She made a small sound like a whimper or a hum and led Storey forcefully from room to room. She stopped short at the shelf with the three photos and pulled off the one of her and Crystal in the leaves and she brought it to her face and rubbed her nose against the print. "Crystal," she said simply. She stood it back up the best she could, and Jess helped her. Then she picked up the one of the whole family and she freed a hand and touched the man and said, "Papa." She didn't cry. Then she pulled Storey through the whole house. She made a full circuit and went straight back to the kitchen and released Storey's hand. She crouched beside the worn and stained braided rug beneath the farm sink and pulled back one corner. Jess noticed a thread of clear stout fishing line extending from one end of the rug and going through a hole in the planks. Countersunk flush to the floor was a heavy ring handle to a trapdoor. Breathing hard, almost hyperventilating, she grabbed it with both hands and tugged.

"Hold on," Storey whispered. "Hold on, Collie, I got it."

The hatch was big enough for an adult to slip through, no bigger. The stairs were steep. Storey felt for a light at the edge of the hole and there it was, a bright battery-powered LED. He went down and lifted her after him.

Musty, but neat and clean. There was one expected wall of canned food and Ball-jar preserves and plastic buckets of probably grains; three cots with thick synthetic mummy bags; a shelf of books; rows of five-gallon water jugs. Jess remembered the rule of thumb—one gallon per person per day—and multiplied the thirty jugs by five and divided and figured they were set up to stay almost two months. The provisions were no help now. But what most interested him were the two marine batteries on the floor beneath a long shop bench, and the radio set on top.

Chapter Ten

Jess's Uncle Harvey, who lived a few miles up the road on Putney Mountain, was a ham-radio nut. He had "friends" all over
the country, all over the world, with whom he stayed in regular contact. "Friends" was bracketed in Jess's mind, because
he didn't understand how one could consider anybody a friend
whom one could not touch. Whose breath one never felt against
cheek or arm, whose smell was as unknown as the true richness
of a voice unmediated by radio waves or digital transmission.
Someone with whom one had never broken bread or shared a
consoling hug didn't seem a bona fide friend.

Jess had classmates whose regular buddies were a thousand
miles away, on the other side of a video-game console. He
understood the need for human contact, but he did not understand the social-network "Friends" thing; claiming scores of
strangers one had never met seemed cheap and somehow sad.
He thought his uncle was truly odd. Harvey lived amid what
Jess thought must be some of the most beautiful country on
earth and he rarely went outside except to roll his garbage bin
back and forth from his carport to the edge of Osgood Road. He

spent all his time at his radio bench or in a recliner that looked like a NASA spaceship seat. He drank Diet Dr Pepper nonstop. He shaved intermittently. He was a cipher.

Jess liked him. For one, Harvey had an easy laugh and he seemed to truly enjoy Jess's stories. He was interested. He prompted Jess to tell him what was going on in his life, what characters he'd met lately who intrigued him. He leaned forward, elbows on skinny knees, and gave Jess his full attention. Skinny knees. That was another mystery: he was rail-thin. The stereotype of a man with his passions was someone overweight who moved more like a parade float than a big cat. Not Harvey: he seemed agile. Was he a drug addict? Sedentary and corroded inside but unable to keep on weight? Jess looked for signs, and except for Harvey's occasional bleary, bloodshot eyes from staying up into small hours—so he could converse with a buddy in Sulawesi—he found none.

One May afternoon when Jess was sixteen and visiting, his uncle took a scheduled call from a regular in Norway, and as he began the trading of call signs and frequencies that were prepa- ratory to a less formal conversation, Harvey glanced over at his nephew and caught him watching with an expression maybe of distaste or even disgust. Maybe Jess just looked perplexed. When Harvey was done with the call, which lasted ten minutes, and included the revelation that Jørgen was at sea on his ketch at the moment, Harvey hung up his headset and swiveled his chair toward Jess and smiled, mouth compressed, but his brown eyes were serious, even grim. He rubbed the graying stubble on his jaw and said, "You think I'm a freak, huh?"

Jess was aghast and mute. His jaw might have fallen open. That was kind of exactly what he'd been thinking.

"You think a man who spends his life on a radio and has few friends but those that come over an airwave is not a man, or at least not living a real life. You think I'm a shell. Right?"

His eyes roved over Jess's face and he continued: "A shell of a man you can't help but like." Now Harvey's eyes creased and his smile became real. "You can't help it. Family is family."

Jess was stunned, more by his uncle's accuracy than by any sense of confrontation, and he could still not speak.

Harvey scratched his chin with one finger and glanced down at Jess's feet. "Are those your running shoes?"

Jess nodded.

"You're wearing shorts. Good. Wanna take a run? Blueberries?"

Blueberries was a three-mile loop that climbed steeply through woods up a rock-slabbed four-wheel-drive track, crossed a stone wall and a meadow crowded with low-bush blueberries, and descended to Sawyer Brook, where it was often thick with ferns and wet.

"Run?" Jess stammered. Not that he didn't know what the word meant, in a very visceral way. He was a born runner. He ran the loop often, sometimes in the morning before school and the same day as a big soccer match. He was known for his speed up the right side.

"Be right back." Harvey pushed out of the chair and disappeared through the kitchen and came back a couple of minutes later wearing nylon too-short running shorts, tube socks, and shoes

Jess recognized as a hot item when he was probably nine. Suddenly Jess was overwhelmed with sadness and compassion; he felt sorry for his uncle and was about to make some lame excuse when Harvey said, "Whoever loses buys the milkshakes," and was out the door. He waited for Jess on the driveway and bent to touch his toes, bouncing in some awful archaic stretch, and Jess felt worse. Harvey seemed amused. "Not gonna stretch?"

Jess shook his head. He felt queasy.

"Suit yourself." Harvey lifted one foot behind him, than another, in the classic quad stretch, shook himself all over, took a deep breath, huffed it out, and said, "Okay, let's go. We'll warm up nice and easy to Florence's, then the race is on. 'Kay?"

Jess felt he was being sucked into doing something he really didn't want to do. He intuited that his relationship with Harvey was about to change forever. He couldn't look at him. Even at that tender age, he knew that once he humiliated his uncle there was no going back.

They trotted up the climbing dirt road. Very slowly. They passed the old overgrown tennis court at the edge of Frazer's hayfield, passed Shumlin's and Doc Brookhauser's. There was a near-level quarter-mile of good dirt road to Florence's Japanese teahouse, which Jess's father—Harvey's brother—had designed, and Harvey began to lengthen out his stride. At Florence's carport there was a hayfield ahead and a sharp left turn; they took the bend, and immediately the county maintenance ended and the road became a steep rocky climbing track that at times more resembled a streambed than a road. As soon as they rounded the turn Harvey said, "Okay, race you back to the house." And he put on the jets.

"Damn." Jess remembered saying it to himself, and then he leaned hard into the climb.

He had run cross-country. In middle school, when the team was short runners, he ran races that didn't interfere with soccer games. He knew how to hang on up a hill and then push over the top and break a competitor. It was one of the great satisfactions of the sport. But he could barely hang on to Uncle Harvey. He could hear his own breathing, not the regular chuff of a good run but the gulps of hitting a pulse rate too high. They jumped roots and slid on water-stained granite slabs. They pushed up a very steep cobbled straightaway and crossed the stone wall and contoured through the blueberry meadow and got hit with the sweet smell of apple blossoms wafting up from Darrow's orchard. Jess had not tasted blood in his mouth for a couple of years, but now he did. The coppery signal that he was pushing too hard. Maybe Harvey had been listening to his breathing. Suddenly he slowed and dropped back, and Jess felt his uncle's hand briefly on his sweat-soaked T-shirt, and Harvey said, "Wanna jog? Get our second wind?"

Jess thought he might be dreaming. None of this added up. He was certainly not gonna take charity from his freaky but lovable uncle. "Shit, no," he breathed.

"'Kay. See ya at the house." And then Harvey lengthened out again, and, as smoothly as if he were just hitting his stride, he took off. Into the trees on the other side of the meadow. Jess didn't see him again until he got to Harvey's mailbox. Where he was pushing against a maple tree in a stretch he probably learned in the last century. When Harvey heard the pats of Jess's footfalls he straightened, turned, grinned. "Let's go to Darcy's and get the shakes. You still like malts? You can buy next time."

On the way down the hill in Harvey's old Bronco, they were silent until Jess finally turned in his seat and said, "How . . . ?"

He didn't know exactly what he wanted to ask. How could Harvey run like that, certainly, but also *How . . . everything?* Basically, he wanted to say, *Who the hell was that masked man?*

Harvey read his mind. "I run at night," he said.

Jess felt himself wince as if he were looking into the sun.

"You knew I was in the war, right?"

Jess gaped, nodded.

"That's kinda why I stick around home. I don't like most people. Hard to explain, but that's how it is. I run at night because I don't want to run into the Brandts or the Brookhausers or the Hollisters. Nothing against 'em, it's all me." Harvey reached over and put a hand on Jess's hot head. "You're one hell of a runner," he said. "You have your old man's toughness."

Jess woke out of his daze. He sat up and turned in surprise. *"Pop?"*

"I knew you'd say that." Harvey laughed, stuck his elbow out the window. "Your old man is one tough honcho."

///////////////////////

So Jess knew a little about ham radios, by osmosis. He approached the bench from the side so as not to throw his shadow over the receiver. A headset hung on a wrought-iron fishhook; even Collie's folks weren't immune to a little kitsch. Jess stood. As if to sit on the padded stool was to commit fully to receiving information he did and did not wish to know. He reached forward and flipped the power switch. Nothing. There was an old steam-gauge amp meter and it did not light up and the needle did not budge. Dead. The batteries were shot. He bent and looked under the bench. Odd. There were the two marine batteries, there was the wire heading up to the radios, but there was no trickle charger on the posts, nothing leading to an outlet. Who knew how long they had been sitting on cold concrete, draining out.

Storey said, "What?" He was at the wall of provisions, scanning for anything useful.

"Batteries dead."

"There's a truck across the street."

"Yeah, I was thinking that."

"Hey, what the fuck. C'mere." Storey had been kneeling on the concrete and he'd pried off one of the lids on a bucket labeled "Beans/Pinto." Now he was holding up a phosphor-white brick wrapped in cellophane. He handed it to Jess, who hefted it. "Not beans," he said. The bucket was packed with the bricks, and a sharp tar-smell rose out of it. He pried off the lid of the pail next to it, the one labeled "Rolled Oats," and it, too, was full of the packets. He dug a thumbnail into the top of one; the contents had the consistency of marzipan, but stiffer.

"I'm thinking some kind of explosive?" Jess said.

"Yep, C-4."

"Is that a shitload of C-4?"

"Yep."

"Collie's dad does more than fish."

"Huh?"

"Nothing," Jess said. "You think these guys blew the bridges on all the roads going south?"

Storey shrugged. He looked dazed. "Dunno," he said. "God-damn. Seems like we know less every minute."

"Hold on," Jess said. "I'll get the battery from the truck."

He climbed back up the ladderlike steps and squeezed up through the hatch. He jogged out the wrecked front door to the green Tacoma pulled in front of the cottage across the street. There were bullet holes in the side of the bed and two of the tires were flat, evidently shot out. Whoever did all this really did not want any serviceable vehicles left. The driver's door was not locked. He yanked it open, popped the hood lever. He felt under the seat for a crescent wrench, socket set, even pliers. He could use the needle nose on his Leatherman if he had to, but it'd be tougher. There'd be nuts on the battery posts and one or two on the bracket. He didn't feel any tools, but under the seat springs his hand ran over a set of keys. He had a sudden thought: *Who needs ham radio?*

He inserted the key into the ignition and turned it until the warning lights lit. He turned the knob on the old truck radio. Sudden static. The digital tuner read 90.9 FM. Probably the one local station out of Randall. Given how low it was on the dial, it was probably a public volunteer station that played indie, folk, classic rock, bluegrass, you name it, throughout the day, and *Morning Edition* right about now—that would have been good. Or maybe, given the apparent secessionist sentiment along the lake, the local station had been more right-leaning, maybe a Christian outfit that played country and inspirational songs all day. Didn't matter now, because of course the station was ashes, like everything else in Randall.

Jess hit the AM button. Static. Made sense—they were way up in the middle of nowhere. He pushed the scanner and watched the numbers tumble on the tuner. It snagged on a couple of frequencies—nothing but snow, a stutter that might be a voice or just interference. He was about to give up, twist the key back, when the scanner stopped on 1485 and he heard a voice. Clear enough. It was French. A newscaster. Must be out of Quebec. Jess had studied French pretty much from first grade, all the way through comp-lit classes in college. His speaking was horrendous but his comprehension was good. He leaned in and heard, all in French:

". . . Do you believe, Professor Laurent, that *la décision* in Ottawa to fortify the international border in Quebec has been met with continuing resistance by the provincial government in Quebec City, because there is fear the federal administration may now feel empowered to exhibit some of the same strong-arm tactics as our neighbor to the south?"

Jess lay half over the driver's seat, ear to the radio, riveted. An electromagnetic whine blew through in gusts and obscured words, most of sentences at times, but he was having no problem translating. Now another voice, a woman's: "No one believes Ottawa is going to wage a war on Quebec—"

Man again: "Of course, the assassination of the American President Schoeffler by the Maine secessionist Lamar Blodgett prompted a swift response, but Washington staunchly denies there is"—static—"kind of war. There is a police action to calm the riots and restore the peace—"

Woman, with disdain: "Paw! We have indisputable proof that two Marine battalions"—whine—"many as two thousand U.S. soldiers, both armored cavalry and infantry, were sent into the Kennebec River Valley on the twenty-sixth of September. Is that not a war?"—whine and snow—"cannot know what the federal government is doing now due to the most severe information blackout in modern times. Even private satellite companies, whole computer systems have been disabled. But you can bet this is no 'police action' to keep things calm, this is—"

Man: "Well, the threat to the republic is very real, we cannot deny"—dopplered whine—"day the Legislatures of both Vermont and New Hampshire took up emergency motions to express accord with the Legislature of Maine and to empower their national guards to deny entry to any other branches of the U.S. military. Don't you think—"

Woman: "I think Washington has been deaf to the concerns of rural northern New England for too long and that the pigeon

has come home to roost. I think we can cert"—blast, like a
sandstorm—"parallels in our own country"—a keen of interference rose and broke into a storm of snow. Jess muttered,
"Damn," and turned the knob two digits up and two digits back.
Gone. He worked the dial again, thought he heard maybe the
man again out of the gale saying, "I'm sorry, we have urgent
news out of Augusta . . ." But maybe not. Maybe it was his own
hunger to know more. One thing was certain, they needed
to hoof it. The world was blowing up around them and they
did not need to take an hour to hook up the radio in the base-
ment to another battery and get the thing fired up, and take
another hour trying to locate some operator that had more spe-
cific knowledge. Jess didn't even have an idea how to do that.
What was clear was that the 49ers, or the rebels, or whoever they
were, had a center of operations right here, in this village, and
that they had ignited a full-blown civil war, and that the three
of them needed to get gone now. Also, Collie's father was part
of it all. Jesus. It occurred to him then that maybe the Marines
hadn't leveled the town because they were searching it for intel.

He did not even turn off the key or the radio or slam the door.
He just ran. Back across the street and into the house, through
the kitchen. He put his head down into the hatch and called,
"Store. *Store.* We're gone. Come up! We gotta leave. *Now!*"

Where do we go?

That's what he thought as he stood in the yard, feeling gratefully
the warmth of the morning sun on his face. *I don't even know
what direction.*

He badly wished right now that he could turn back the clock some eight weeks and be on the fishing trip to Montana he had offered Storey as a prequel to their hunt. They would drive from his house in Denver up to Missoula, where he had a couple of good friends. Adam was a poet and a fishing guide, and he'd set them up with three or four days of driftboat trout fishing on the Blackfoot, the Clark Fork, the Bitterroot. Then they could drive into Yellowstone and fish the Lamar Valley and check on the wolf packs, which had been so recently devastated by Montana's loosening of hunting and trapping laws. One of his favorite places on the planet and favorite things to do: to hike up the creeks that fed the Lamar, hike up and away from the crowds and into the spruce and pines, and fish the creeks, where they were small and you were as likely to run into a grizzly or a wolf as a person. Nothing he loved more. And nothing on earth more invigorating than to be casting into a clear run at dusk with the Absarokas leaning against the first faint scattering of stars and hear the wolves begin to sing. He wanted to be camped outside of Cooke City, on the border of Yellowstone, and go fishing every day with Storey. Why hadn't they done it? Maybe then they would have decided they could forgo the moose hunt this year and none of this would be happening. To them.

Well, now they were truly fucked. Should they head west . . . try? To New Hampshire? And thence to Vermont and Storey's family? It sounded like there were tensions coming to a head there, too. Like a military buildup. Like the fire of secessionism was spreading. How on earth? They might simply be shot on sight as spies at the New Hampshire border.

He heard talking, turned. They were walking toward him. She was not holding Storey's hand now, she was clutching a ratty plush loon. To Jess, that was a good sign. She was coming along of her own free will, she was trusting Storey now, who was telling her, "We're gonna go look for them now. That's what we've gotta do, right?"

Her nod. Her gripping the loon more tightly. She was out of the lion suit and wearing synthetic black pants, a rose-colored fleece sweater. She carried a small pink daypack sewn to look like the head of a Saint Bernard. Good. Though the day was warming fast, Storey had understood that rain and cold would be their companions. Jess bet that if there were clothing items in the little pack it was her rain gear and a down jacket. And a Saint Bernard was as good a mascot as any. Right now Jess could really use the brandy in the little barrel they were purported to carry.

"'Sup?" Storey said, trying to sound casual.

Jess didn't know what to say. If he spilled now, Collie would hear it all. He blurted, "Look at this truck bed. Never seen one like it."

Storey turned immediately to Collie. "Here," he said. "Sit in the shade of this maple tree for a second, okay? Jess is going to show me the truck. I don't know, he's crazy about trucks."

"That's Hartley's." She frowned. "He's got flat tires. Oh boy."

"Yep. What a pain. We'll be back in a sec."

Jess told him everything. Tried to replay the conversation as he had heard it. He began, "It was a station out of Quebec. The only one that tuned in. FM was all out."

"Sure. Much shorter range, depends on repeaters."

"Yeah, so it was some kind of news talk show, some interview with a professor—political science, I guess."

"You understood it all?"

"Pretty much."

"You always surprise me."

"That a compliment? Listen, it's bad . . ."

He told him. That three days into their hunting trip the president had been assassinated. By a Maine secessionist. That the Maine Legislature must have voted to secede from the union in the days before, because the Legislatures of New Hampshire and Vermont were apparently throwing their hat in with Maine, sympathizing if not seceding. That the response from the feds was apparently swift and overwhelming: the United States sent two battalions of Marines rolling into the Kennebec Valley. Which meant that the heart of the insurgency must have been in central, very rural Maine. "Which we knew from all the upheaval before we left. Some guy, Krichner, from right over on Moosehead, started the whole movement, remember? Don't they always have names like that? Like 'Grinch'? Sours them from birth. Anyway—"

Storey did not blanch, he flushed. "Two battalions?"

"Yep. That's, like, two thousand troops. Infantry and armor, apparently."

"Whoa." Storey glanced back at Collie, who was sitting dutifully in the shade of the maple, having a conversation with Loony. He said, "It's extreme. Armor is tanks. Extreme response. These are U.S. citizens, right? Why would they do that?"

"Because the VP, now POTUS, is DuPonte?"

"Right." Storey rubbed his eyes. "The general. Hawk of hawks. Wasn't he commandant of the Marines or something?"

"Yes."

"Sonofabitch probably wet himself. Wanted his whole life to be a wartime president. Probably figures now he'll get his head on a coin. Fuck. Still . . ." He swung his chin toward the half-destroyed village below them. "These are Americans."

"So what?" Jess said.

Storey blinked at him.

Jess said, "What did Sherman do, burning through the South? Or the Russians to the Ukrainians, their 'true brothers'? Or Pol Pot to his own people? Nobody held back."

"What about the Maine National Guard? Were they radicalized, too?"

Jess shrugged.

Storey said, "They take orders from the governor, right? But the president has ultimate authority. What did they do? Sit it out?"

"I don't know, they didn't mention it."

Storey winced his eyes shut. As if to squeeze the news into a strip he could store away somewhere. "So . . . that's everything we've been seeing? The work of one radicalized militia that assassinated the president and an avenging general now in charge? Doesn't quite add up."

"I don't know. It's so fucked up." Jess looked past Storey to the house, as if some answer might be found there. Then he let his gaze drift toward the climbing street, the rest of the town. He said, "DuPonte must have sent in air cav, too. The choppers . . ."

"Yeah."

"How else could they have blasted those towns to the roots? That was from the air. Indiscriminate. I guess nobody knows how bad it is. The professor on the radio said there was a total news blackout; even the private satellite companies went dark. Nobody knows."

"But us." Storey waved toward the village center, the lake. "And these poor bastards."

"Yep."

They were leaning against the truck bed, elbows on the rail. Suddenly Storey straightened. "Wait. What did you say before? About Vermont?"

"They're throwing their hat in. They and New Hampshire. With Maine. I guess the state Legislatures voted on motions of 'accord.' That's what he said. They are mobilizing state national guards to the borders to keep out any other branch of the U.S. military. Those were his words. Till they sort it out with the feds, I guess."

Now the heat or emotion did drain from Storey's neck. "So . . ."

"So I guess there must be checkpoints all along the New Hampshire border to keep U.S. Marines from coming in from Maine. That's some crazy shit."

"So . . ."

"So I guess two dudes wandering out of the woods might get shot on sight. At the border. Or two strangers in any small town. The way everyone else has been acting." Jess suddenly felt the weight in his gut—the constriction along the limbs, in the chest, neck—of dread. Leaden and contracted. As he had not quite felt before. The solid dread behind the fretwork of fear—of all options closing down.

"What's in her little backpack?" he managed to say.

"Her lion suit. I put long underwear and rain gear in there, but she made me take it out."

"It's like her superhero Wonder Woman suit, huh?"

"I guess. I took the stuff she needs. Also, the family were campers. I found her little sleeping bag and pad." He glanced at the plastic bag on the ground. "I rolled up the lion suit tight and tucked it in her dog pack."

"Wish I had a suit like that about now."

"No kidding."

"Let's eat something. I feel kinda queasy."

"Okay. We'll go back down to the packs and the wagon. Maybe eat something on the porch."

"Or maybe that crazy old dude has possum stew on the stove."

Chapter Eleven

"Weird, huh?" That was Jess at the old man's stove, stirring Campbell's canned clam chowder.

Crazy old dude did not have possum stew, but he did have a wall of canned soup and chili in a closet pantry off the kitchen. He had a propane tank in back and an ancient rack of three gas burners with brass lever valves on a narrow counter. No oven, but this would work. He had a red Formica table with white flowers twined into the corners, probably from 1950. The walls were papered with a repeating scene of a three-masted schooner breasting a storm, and they were heavily grimed with spattered grease. Two pictures hung on nails: a chocolate Lab smiling above a row of dead geese, and a young woman holding a straw hat to her head in a brisk wind and laughing. Both looked to be prints of Kodachrome, faded by the years. Jess wondered how long ago the Lab had gone into the perpetual predawn dark of hunting-dog heaven. Probably decades. The woman, too. Who was she? His wife, lover, daughter? There was no clue. Otherwise, there were pots and pans on hooks, three chairs—that seemed odd—and a well-scrubbed floor of wide oak boards. A smell of pipe tobacco, cherry or vanilla, but no ashtray or pipe.

"Weird?" Storey repeated. He sat in one of the chrome-and-vinyl chairs. He was flipping through an ancient phone book for the Lake Region. The cover had a couple fishing out of a canoe on a lake backed by woods in brilliant fall colors . . . of course. "Weird that the old guy seems to be sponsored by Campbell's?"

"That, too," Jess said. "I mean it's strange sitting in a kitchen, preparing a meal."

"You mean like the world is normal?"

"A little." Jess reached up and opened a painted plywood cupboard—maroon red, like the table. Bag of brown sugar, spaghetti boxes, Cream of Wheat, handful of spices, can of Folgers coffee and a jar of Nescafé instant. Two boxes of twelve-gauge double-ought buckshot. He pulled out the can of coffee and held it up on a flat palm with a big grin, then opened the next cupboard and slid down three bowls. "Did I ever tell you about Mom's search for the best clam chowder in Maine?"

"No," Storey said.

"Two summers ago, she and Pop went up to visit her cousin Pete in North Haven. They drove over, took a couple of days going up Route One. She was determined to find the very best chowder, the *crème de la crème*. They spent five days on the island with Pete, drove home for another two days. Super-relaxed, like retired people. Stayed at the Freeport Hotel and toured L.L.Bean like it was a museum. So, in Bath, in a hole in the wall under the highway bridge, they found it. Jackpot. Not only the best clam chowder in Maine, but the best she'd ever had. The owner, who was the cook, came out of the kitchen in a stained apron to take the compliment. Mom said he needed a shave and had what looked like eczema on his forearms. You know Mom is fastidious, right? Still, she overlooked it all. The best is the best, right? 'The soup is really superb,' she said. 'Where did you get the recipe?' The cook frowned. I guess he had zero sense of irony. 'It's Campbell's,' he said, looking puzzled. 'You never had Campbell's soup before?' "

Storey tried to smile but failed. He was not in the mood.

Jess added a half-cup of water to the soup, stirred. "We could stay here," he said.

"Stay? What do you mean?" Storey said.

"Dunno. Just a thought. With everything exploding. I was thinking that if we're in a full-on civil war we've gotta get going. Find someplace safe. But nobody's here. I mean, to our knowledge. The military or militia or whoever already came through—"

"And then we came through," Storey said, not without bitterness.

"We came through," Jess repeated. But he would not be derailed. He said, "Listen. They're not coming back, is my guess. We could hang out. Wait until things quiet down a little."

"Hunh" was all Storey said.

Someplace safe. Jess stirred the soup, let his eyes travel out the small curtained window. Someplace safe and warm was what he had seemed to be seeking his whole life. What he had found with Storey's family, for most of his childhood. And then he had tangled with Storey's mom and tried to pretend nothing had changed.

Why was he thinking about that now? All of it? Because this felt like some reckoning, like the end of a dream or a book? He didn't know. But it rankled—the memory he had had on the road just an hour ago, of him and Hannah making love, and how he had tried so hard to believe that they could all go back to the way things had been.

The first ripple was when Jess finally made love to his girlfriend Gwen after three months of dating: he was horrified to find himself imagining that he was entering Hannah. Gwen was very nervous and it had taken him a while to get her ready, and so, when he finally did push inside her, he conjured Storey's mother and lost himself in the ease and delight of the only other time he knew. That was the first thing.

Another was that once in a while, especially after dinner and after two glasses of wine, Hannah looked at him with an expression he could not read. It was always fleeting and it seemed to be shuttered quickly by an act of will. But it disturbed and upset him. Because, let's admit it, he got off sometimes to the memory of her, especially the image of her standing in only her shirt in the light of a window that held trees and sky. The picture was burned into his soul like a brand.

The third thing was that he caught Storey looking at him sometimes. Puzzled and a little wary. He could never say, "What? What's up?" because it was the one thing in his life at that moment he didn't want to know.

If Hannah was also troubled she never let on, except in those rare glances, which Jess read as desire. She was as warm and lighthearted with Jess as she had ever been, and she was exuberant with Gwen. So she must have constructed a reality where it was all okay.

That was Hannah. Cecily built a world where her handicap was an asset, not a liability. Maybe it was. The littler sister, Annie, pretended to be visited by fairies in green hats so that she could feel special in a family that often seemed to be galloping headlong without her. And Storey shrugged off the sense of every impending disaster and pretended that soccer was what he cared about, and hunting and fishing. Jess knew that what Storey cared about most was what was true in the world, but he hid it because it made him very vulnerable—that's what true things did—and the sensitivity in his friend made Jess want to protect him.

Well. He, Jess, got a girlfriend and pretended to be in love.

"Hey!" Storey straightened in the chair, looked around. "Where's Collie?"

"She was just here."

"Hold on." Storey rose. He went out through the screen door, let it clap shut. Jess heard his boots descending the steps. Which meant she wasn't out on the porch. Storey would be in the street, looking uphill and down. He wouldn't call because . . . because who knew. They were in a world now where you didn't shout, ever, unless you had to. Jess set the empty pot in the sink, half filled it with water, as if they might stay, as if he had reason to wash a pan, and went out after his friend.

The morning was nearly hot. He flew off the porch into bright sun. Down four steps to the street.

Despite his hurry, he was hit with the smell of the lake—cold stones and warming slabrock, and sediment—and the certain scent of an Indian-summer morning in the North Country in late September—the fragrance of yellowing ferns and leaves turning, and toasted hay grass. It hit him like a strong draft of his youth. He stopped for a second, closed his eyes. The trans-migration was so visceral it was as if for a moment he inhabited two lives at once, the one in which he was a teenager stepping out into a glorious Maine autumn morning—and every love and every possibility was waiting to be tested—and the one now, in which heartbreak ruled and survival was the best hope. Two musics thrummed in the same heart and wove together without discord. As if every life was an instrument meant to play them both.

He must have turned as he inhaled the morning, because his reverie was broken by the sight of Storey running up the hill and rounding a corner. *Damn*. He ran after.

///////////////////////

When he found them Storey was covering her. They were across the street from her house and she was behind the trailer. She had gone home to look for her dog. She was lying over Crystal, arms hugging her ribs and face in her bloodstained ruff, talking to her, asking her to wake up, she didn't have to be so tired, it was time to stop sleeping. And Jess saw that it was Storey sobbing in her stead, wrapping her as she wrapped the dog, and his back was heaving and he was trying to stifle it and was helpless. And Jess knew that Storey was crying for the dog and for the girl and for his own daughters and wife, and for the odds of getting home to find them safe or getting home at all. Jess stepped back into the shade of a pine and let them grieve. They were in no hurry now.

No hurry when the compass is spinning. When you are rooted to earth. When living means taking a step but you have no idea toward what. You are alone under the wheeling season, and the best memories are drained by loss.

Chapter Twelve

They left that afternoon. Not because they had a plan of action but because they could not stay. Collie would not leave Crystal. Storey had to tear her fists from the dog's dark fur. Her screams pierced the morning. Between screams and sobs she insisted that the dog would wake and they could not tell her no.

In the end, Storey carried her back down the hill, over his shoulder, rolled tightly in a blanket Jess had fetched from her house. Again like a crazed cat that clawed. That such a small being could wail with such volume. They could not shush her, but what did it matter, with the old man shouting and shooting, the blare of his engine as he fled? The woods, the empty houses absorbed it all without comment.

The decision to leave was made as she napped, finally, in the old man's daybed, a pillowed platform under his one big window. He hadn't seemed like a daybed kind of coot, but maybe it had been his wife's. Maybe the old man slept there in her scent, curled like a hound.

They ate the cold soup in the bowls and heated more. They woke her to eat, and when she was done she insisted on wearing the lion suit. Storey helped her put it on over her fleece, and then she fell back to sleep. Good. Jess made a pot of coffee. The cream in the fridge had soured after days of no electricity, but Jess found a can of sweetened condensed milk and they stirred it in gratefully. They each drank two cups, and packed the rest of the Folgers in the wagon.

Storey said, "East is where the cities are, the coast. The biggest roads. The money. So I'm thinking it's unionists probably. East and south. By all rights, that's where we should go."

" 'By all rights.' So you don't think we should go there. You think we should go west."

"Yes."

"Why? We could take the boat south. A couple of hours to the end of the lake, and then get on a new highway."

"Too exposed," Storey said.

"We could go tonight. Hug the shore. Go back past Randall, Green Hill. Cut across to a new road."

Storey set his cup down so it wouldn't tremble. "The lake has been nothing but . . ." Jess could tell he was seeing some filmstrip of memory.

"Hell," Jess said.

"Right."

Jess said, "You've gotta think there are sane people on the coast that can help us. And maybe the highway west from Bangor is clear."

"We don't know what's happening over there. Could be total civil war."

"So—what? Could be anywhere. Everywhere."

"So we stay out of sight. Go west little by little. Move the way we've been moving. On the road and off it. The New Hampshire border's all woods. No way they can secure the whole thing. Whoever's fighting probably has no interest in what's west of here anyway. It's mostly empty."

"What about Collie?"

"What about her?"

"She's not exactly discreet."

"We'll play the quiet game," Storey said.

"How does that work?"

"If she's super-quiet the bad men won't come."

///////////////////////

They left just after three, Storey carrying the girl, Jess pulling the wagon. They went straight across the fields, up the good road. Nobody shot at them now. By five they were in Randall, where the ashes no longer smoldered, and they met the paved two-lane highway and followed it as it curved west.

Chapter Thirteen

Jess's mother, Carol, sensed something was up. She and Jess were not close. Carol was kind, she helped him with his home-work, especially math, she cooked about half his meals—neither she nor Jess's father, Jay, loved to cook, but they split the chore and made passable, or at least edible, meals. Carol had played violin in school, mostly old-time mountain music, and so, when Jess was learning guitar, she helped with chords and keys and kept time in lieu of a metronome, but she never pulled out her old fiddle to accompany him. She could still play, though. Once in a while, at the end of a training run, as he leaned into a last push up the incline of their long dirt drive—with nothing in the world in his awareness but a row of huge old maples and a stone wall, and his own exhortation to hold the pace, *hold it, hold it*—he heard the strains of a fiddle playing "Fox on the Run" or "Blackberry Blossom" and it broke his heart—in the quiet, gentle way a heart can be broken by the same person again and again. Not because the songs were painfully beautiful, which they were, or because the plaintive, climbing arpeggios were winged with longing, but because she might have taught him these tunes and they might have played them together. She never did. Either she was shy about her proficiency or she was protecting a pure, sacred part of herself from her husband and her son. Jess suspected the latter.

Sometimes he pulled up short of the house and leaned against the great rough trunk of the last sugar maple, leaned into it with a hammering heart, and felt somehow the tree's large accepting spirit, and he listened. Listened for the end of a song, and as she began another, maybe "Tennessee Waltz" or "In the Pines," he might close his eyes and let the sadness overtake him. It was a grief he could not name, but had to do somehow with a mother who made choices he would never understand. Who at night would choose a book on Celtic history over a game of cribbage with her son; or choose her reading over a simple conversation about the things she knew best, like the platting of the old farms when all these hills were bare of trees and flocked with sheep, or sharing stories about the tribes who once hunted and traded here, of which she knew many. And why did she call him "Son" half the time? The formality of it stung him.

As reserved as she was, Jess's mother seemed to know that he was going through a life change. Almost as if she could smell it on the air, like an incoming tide. His allegiance may have been divided over the years between her house and the house down the hill, but his heart had never been lost. But after he made love to Hannah he found himself daydreaming more. Not just about her, though those fantasies abounded; he mused about travel, about losing himself up in Alaska, building a cabin on the banks of some river accessible only by boat, getting his moose every fall, and laying in cords of firewood. Sometimes the fantasy included a woman—okay, it was often Hannah—and they would discover that a life in the wild—ruled as it was by the iron-bound march of the seasons—also held bounties of open time in which they would explore each other and exhaust themselves in lovemaking. Was he in love? With his best friend's mother? He scolded himself and made sure he wasn't and directed his imagination by force of will toward a pretty classmate. This was before he had hooked up with Gwen.

And sometimes in these flights of romance he would abjure any partner and find solace in a spartan solitude, in braving the storms on the tundra, hunting the taiga, paddling the streams with wind and rain and raptors as his best companions. Even then he had intuited that this was how he would give to his life the best of himself. And later he would understand that hunger for wild country and solitude might have been why he had lost his wife, Jan. Apparently, she was sick of sensing that there were other worlds in which he felt much more at home, and it occurred to him after it was too late that she was feeling something like what he had felt with his mother, Carol. That many parts of the person she loved most were being withheld.

One evening, after a soccer game down in Northfield which Hannah had attended—she didn't come to many, but this was a qualifier for the state championship—she dropped Jess off at home. Carol must have seen the headlights, because she came out the front door and waved Hannah in. Hannah, hand on the shifter to back up, blew out her cheeks, huffed. It was brief but he noticed. Then she forced a quick smile and nodded and flicked off the lights, turned off the engine, pushed out of the car.

"Why don't you come in, Hannah?" Carol was saying. "Do you have time for a cup of tea? I was thinking it would be nice—we haven't seen you in a while. Jay is at a meeting with a client, it's just us."

Just us. Though they were close neighbors—close for these hills—and their sons were best friends, the two couples rarely socialized. Jess understood that Storey's family thought his own parents reserved and dry, if not stiff, and his own father and mother thought of the Brandt clan as . . . what? Undisciplined? Sloppy? No, Storey's parents were a working doctor and an accomplished equestrian. Bohemian? Not exactly. Jess's father and mother thought of the Brandts as whatever it was that was raucous and unpredictable, whatever made a habit out of disturbing the peace. That was enough to keep social interactions to a polite and sparse minimum.

Jess pecked his mom on the cheek quickly at the door and said, "I've gotta shower. We got soaked, Mom, in a thunderstorm." He dropped his cleats under the bench by the door, said, "Thanks for the ride, Hannah," and hurried to the stairs in back of the house, and up them to his loft room.

He was grateful he did not have to sit through the rare meeting with a glass of chocolate milk, though he craved one after the hard-won game. He was famished, and he knew that after Hannah left he could dig into the meatloaf that he could now smell. He thought, from the way his mother had been looking at him lately—the way Hannah had, too—that the conversation might be halting and tense. That his mother, who was not the most socially adept person on earth, might be awkwardly probing Hannah for whatever she knew about the changes in her son. Was he in love? Finally? Did she know with whom? Or was it something on the team, with the boys, or some experimenting with weed, or alcohol? Did she know?

He took a shower and let the gushing hot water obliterate him for a couple of minutes; then he toweled off and pulled on jeans, flip-flops, a flannel shirt. He kept listening for the sound of the car starting up again and he kept not hearing it, and finally, starving, he came back down. The two women were at the table leaning together, his mother's hand on her teacup, Hannah's hand on Carol's forearm. Hannah was in profile, head tilted down into its own pleasure at something just heard, and he saw something on her face he had never seen: eye delighted, a smile so relaxed, so relinquished of expectation or hunger or disappointment, a smile just glad to be floating there in another's company. He heard the laughter—not the hilarious hoots of Hannah's family, but a gentle chiming of mirth. He stopped still, unsure of whether to go forward or back. Was he jealous? A little. He realized that *he* would badly like to prompt Hannah to this species of pleasure. It was the sense that nothing else at all right now was wanted or needed. How had his reticent mother done it? To Hannah? And his mother—why would she not share this strangely free-flowing contentment in *his* company?

He backed away. Whatever he needed from both women was somehow strangely present at that table, and inaccessible, as if behind bulletproof glass. He climbed back to his room, ate a power bar he found in the CamelBak he wore on long runs, and curled up on his bed.

Collie was asleep when they passed through Randall, thank God. They found another marina wagon on the second dock and they padded it with her blanket. Jess rowed a dinghy out to one of the nicer weekend sailers and found the hatch unlocked and he fetched some foam pillows from the V-berth. They made her a rolling nest as shockproof as possible. They barely spoke. Each understood what needed to be done. A little over an hour until sunset, and they did not need a conversation to know that they had to get the scorched town behind them and beyond her sight, and that when they got over the first hill they would look for water and a place to camp. They got her into her child's sleeping bag, which had some kind of polyester fill— good, it would keep her warm enough if it got wet—and they nestled her into the cart. She whimpered, brow furrowed, and Jess thought he heard her murmur "Crystal," but she curled on herself and stuck her thumb in her mouth and Storey took up the handle to her wagon and they climbed away from the ashes and the lake without waking her.

Forty minutes later, they came over a wooded hill and looked down on what once must have been the prettiest farm.

Below them were pastures the farmer had let go: the grasses and clover were tall and golden and flecked with Indian paintbrush and wild pea flowers and black-eyed Susans, Queen Anne's lace, fireweed. The road followed a stone wall, and in places the rocks were grown over with wild mint and the heady scent wafted up the hill. Jess stopped and let the wagon bump his legs. For a moment he just inhaled the fragrance and let his eyes rove over the reds and magentas and yellows, the soft tawny golds, and he untethered. For a moment he felt he was in a painting and remembered the sudden and uncontested peace of looking through a Bonnard doorway to a country garden. That a place like that existed, a life—in France or anywhere else. The sense that simple beauty might hold so much of what was needed, and that it was just as true as all the shadowy architectures of thought.

It was beautiful now. Below—in the pocket of a little valley, through which he could see the silver thread of a brook—were fenced pastures and a hayfield on which the windrows of the last cutting lay waiting to be tedded and baled. He could see the spot where the farmhouse had stood, now burned but offset with islands of flower beds, and a pond with a red sugarhouse on its bank, intact. In the meadow behind it was a leaning outhouse. Jess counted a dozen Guernseys and four horses grazing, heads down. If he were ever to have a farm—which he wouldn't, because he knew from summer jobs how much work it was—it would look like this. It might be right here. It could be. Nobody was coming back to claim this. The courthouse at the county seat, wherever that was, would no longer have record of deed, because the courthouse and the clerks who tended it would no longer exist. The thought raised the hair on his arms like a cold wind.

Why had they left the sugarhouse standing? Maybe for the same reason they had left the boats. Because the attackers were capricious, or had a malevolent sense of humor. Or simply that whatever was recreational wasn't worth the effort.

Jess stood in the road as Storey stepped past him, his wagon and the girl bumping over the frost heaves. "You thinking what I'm thinking?" he said as he passed.

"Yes."

"Unless it's booby-trapped, the sugarhouse looks good to me."

"I don't think it's booby-trapped. As far as they're concerned, there's no one left."

"Right."

Jess followed Storey down the hill, pulling his own wagon.

////////////////////////

Storey knew his way around a sugarhouse. His father, Daniel, had built a small one on the bank of Sawyer Brook. Before they had children, he and Hannah had gathered the maple sap together and made enough syrup for themselves and their friends. They did not run plastic tubing like everyone else in the country, they tapped the old trees with steel taps and they hung metal buckets. The buckets had peaked metal lids that gripped the lip of the pail and flexed free when you banged the top. Daniel and Hannah walked tree to tree and unhooked the brimming pails and popped off the tops and dumped them into five-gallon pickle buckets, which they carried down to a tank on the back of a four-wheeler. They were in their twenties and they were tough and strong. Hannah could carry two buckets at a time, each no more than two-thirds full to prevent sloshing over rough ground, but still weighing almost thirty pounds apiece. They parked the ATV on a rise above the shack and let gravity empty the tank into the storage cistern. They didn't make a ton of syrup, usually around twenty gallons, enough for them to sweeten everything they could think of, from coffee to pies, and to give away to neighbors and friends and send a couple of gallons to Hannah's parents in Annapolis. Her mother had been a career diplomat and they had always lived, when they were in the States, near D.C.

When Storey was old enough to carry a single half-bucket of maple sap he began to help his father. Hannah had stepped away from sugaring a few years before, and Daniel welcomed the extra hands. And Storey enlisted Jess, of course. Who would have worked for free, because he loved doing any project with the Brandts, but Daniel insisted he get paid two gallons of finished syrup a week and all the bratwurst he could eat. Jess was crazy about grilled bratwurst and he could never get his parents on board. His mother cooked it a few times, with evident distaste, either fried in a pan on the stove or boiled, and it was not at all the same.

By the time the boys were fifteen they were each swinging two buckets of sap down the snow-patched hills, and stoking the firebox with cordwood, and helping Daniel boil. That was one job Storey's dad would not hand over. Daniel often boiled all night, riding herd on the long, open evaporator as the steam poured out of the vented cupola in the roof and dissipated among the stars. The puddles of snowmelt in the tire tracks reflected the cold constellations and froze over. Daniel liked to smoke a cigar and drink black tea and eat pickles—which cut the sweetness of the near syrup in the pan, which he *had* to sample continually—despite having a hydrometer that told him exactly when the liquid reached the right consistency.

One March night, Jess couldn't sleep. It was senior year and he and Storey were on spring break and helping Daniel sugar. There was a lot of snow that year, and though it was melting fast the woods were still mostly covered, and after a day of gathering sap the boys had clipped into cross-country skis and raced through the woods and up the flank of Putney Mountain. They contoured the ridge in a rolling rhythm, switching leads, and swooshed down the cut by Banning's and flew over the log bridges and the swollen brook. It was dark when they skied out into the field above Storey's. The snow-covered clearing gave off its own light, as bright as a shaded lantern, and they skied right into the yard, slaloming around patches of mud, and they kicked out of the skis and leaned them against the outside of the barn. They were soaked with sweat, and the freezing night and the downhill run had chilled them, and they pushed inside gratefully to the warmth of the house, the popping woodstove and the smells of baking bread. Jess always ate dinner with the family—it was part of his pay—and he slept most nights in his room in the barn, and he would remember those three weeks as some of the happiest of his life. He and Gwen had broken up just before Christmas and he was surprised to find that he was okay with it. He and Storey had grown so close, matching strides through the daily rhythms of school and work, that they might go several days barely saying a word.

So that night, after working the sugar bush, after skiing, after a big meal, Jess lay awake for hours. Through the window of his bunk room he watched Orion rise over the trees, flexing his longbow toward the Bull, which he would never kill. Jess felt deeply uneasy. He was doing fine in school; he loved the days of this spring break and he could think of no better way to spend time and he wanted for nothing. But he lay on his back and drifted. What it felt like—like he was on a raft that rocked over an ocean swell—and he wondered if this was what life offered. Just this. Days of good hard work, a friend, a sense of family, a winter constellation rising late in the infinite silence of an early-spring night. Why, then, did he feel sad? A hollow ache he could not name? And why, though his belly was full and his best friend slept yards away, could he not shake it off?

He pushed off the duvet and pulled a thick sweater over his long johns, stepped into his work boots, and pulled open the door. He stepped outside. Delicious shock of cold. He could see his breath. He walked across the muddy yard, breaking the thin glass over the standing puddles, and took the track into the trees and down to the brook. Only two hundred yards and he could see the clearing by the stream and the sugarhouse bulked against the leafless woods and the thick plume of steam pouring from the cupola. There was no wind, and the steam boiled and rolled straight up into the current of the Milky Way. He could see light in the window, and he walked on and pushed through the heavy door. Daniel was sitting on his high steward's stool at one end of the evaporator pan. He wore a red union suit with the sleeves pushed up to the elbows and a battered Brattleboro Art Museum cap. It was not a big room and Jess was close and he could see that Daniel was not smoking a cigar or eating a pickle—he was staring at the bubbling sap and he was crying. He turned his head to the opening door and did not have time to hide or wipe his tears. And Jess saw on the plank bench beside him a torn envelope and an unfolded sheet of stationery, and he recognized the hurried script of Hannah's hand.

He thought maybe his heart might have stopped. The unshielded sorrow on Daniel's face, this man he loved as much as anyone on earth, the tears that sopped into Daniel's ginger beard, the usually spirited eyes that most often sparked with mischief or humor—they may have broken his heart. Daniel registered Jess, and tried to smile but could not, and Jess hurriedly mumbled a lame "Sorry, I thought I left my Leatherman," and backed out of the door and let the heavy spring swing it shut.

He did not mention it to Storey the next morning, or ever, and Daniel never spoke of it, but in the last week of April, Hannah sat the family down and told them that she was moving to Dummerston.

She was taking the horses. She told them that Annie would be with her during the school year and Cecily would live with her half the time and Storey could of course stay wherever and whenever he wanted, he was a young man now. Jess was there for dinner that night and Hannah had asked that he stick around for the talk, as he was part of the family.

Afterward, he walked home up the good dirt road, the road mostly covered with the reaching limbs of big old trees, and he smelled the first apple blossoms in Darrow's orchard and heard the brook drumming in its bed, and he let himself sob all the way home. Sometimes he had to stop walking, he was crying so hard. And he never knew if what had happened had anything to do with the afternoon in the barn, but Hannah had the consideration to call him a week later—the caller ID on his phone surprised him—and she told him firmly that the separation had not a shred to do with him, that it was a long time coming. She made him repeat twice that he understood. But always after that, for the rest of his life, he suspected that he did not know how to properly read the emotional landscape of those around him, and that what seemed solid and eternal probably wasn't, and that love could run very, very deep and also end.

///////////////////////////

Tonight they walked through the farmyard past the charred ruin of the house, past flower beds blooming with cosmos and shrub rose and purple asters, the colors pulsing in the early October light. Past a training ring with rail jumps still standing, waiting for the ground thud of horse and rider, the knock of a hoof, the heavy breathing of the two living animals conjoined in the rush. The red-and-white-striped rails would wait now for a version of eternity in which days would follow nights and the paint would fade, and a winter storm or a spring gale would knock them off their posts one by one and the snow and mud would cover them.

They pulled their wagons to the pond and around it, past a dock with a life ring mounted on a piling, to the sugarhouse. Collie still slept. The trauma of the past couple of days had caught up with her. They would wake her before dark and feed her a full meal, which Storey knew she needed.

He set down the handle of the wagon as quietly as he could and pushed through the door of the shack. Jess was right behind him. Like the rest of the farm, it was well kept and had been designed with an eye for the long view: a row of muntined windows faced the pond side, and from the boil master's chair on its low platform the windows looked over the water and the climbing fields to the ridge. Jess noticed for the first time the spreading of color up there, hues of vermillion and blood orange and ochre bleeding through the tender greens and yellows of the woods.

The shack was one open room. The concrete floor had been recently swept and no spiderwebs shimmered in the corners. Enough space to lay out the sleeping pads and bags. A full half-cord of wood was stacked against the unwindowed wall and they could start a fire under the evaporator. They could heat food in a pot on the long pan itself, for that matter. The pan was a heavy steel rectangular tub with a firebox beneath it, and they would not warp it by burning it empty of sap. Probably. If they did, who would be upset? Who would come into this country again? With no towns to support them? Still, Jess thought that tonight they would be careful not to stoke the fire too much, not to damage anything; a sugarhouse this well loved should not be wrecked.

He was thinking that and surveying the placement of the storage tank, the shelves of canning jugs and tools, admiring the layout, when he heard Storey whistle. Long and low, a whistle of approval. Jess turned. "What?"

Storey stood from a cupboard by the slat-backed chair and said, "Look what I found."

He held up an orange plastic radio with a heavy analog tuning dial and a crank handle. "Just AM/FM, but still. If the batteries are dead it's got this crank."

"Nice."

"Maybe someone will let us know what the hell is going on. And not in French. Also, there was this deck of cards."

They fed her half asleep. When they gently woke her she blinked open limpid brown eyes and gazed from one to the other and past them, as if not remembering, and she called for her mother and father and for Crystal. The fire cricked the dry boiling pan, and wheezed, and cast an orange glow through chinks in the plate steel. It warmed the shack, so they stripped to their light wool T-shirts. Storey gently told her that they were looking for her parents now, they would journey till they found them, he promised, and that Crystal would probably come after them soon, once she had a rest, and she, Collie, needed to eat. Jess watched her take in the words, watched her chest heave once, and she made a decision or was completely cried out, because she compressed her lips and nodded and let Storey spoon the reconstituted freeze-dried beef Stroganoff into her mouth. She ate two bites, and pushed his hand away. "I can do it myself," she said.

So the three of them sat on upturned sap pails—there was a stack in the corner from the olden times before tubing—and they ate their dinners in silence, she in her lion pajamas with the hood pulled up and ears erect and the full mane shagging her head and neck. When they were done Storey took her hand and they went outside to pee under the stars, and Jess took the pot and bowls to the dock and washed them as the frost thickened on the grass of the bank.

They made her nest again against the shelves with pad and blanket and her pint-sized sleeping bag and she fell asleep instantly.

"Whew," Storey said. He glanced at the glowing evaporator. "We'll let it burn down. It's too hot in here."

"We could prop open the door."

"Yeah, let's do that." Storey rose from his bucket and swung the door and with the toe of his boot he slid a heavy iron bootscraper against it. The fresh current of cold air was a relief. "Shall we go out onto the dock and have news hour?"

"Sure. I want to and I don't."

"I know. Me, too."

Jess picked up the radio and Storey checked on Collie one more time. "She'll be okay for a few minutes," he said. And Jess thought that, after what she'd survived, he'd bet she could hold her own for much longer.

///////////////////////

They sat on the dock side by side, legs swinging over the water, as they used to do when they were boys on Mean Beaver Pond. What they called it. It was in an old abandoned orchard just off the ridge, a brook-fed swimming hole below a neat cabin, owned apparently by a professor at Amherst, but she rarely came up. The derelict gnarled trees still blossomed and still fruited with apples, but they were never pruned or sprayed, and the apples were scarred and small and mostly worm-eaten. The clean ones were firm and delicious, as if the wildness had distilled their sweetness. The boys loved to run there and swim, and one summer afternoon they were surprised by the owner. They heard the car door slam just above them, and had not time to put on any clothes before a slender young woman in a cotton skirt and linen sleeveless top came over the bank and burst into generous laughter. She propped her sunglasses on her loose cinnamon hair and declared, "Gracious, what do we have here?" They must have been about twelve then. They looked in panic from her to their shorts piled at the head of the dock and without a word both toppled into the pond, which was freezing. They treaded water.

"I'll turn around," she called. "Promise I won't look. You all can get decent and then tell me your names."

Her name was Frith and she *was* a professor—of Latin American literature, she said—and she *was* extremely pretty. They stood dripping on the dock, dressed now, side by side, awaiting the verdict, a little like two captured prisoners of war. They told her their names. She looked them over and laughed again, warmly, and she said, "Don't worry, you guys are welcome here anytime. Just promise not to disturb the beaver, who is my friend. If he's in here, just wait him out. Now I'm going up to the cabin and you can finish your swim."

She did go up and they did jump back in, and they did both hope that they would see her again.

Now—though this dock was not so idyllic, and no one was going swimming—Jess felt a certain comfort in sitting on the planks over dark water and swinging his legs beside Storey. "I guess," he said, and reached for the radio beside him and thumbed the On switch.

Again nothing. He rolled the tuner up and down the dial. Again a stuttering in static that may have been music, and again he caught on the shred of a voice and tuned back to 1485. French again, a woman narrating in a newscaster's lilting monologue, Jess for some reason having no trouble understanding now, not translating even, just listening as she said, "The band will reunite on the twenty-second of October, at the Videotron Centre, and, sad to say, she is already sold out. *Merci bien*, Marie Blanc, for joining us in the studio, and we wish you luck! Stay tuned for *Cuisine Formidable du Québec* with host Yvette Leroy, and in half an hour we bring you *World News* and the latest updates on the conflict to the south. This is Myriam Anders wishing you all a good night . . ."

Jess clicked off the radio. Storey watched him anxiously. "What did she say?" he said.

"She said the band will reunite for a big concert, but don't get all excited because it is sold out."

"What band?"

Jess shrugged.

"That it?"

"Yep. World news in half an hour."

Storey glanced at his watch. "I guess I can stay up that late. You cold?"

"No. It feels good."

"Me, too."

They sat in silence and swung their legs. Storey pried splinters from the boards and dropped them into the cold black water. There was little breeze, but what was there stirred down from the hills behind them and they could smell the smoke from the shack's stovepipe. They'd banked the firebox with the cordwood stacked against the wall, mostly split lengths of seasoned oak. The scent was as comforting as sitting on the dock.

Jess said, "I was remembering the time we were skinny-dipping at Mean Beaver Pond. That little swimming hole in the old orchard—"

"Dude, I know the pond."

"Right."

"You were thinking about the hot professor, Frith Cormier."

"How did you know?"

"Duh."

"Yeah. She really was hot. And she caught us—"

"With our little peckers in *plein air,* I know. Do you know how many times you have retold this story?"

"C'mon. Really?" Jess said.

"You were totally smitten. Like devastated."

"Weren't you?"

"Probably."

"Yes or no?"

"Yes," Storey admitted.

"Okay, then. I wonder what happened to her?"

"A couple of years after, she had a daughter and they moved back. To the cabin by the pond. Most of the time. She still taught at Amherst, but the girl went to the Grammar School. I've met her . . . Hailey. She's just as cool as her mom and just as pretty. I think she goes to Berkeley, or just got out."

"Whoa, you know a lot."

"They're our neighbors. In a way. Yours, too."

"In a way." For a moment Jess was transported to the ridge where Storey's dad, Daniel, still lived in the old house, next to the old barn, now empty of horses. And up the sinuous dirt road to his own place, where both his parents now cooked together, mostly wordlessly, each humming their own tune, and spent most evenings quietly reading—he saw the two homesteads as a night bird would, flying over the dark roofs and lighted windows, the trace of wood smoke drifting out of each chimney just as it was here, now. A vast unnamable sadness moved over him again. Without thinking he said, "Did you ever find out why your mom left your dad?"

Storey's hand, which had been stacking the dock splinters like pickup sticks, stopped. "Yes," he said.

"Was it—?"

"No."

"What?"

"It was not because she seduced you."

Jess stopped breathing. The night thickened—hardened and stilled as if crystallized, like maple syrup boiled too long.

Storey said, "You didn't think I knew?"

Jess could not breathe, much less speak.

"Jess?"

"No," Jess croaked.

"I knew that night. At dinner. You were acting so weird. Like you'd been hit on the head with a cow. Also kinda like you'd just eaten gelato for the first time."

"Gelato?"

"Or panna cotta. I don't know, something out of this world."

"But—"

"But I didn't kill you?"

"Yes," Jess croaked again.

"Mom, Hannah, had that problem. She did it with the guy who hayed the fields—"

"Frazer?"

"Yep. And the guy at the bottom of Tavern Hill, where we'd buy a side of beef."

"Glen?"

"Right. That guy."

"Holy shit."

"Yep. To tell you the truth, I was always dreading when she'd figure you were old enough."

Jess's breathing shallowed. He felt hot tears on his cheeks. He could not control them and he wasn't sure why. Was it that Storey had been a better friend than he'd ever imagined? Or that his first love had maybe bagged him like a deer and notched her belt? Right now there were many reasons to cry, and so . . . he cried.

He felt Storey's hand on the back of his head, palming it like a basketball. It was firm and forgiving, and then it was gone, and Jess cried harder.

"Sorry," Jess said finally. "I was the one who fucked up."

"No, you didn't. I would've . . ." He grunted. "I guess that's not the way to put it. I . . . anyway. It's almost time. Let's fire up the radio."

And that was it. End of discussion. Jess wiped his face on his sleeve and reached beside him and took up the radio. He set it in his lap and switched it on.

///////////////////

Nick of time. The French was rapid, but mostly understandable.

"—return to the headline story of the day, the reports of fierce fighting south of the border in the U.S. state of Maine following the assassination of the American President Schoeffler by the Maine secessionist Lamar Blodgett. And the confirmation that one week ago today, on the twenty-eighth of September, partisan operatives in support of secession exploded the dam on the river Kennebec, unleashing a flood that wiped out two battalions of federal soldiers. The death toll has been estimated by Canadian military intelligence to be more than two thousand men. No word on civilian casualties, but there have been unconfirmed reports that news of the plan somehow spread down the valley and that most of the residents sought high ground just before the explosion. I have here in the studio Lieutenant General François Schwab, Canadian Special Operations Branch, to talk about the action and the response by the U.S. military. Good evening to you, General."

"Good evening."

"Can you tell us, first of all, what you know about *le barrage* Kennebec and the resulting massacre?"

"You mean the destruction of the U.S. assault units? Eight hundred infantry from the Marine expeditionary force and five companies of cavalry, also Marines—but excuse me, this was not a massacre, Ms. Anders, this was the complete and total neutralization of an armed attacking force."

"You sound impressed."

"I am stating the facts."

"Yes, well, can you describe what we know of the federal government response?"

"Well, we don't know much, due to a very effective information blackout, but the report we are hearing is of a scorched-earth campaign in the counties that support secession. Some would say the response has been . . . disproportionate . . ."

They listened. Or, rather, Jess listened and Storey heard, grasping at the few words he understood—like "massacre"—and he watched Jess's face intently for some import, as if he might read the narrative there. When the interview was done and Myriam Anders thanked the general and turned to economic news and the impact the war was having on the markets—*"Parce que, enfin,"* she added soberly, *"nous devons appeler un chat un chat. C'est une guerre, une guerre civile . . ."*—because, in the end, we must call a spade a spade, this is a civil war—when she turned to collateral news, Jess turned off the receiver and set it on the plank beside him.

He blew out. There had been a lot to digest in the last hour.

"Bad?" Storey said. He could not hide his dread. And Jess knew it was not for himself but for his family, and maybe for Collie, too.

"Bad."

"You need a minute?"

"No." Jess zipped his shell jacket to the throat. "You remember I told you this morning—" He interrupted himself. "Was that really this morning? Fuck, these days are long."

"No shit."

"Well, I was telling you that the government—the U.S., the feds— sent a couple thousand assault troops into the Kennebec Valley."

"I remember."

"The secessionists blew the dam."

"The dam? Harris Station? Below Indian Pond?"

"Yes."

"Whoa. That's a mega frigging dam. And isn't the 'pond' like ten miles long?"

"Yes. I guess it was apocalyptic. It wiped out the two battalions, like two thousand soldiers. I guess no one expected it, for some reason."

"Whoa."

"I guess it's why . . . why what we've been seeing . . ." Jess trailed off.

"Yeah," Storey said. He was gazing at the ridge across the lit- tle valley, to where it bulked against the stars. Jess heard him whistle without tone, just air, which he did sometimes when he was stressed. The whistling cut. "What about all the people that lived there? The residents downstream? Waterville, Skow- hegan? Didn't it kill a ton of civilians?"

"Water probably spread out by then. And apparently word got out just in time, and almost everyone who needed to got to higher ground."

"Fuck," Storey whispered. He said, "These guys are way serious. They all are. No one is playing games. I guess we can see that for ourselves."

////////////////////////

Nobody was playing games, that was a fact. But tonight the three of them were snug in a well-built sugarhouse with enough firewood to last weeks, and probably food, too, but they would not stay.

They left the door cracked open and Jess lay on his back on his pad on the concrete floor and let the news sift. All of it. He heard Storey snoring softly and heard Collie whimper and huff, and heard the fire ping in the evaporator, and the sheet metal creak and sigh. And after a while he heard the soft call of a great horned owl, hollow and insistent, and it sounded doleful, muffled by distance, and he heard maybe its mate answer with a matching sorrow from a place even deeper in the night.

He was being stripped, little by little, of all he carried that meant anything. That's what he thought. His wife had gone, had left him standing in the middle of their street not knowing if he should wave. His dog, and now his first love. The memory of Hannah had always warmed him; it was, oddly, a touchstone, and now he was supposed to toss it, too. He refused. She had loved him. She may have screwed the neighbors, but she had loved him, he was sure. Wasn't he?

And what did any of it mean if a helicopter or a sniper's rifle cut him down tomorrow? And could an owl's call carry the grief, echo it down the freezing valley and soothe the spirit? And why could he not love his parents with the same warmth with which he loved even the horses in Storey's barn, who had also been taken? Andandand. Again he floated. His sleeping pad was a raft and it drifted, spinning slowly, and at some point he realized that the owl's call had ceased and he heard now only the brook that fed the pond and he slept.

Gray dawn. Sometime in the night the clouds had moved in and lidded the valley and they woke to the smell of fog and rain drumming the metal roof. The men did; Collie slept. Jess stepped outside and could see even in half-light the mist clinging to the ridges and the paler streaks of sleet mixing with the downpour.

Respite and relief. For now they had no decision to make except whether to add cinnamon to the oatmeal (yes), and guess what else? They found on a shelf one unsold and unopened quart of maple syrup. The dry evaporator pan was like one giant stovetop, and while Storey stirred the oatmeal, Jess made coffee. They'd add syrup to that, too. Not the precious cans of evaporated milk, though; those they'd save for Collie's oatmeal.

Rain day. They wouldn't move, at least not this morning.

They woke her and Storey got her into her raincoat over the lion suit and they went out into the rain to the outhouse. When they returned they shook off their rain gear side by side— "Whew! Shake-shake!" Storey said. "Whew! Shake-shake!" Collie repeated—and they scraped their boots ceremonially on the toothed iron scraper.

Jess had three full bowls and three full hot cups waiting by each bucket and he said, "It's like Goldilocks and the three bears, right?"

"Right," Collie said. For a second Jess panicked, thinking, *Wrong thing to say,* but she didn't, thank God, ask where was the mama bear.

The oatmeal with syrup was delicious, and hers with milk even more so, and they ate hungrily and in silence, and she asked for more. When they were done he gathered up the bowls and the pot and Collie said she wanted to come help do the dishes, she liked it, and Jess said it was raining, and she said she liked that, too, and so the two of them went back out into what was becoming a deluge and they walked to the upper end of the pond, where the brook flowed, and they squatted in the sleet and scoured the dishes with the half sponge. Jess did, and Collie rinsed. She held up one bowl and squinted as the rain pattered on her eyelids and said, "You missed a spot," and handed it back. Jess was pretty sure she couldn't see anything in the spray, but he held it up and turned his face blindly into the downpour and said, *"Did not,"* and she grabbed it back and held it up and pointed at a spot neither of them could really see and said, "Did *so.* See?"

So Jess sighed in defeat and said, "Are you Mrs. Clean or what?" and she nodded, emphatic.

He took the bowl back and rewashed it and when he handed it back to her he saw something like glee in her triumph. He thought then that this five-year-old had more resilience than he and Storey by an order of magnitude. He did not think that she was willfully ignoring her recent losses, or had somehow skillfully forgotten, it was just that she was little in a mean world and she needed her agility and she would protect it. She would stay rooted in the present whenever she could. He felt admiration.

In the shack Storey untwisted the plastic band from the tattered deck of cards and he taught her how to play Go Fish and three of them played it for hours. She loved saying, "Go fish! Go *fish!*" which she accompanied sometimes by clapping her hands and spilling her cards. When she dropped her cards she said, "Whoops," and made them not look while she gathered them. Storey somehow found a faint classic-rock station on the AM dial and they listened to "Wild Horses" and "Cinnamon Girl," the songs coming through in swells, as if pushed by a capricious wind, and Collie said, "I love horses. *And* fish." And Jess saw the logic in it and said, "Me, too," and added, "and sometimes beavers." And she said that there was a beaver in the lake that had something wrong with him and he swam in circles, but she loved him sometimes anyway.

They kept the stove stoked and the door cracked for fresh air, and the rain abated to a steady whisper on the roof, the kind that might last all day and into the night, and Jess didn't care. A part of him unclenched, and when she shouted, "Go *fish!*" and clapped her hands and scattered her cards for the third time, he found himself laughing. It surprised him. And then he couldn't contain it, and the more they stared at him the more he uncorked.

Collie was staring and moving her lips around, and when he finally sputtered out and blotted the tears from his eyes with the back of his hand she said, "You got the fits, mister." And then: "I'm *fam*ished!"

Now Jess stared. "*Famished?* Where'd you learn that?"

"Means starving, dummy."

"Well, *okay*. I'm gonna go outside and see a man about a horse. Then I'll whip us up some lunch."

"A horse?" she said. She started to stand. "I wanna come."

Jess said, "It means I gotta pee. It's a polite way of saying it."

"Oh." She sat back down.

"Just a sec," he said.

His Gore-Tex slicker hung on a peg by the door. He grabbed it, shrugged into it, and went out the door. He walked down to the dock. Not for any reason except that he liked it. It comforted him. The rain was gentle but steady and it drummed the dock and hissed on the water. He could so easily imagine the storm tapering off, the clouds breaking to a hot autumn sun, the afternoon warming; then: stripping to boxers and running off the end of that dock. No beaver to scare off. The water would be freezing and delicious. It occurred to him that they'd spent days walking the edge of a lake and hadn't been swimming once. Well. Neither had been in the mood.

He peed in the grass where the dock met the bank and let his eyes travel the pocket of valley, the wooded hills and meadowed slopes striped with ravels of mist, and he inhaled the scent of sodden pasture. The smell of rain sifting on cold black water. His gaze swept up to the higher fields, and he saw the ribbon of road where it emerged from the woods at the top of the ridge, and he shook himself and zipped up and froze.

At the top of the road, fog merged with low clouds, and out of it he saw the bulk of a vehicle descending. Then another behind it, and another. Pickup trucks maybe, one larger, size of a farm truck, a troop truck maybe. Three. Jesus.

He ran. Hit the door so hard he almost fell inside.

"Trucks," he said.

Collie blinked at him; she was trying to straighten the cards into a square deck. Storey was crouched at the wagon, prying cans out of the stack. He dropped them. "Where?"

"Top of the ridge. Road we came on. Coming down."

Storey was already moving. Storey had the fastest reaction time of any person Jess had ever met, and he had ice in his blood when it counted. "Grab the pot," Storey said. "The sleeping stuff. Shove it in her wagon. Baling twine on that peg—it'll get wet but fuck it. I got the food and the girl."

Ninety seconds later, they had the packs on and rifles slung. Jess remembered his binocs on a hook. Storey yanked open the back door—lucky thing there was one—with his left hand. He looked down at Collie and said, "Can you hold my hand and run?" She didn't balk or cry. She nodded. She reached up for his hand and he said, "Okay, you're the leader. You run in front of me. Straight through the grass to those trees. Okay? Three-two-one, go!"

Jess pushed through after them and tugged the door till the latch reseated. The grass in the narrow pasture behind the sugarhouse had been recently mowed, thank God, and would not leave an obvious swish of trail. Plus the heavy rain, which blurred everything and filled the hoofprints of the cows and horses. The meadow was a mess. They ran. It was only forty yards across and then they were in thick woods, pines and hemlocks and untapped maples. A blowdown yellow birch had snapped an old pine, and the fallen trees lay broken and tangled at forest's edge, and they skirted the ragged stump and threw themselves in behind it. The convoy of three trucks had hit the flat and were turning in on the drive to the cinder pile of the old house. Good. The drivers could have seen them running from the high road but from the level of the valley floor they would not have had the vantage. But they were close now, and there was nothing between them and their pile of dead limbs but open ground.

The three trucks ground on into the farmyard and around the charred timbers of the barn. They turned onto the rough tractor road to the sugarhouse, *fuck,* two pickups followed by a tarped farm truck with staked wood sides. There were six or eight camo-clad soldiers in the second truck. The first truck had a .50-caliber mounted high in the bed and a man in a green slicker leaned into it. The gun was aimed at the shack as if ready for anyone who came out the front door. Because of course there were people in there: a kerosene lantern glowed through the windows in the storm-dark afternoon and smoke leaked from the stovepipe.

Jess glassed the man. The only mark on his slicker was the Carhartt "C," but he wore a baseball hat, not a helmet, and on the crown was a red-and-white patch, the shape of Maine outlined in crimson with the number "49" in the center. The man and the pickup passed out of view behind the sugarhouse, where it evidently parked, because the two other trucks jounced to a stop still in sight. Jess heard shouting. Then a burst of automatic fire, percussive. It seemed to shake the rain out of the trees above them. Collie was squeezed between them where they pressed against the birch trunk, and Jess felt her shaking hard. He felt Storey's arm come around her, heard his quiet "Don't worry, they won't hurt us here. I promise." And Jess felt him push her head down gently and heard him whisper, "Super-quiet, and cover your eyes, 'kay?"

Now out of the back of the farm truck jumped men. A stream, un-uniformed, in rain jackets and oiled coats and surplus ponchos. Carrying long guns, mostly AR-15s and scoped hunting rifles and a few shotguns, pump and auto. On the caps they wore the same patches. Jess counted eleven. He swung the glasses back to the second pickup and was surprised to see that the uniformed soldiers hadn't moved. Then he saw why: two of the dudes from the bigger truck jogged up and prodded them with gun barrels, and the men tried to stand and jostled each other and two fell over, and Jess saw that they were zip-tied and he saw one of the guards strike the fallen ones with the butt of his rifle. He heard more shouting and the men climbed down too slowly and shuffled, hatless on the mud, and he could see that they were broken, probably beaten to within inches of not being able to walk at all. The two prodded the line of one-two-three-four-five-six captives out of sight behind the sugarhouse. Then, evidently, into it, because they saw in the big windows a crowd of shapes moving. Moving at first chaotically, and then forming what looked like a solid phalanx blotting the light all the way to the ceiling, shoulders maybe, and heads, and then the crashing cavalcade and the windows exploded and men flew through them, airborne in a red spray like so many rags. Jess heard Collie cry out and felt Storey squeeze her, heard his "Hush-hush-hush, Collie, bad men, we've gotta stay quiet," and he heard her stifled shout as Storey covered her mouth and shoved her head down. Jesus. Jess felt her squirm against him as Storey repeated harshly, "Hush, *hush,* please, Collie, *quiet!* Or the bad men will kill us!" And she finally hushed or just abated, and she kept her head down and whimpered and shook. They watched as someone arced the kerosene lantern—probably into the stack of split kindling—and someone else must have dumped gasoline, because one side of the room flared and then the flames poured out the windows, despite the rain.

They had stood the prisoners up on the boiling pan and shot them point-blank. They probably had orders. They had fulfilled them and just left the bodies out in the rain. God. They clearly did not have time to search for whoever had been enjoying a pot of coffee, they had bigger fish to fry, they just offed the soldiers and ignited the slaughterhouse and now they were loading back into the bigger truck, and now Jess and Storey heard the engines rev and saw the vehicles back around. They saw the pickup with the machine gun bounce forward and skirt the others and retake the lead. The convoy jounced up the farm track past the remains of the house and turned left on the country road, and Jess lost them in the mist and the rain.

///////////////////////

They would not fare well. Not here, not on the road. Not, probably, at the border with New Hampshire, or with Quebec, either. Had they been caught eating their lunch, sitting on the three pails like characters in some country fable, they would no doubt be sprawled now on the blood-painted grass with the six U.S. Marines.

They huddled behind the blowdown in the steady downpour, and it seemed the shots still echoed down the valley. For a while, no one spoke or moved except for Collie's shaking, which Jess could feel against his shoulder. She was beyond crying and only trembled as if cold, and Jess heard her whimper to Storey that she was hungry and he heard Storey say, "Sure, sure, hold on," and Storey squeezed her hard and dropped back to his wagon, where he dug out a can of Mexican flan of all things and found a spoon in an outer pocket of his pack and offered it to her. "Pudding," he said and she took it and spooned it slowly at first and then more avidly and then with an animal hunger. "More," she said, and Storey found another can and . . . *repeat.*

Their sleeping bags were getting drenched in the other wagon, but there was nothing for it. Though Jess had spread his extra blanket over the top, it was just wool and wasn't helping much. They needed shelter and a fire to dry things out, but their shelter was being devoured by flames.

They would string up the tarp and rake burning timbers out of the edge of the pyre and start their own fire and try to dry out the sleeping gear. They did. They ventured out and skirted the dead men and went to the dock side of the shack. The burning building threw enough heat that it seemed to evaporate the drizzle, and they could not get closer than about thirty feet. The wall there had collapsed and spilled outward. Good enough. Storey found a stack of steel fence posts in tall grass beside the riding ring. They each had a triangular blade at the base for driving into dirt, and he used one to rake back a pile of embers and scraps of flaming two-by-fours and siding. Then he and Jess headed to the brook at the top of the pond and Collie cried out that she was coming, too, and the three walked together. Storey and Jess found heavy round stones just small enough to grasp, and Collie found one she could carry; they could not walk on the pond side of the burning shack because it was too close to the flames, so they took the meadow behind it and swung way wide of the dead men.

Jess and Storey used the rocks to pound the stakes into the grass, and the ground was sodden, and they drove easily. The two men worked in tandem, but they couldn't look at each other. They strung the parachute cord four feet up and staked out the tarp into a lean-to and they put Collie underneath it. She sat in the center, in front, like a Buddha in a flickering stupa, and just behind her, under cover, they pounded sticks and strung more line and draped the sleeping bags as best they could. The heat was intense, just bearable, and it warmed and dried Collie and the synthetic bags, too. She peeled out of her raincoat and shook her mane like a true lion, and once Storey gave her the last can of flan and the spoon she lost herself in the fire's wavering light and the exploding flares of sapwood, and her eyes focused on nothing, and she looked abstracted and not unhappy.

Mid-afternoon but already evening dark. Sky black with storm, and pale fog rolling along the ridges. Jess thought it looked like a classical Japanese pen-and-ink landscape. They stood outside in the rain. There was not room enough under the tarp for her and the drying gear and both of them, and also they needed to talk and not in code.

Jess squeezed his eyes shut against the gusts and hugged himself.

"You okay?" Storey said.

"No."

"Me, neither."

"Fuck," Jess breathed. "*Fuckfuckfuck*. You hear about stuff like this, in other countries."

Storey grimaced against the rain, turned his face away from the wind. "It's not real."

"It's real." Jess shook himself like a dog shedding water. He straightened and tapped Storey's rain jacket where the shirt pocket of chew would be and he struck the can.

"Thank God," Storey said. "Good idea." He unzipped enough to get two fingers down to the can and he slipped it out. He rapped the lid and twisted it off and held the can out to Jess. "We're gonna run out of this tomorrow. You think any of those poor guys have any on them?"

"You wanna look?"

Storey shook his head.

"The Forty-niners woulda searched them anyway."

"Right."

Jess spat. "Everybody's crazy. Berserk. Everybody's killing everybody."

"Yeah."

"Where did they *come* from?" Storey closed his eyes as he felt the nicotine hit his bloodstream. He said, "I didn't even get a chance to finish my coffee. About the best cup I ever had."

"It's not safe on the road," Jess said.

"It's not safe on the lake. Just ask the *Clawdette*."

"We could move through the woods."

"No, we can't."

"I guess not." Jess turned so that the heat and light of the fire was full on his face, almost the way he would have turned his face to the sun on a winter day. Does one became inured to death? No. But one turns one's face to the fire, closes eyes, and becomes suspended. Does time work like that? Can we suspend it? Yes. Seems so. Time present and time past.

He drifted for a moment. Without expectation. It was as if whatever the future held passed beneath like an ocean swell.

"You look nuts," Storey said.

Jess startled.

"You're upset because you were finally winning at Go Fish," Storey said.

Jess smiled, shrugged. Storey's face was still grim but his eyes sparked with the old humor, and it warmed Jess. He spat. "What do you want to do?"

"I don't have a single good idea. They went west. Straight west, no hesitation, as if they knew there were more of them that way. A lot more."

"Right."

"And I'm getting the sense they have zero tolerance for surprises or strangers." Storey turned, spat. "Nor, apparently, do the other guys."

"Agreed."

"So."

"So."

"We go back east."

"We're starting to yo-yo," Jess said.

"I don't know what else to do."

In the fall of his senior year, on a Friday night, Jess got a text from Hannah. It surprised him. He hadn't heard from her all summer, and he didn't know if that was strange or not. He hadn't visited her on his own initiative, because he felt shy and figured she had enough on her plate, adapting to her new life in Dummerston. He had stopped by with Storey a handful of times, mostly so that Storey could pick up something from his new room in the 1870s farmhouse. Once, in July, she had asked them to stay for supper, and they ate with her and Cecily on the back porch, which was screened. The porch looked past a clearing to the swift black water of Salmon Brook. There was a round cherry table back there and she had placed a Ball jar brimming with pea flowers and daisies in the center, and the simplicity and the accompanying burble of the brook and Hannah's familiar bell laugh made Jess feel that maybe she had made the right choice somehow, and he remembered feeling apostate at the thought, disloyal to the union of the family he had loved so much. They ate a cold chicken salad that was delicious, and Hannah gave them each a ginger beer, which was Jess's favorite. If Cecily, who was usually voluble, didn't say much, and glanced over at him swiftly now and then, and between bites covered her curled hand with her good one as if protecting it, he didn't ask himself why.

But now, with the text, Hannah was reaching out just to him. It said, "Hi J, haven't seen you in many moons. Would you like to come over for an iced tea and catch up? I was thinking tomorrow after your game at Deerfield. You've got the old Subaru now, right? Cecily is on the Ridge with Daniel and Annie is at soccer camp. Lmk." Storey would be with his dad, too, for the next week. He had promised to help Daniel cut firewood out of the sugar bush.

Jess should have been glad. Why did his gut contract? He was seventeen and not old enough to know. He typed back, "Okay, sure."

She messaged back, "Great. I know you'll be starving after the game. I'll make something simple."

He typed back, "Thanks."

Thanks. Which was what, truly and simply, was in his heart. Thanks for all of it. For partly, maybe mostly, raising me. For shuttling me everywhere. For teaching me to garden and cook a little. For laughing when my own house was so serious. For insisting on listening to my poems. For guiding me so graciously through that other rite of passage. For—I guess—seeing me full-on, gladly, when my own parents just lowered their reading glasses and looked up over their books.

The next morning, the Saturday of the soccer game, it was raining. A steady, cold October rain not unlike the one that washed the tarp now and dripped off the brims of their Gore-Tex hoods. The field at Deerfield Academy, as perfectly maintained as it was, turned muddy. The rain came in blowing veils. Two players slid and collided and a Deerfield player was taken off the field on a stretcher. No yellow or red card was given, and the game turned physical and then vicious. The ref could not control it. Storey and Jess played hard, in their usual sync, feeding the ball to each other, taking foul hits and recovering balance and pressing attacks. Regular Time ended in a tie, and Putney lost on penalty kicks. The team did not use Deerfield's field house and drove home in the school bus mostly silent, soaked, covered in mud. It was still drizzling and cold when they got to the Putney campus, and the two boys didn't even bother to run to Jess's ancient Outback. They walked slowly, defiantly, together, and let the rain wash off some of the mud. They slammed the doors and Jess cranked the heat and all the windows fogged and they opened them and blasted the defrost and had to wait until the glass cleared.

"That sucked," Storey said.

"I thought it was kinda fun."

"We shoulda won."

"Yeah. Pass me that red rag." Jess tried to wipe the inside of the windshield, but it just streaked the fog. "We've gotta wait a minute."

Twenty minutes later, when they pulled up to Storey's house, Storey said, "You wanna come in and have lunch with me and Cecily and Pop? He said he was making burgers."

"Nah, I better clock in."

That's what Jess said when he felt like he'd been spending too much time away from his parents. It was maybe the first time in his life he had deliberately lied to Storey. He was not going to clock in. The county road was not visible from Storey's house, and Jess was going to drop Storey off at his front door and head down the gravel driveway, but instead of turning left, up the hill to home, he was going to turn right, back down the hill and out Bunker Road to Dummerston. To Hannah. That's what he did. Storey got out and stood in the rain and leaned back in. He said, "Hey." His voice sounded brittle. "I've gotta cut wood tomorrow," and Jess said, "I'll come over and help you guys," and Storey hesitated a second and shut the door.

Jess drove out the good paved road to Dummerston. Mist hung in the trees and over the fields, and he drove with the window half down so he could smell the wet fall woods. He followed a stone wall and passed the old Aiken dairy farm and Pete Dixon's artisan-cheese operation. The car's heat huffed and wheezed and he was warm despite his wet clothes and the rain spraying in. He realized even then that on any normal day he would have felt happy, probably euphoric. He had just played a well-fought soccer game with his best friend, they had played as well as they ever had, his favorite time of year was in full swing, as was one of his favorite kinds of weather, and he was covered in mud. What could be better? Except that inside, somewhere near his diaphragm, he felt a dark churn. Of something akin to shame but deeper in the roots and darker, more subterranean, because it was bound to a willful surrender to something probably very wrong, and the anticipation held a dreadful frisson of excitement and anxiety. All of which squelched any germination of joy. He had lied to Storey, he was heading to meet Hannah, where they would be, by design, in a house alone, and he realized as he drove that he was hard.

It was an old farmhouse with no garage, and so everyone used the back door into the kitchen. She was standing in it when he pulled up and she laughed as he ran in his Crocs through the rain. She held open the screen door and said, "Wow, what a mess! Stop on the linoleum. Some fool put it down in the kitchen years ago, but it has its uses." He didn't know whether to kiss her cheek as he passed—plus, he was really muddy—so he just whisked by and stood dripping. Her smile was wide and relaxed. She was truly glad to see him. And she was not wearing cutoffs, thank God. She wore loose faded jeans with threadbare tears at the thighs and frayed pockets, and a flannel shirt. Her hair was loose on her shoulders. There was not a thing provocative about the outfit, and yet Jess thought she was more beautiful than he'd ever seen her. He was more confused. She was acting like his friend's mother and yet his heart swelled and he wanted to kiss her more than anything. "Hold on," she said. "I'm going to get you a towel. Two towels. Did you bring anything to change into?"

He was speechless. He shook his head. Her tongue went to her upper lip and her glance said, fleetingly, *Still a teenager, but I forgive you.* "Okay, wait a sec," she said. "I'll get you a pair of Storey's jeans and a T-shirt." She walked past him. He smelled her shampoo, same coconut scent as ever. He followed the curve of her hips in the jeans and he wondered why baggy pants with rips on the thighs now seemed so much sexier than anything else. He set up a quadratic equation in his head and tried to solve it. He wondered if she'd noticed that he was excited. If so, she did not let on. She returned and handed him two folded white towels and said, "One is for wearing now and getting muddy and the other is for after the shower you are now going to take." Her smile was bright and somehow sad. "Strip and hand me the uniform. I'm going to hose it down. Here, I'll turn around." She did. She turned her back and held one arm out like a clothes tree, and he could not help but take her in, hair to hips to clogs, and all of algebra went out the window. He peeled off his clothes clumsily and placed them on her hand and arm and he wrapped one of the towels around his waist and she turned back and surveyed him head to toe and he shivered. Couldn't help it. "Okay," she said. "Use my shower. I think the uniform has most of the mud; you alone shouldn't clog anything. You know where it is?"

He nodded.

"Okay, go. I'll put out lunch. We can eat on the back porch and watch the rain on the brook. Sound good?"

He nodded.

He half expected her to come through the door into the steamy bathroom while he showered. More than half. Maybe with nothing on but black lingerie. Slip that off, too, and join him. Wasn't that partly why she had invited him here, alone? He didn't know. He shook, and it wasn't just the gush of hot water driving the chill from his bones.

But she didn't come. He scrubbed the mud off his arms and knees. He had to shampoo twice to get it out of his hair. It took a minute, but the task settled him down and he found himself relieved to be alone, and by the final rinse he was just a high-school kid who had lost a hard-fought soccer game and was about to eat lunch. Nearly. As he came into the kitchen, she was at the counter with her back to him, just setting down a ceramic bowl. He noticed her hand tremble as she reached for a wooden spoon and his heart began to canter. (A) The fall of her loose hair on the red-and-black flannel was crazy pretty, and (B) Why was she trembling? It occurred to him then, with a shock, that she might be just as nervous as he was.

She sensed him and turned. Too quickly, it seemed, because she did not have time to banish a look he would never forget. In profile, in her eye and the set of her mouth, he saw the determination and spirit of the old Hannah, and the sadness and insecurity of the new one. The loneliness. He didn't know why, but he suddenly wanted to cry. Hannah was before him and she was not. The extended family he had relied on most of his life existed and it did not. In the doorway, he was Jess and he was not. He didn't know who he was.

She covered her lapse with a glad surprise. *There you are!* Maybe she read his face. She smiled brightly. She said, "Almost ready.

I know you have a hollow leg, but if you can eat all this I'll—"
She stopped. What? *Give you a prize?* She couldn't find words,
so she reached up to a cabinet and pulled out two tall tumblers.
"The iced tea is in the fridge. In the blue glass pitcher. I mixed
it with lemonade, the way you like it." Relief. Again. Again she
was in charge like the old Hannah, and he had something to
do. He took the glasses and went to the fridge and took out the
fogged decanter, and she said, "Go ahead and set it on the table
on the porch. I'll be right out."

There were two place settings, both on one side of the round
table, spread on a light cotton tablecloth covered in a weave of
blue cornflowers. He guessed it was so they could both see
the stream. The Ball jar was there, overflowing with petunias.
The rain had lightened and barely sifted on the porch roof, but the
brook was boisterous with runoff. She was behind him, carrying two bowls—a bone ceramic, glazed with a simple vine
scrolling the edge, and a smaller blue clay vessel full of dark
olives. In the bigger dish was one of Jess's favorite meals, a
chilled macaroni-and-tuna salad. She set them down in front of
the place settings and she put a hand on his shoulder—warm,
appreciative—and she said, "Here, you sit here."

And he muttered, "Okay," and glanced at her, at the sunburned
cheeks, the pattering of freckles, the turquoise earring . . . He
might have fainted. Not from nerves now, but from a surfeit of
beauty. The simple table with its centerpiece of flowers from
just outside, the stream and the sound it made, the smell of the
salad, her coconut scent and closeness and the way she had just
touched him, casual but receptive—the shadow of loneliness, of
sadness, had somehow been banished. He wanted desperately
to believe it.

He sat down. He was glad they weren't facing each other. She was on his right, almost close enough that their shoulders touched. She took a deep breath, as one about to dive from a high rock. She did not try to hide it. An almost silent "Whew." He loved her for that. She reached for the pitcher and poured his glass. Had she just openly confessed that this was not easy for her, either, but that she was happy he was here? It seemed so. He relaxed.

"*Skål,*" she said, and lifted her glass.

"*Skål.*" The Mexican glasses tinked. A breath of wind shook the trees and knocked heavy drops onto the eaves where a maple overhung. The brook raised a rush of applause. Could it be possible? Could this all be okay? Even sweet and good?

"Dig in," she said. "You first. Just leave a little for me."

They ate. Companionably. She asked about his poems—somehow during soccer season he didn't write many. About college—his mother and he were going on a Western tour in mid-October, he'd miss a game with Vermont Academy, no big deal. He was thinking of Berkeley.

"Why?"

"I like to say it better than Cal Poly."

"Good enough. California, though?"

"Yes."

She didn't ask why. They each ate two helpings of the tuna salad. She scraped her plate gently with the side of her fork and unbuttoned the highest closed button of her flannel shirt. All in one casual motion.

She reached for the pitcher, which was on his side, and leaned over, and he could see the swell of her breasts held by black lace. A frill at the edge and a mesh crosshatched with black thread. Her slender neck was flushed, and he thought he could feel the heat of it as she leaned. The warmth held a scent of apple. He felt the vertigo again. He didn't know what he was supposed to do and he wasn't capable of much, anyway. She twisted in her chair and tipped the jug and filled his glass. She was inches away. She set the pitcher down and lifted her eyes to his. How could he never have noticed that they were a dark gray, slate after rain? They were steady, but where they had always held a game confidence, and a kind of music, as if she were singing to herself, now the shadows there seemed to extend to empty rooms and hallways where the song of her life echoed. And there was determined bravery there, too, as if she knew she could hide nothing and was willing to show him anyway. He was moved, and scared. And then, without dropping her eyes, she unbuttoned one more button. And she reached out and slid her fingers into his hair and urged his face, gently, an inch closer to the lace.

"You can," she said. And he did.

They tumbled to the clean rag rug, on the porch, beneath a wicker love seat. With the up-valley breeze shaking the rain out of the trees and the tuneless, dropping two-note song of a chickadee piping out of the woods, portending the end of storm. Hannah tugged off his sweatshirt and he unbuttoned and shoved down on the waist of her jeans, and as he brushed the smoothness of her lower stomach, and the silk of her skimpy panties, his confusion was swept away in a rush of desire that obliterated everything else. As it had the first time. He lost himself more deeply, more completely than he ever had with Gwen, but this time it was to that dark churn, the current that felt subterranean and powerful and blind. There was fear down there, and abandon. That was it: the sense that he had abandoned himself at the gates.

She shuddered, and it seemed she orgasmed twice. He did not ask. As he came, and after, he felt the crash of relinquishing everything. And a tide of anger swept him that he did not understand. They did not speak. She led him to her shower, and this time she sudsed and washed him. She rinsed them both off, and she led him to the laundry room behind the kitchen and handed him his soccer uniform, which was in the dryer and dry. Not like *Here are your clothes, now get out of here,* but tenderly, like *I love you, I have always loved you, love changes, and here are your old clothes so you can return to yourself, the one I know you just left at the door.*

When he walked down the back steps and turned and saw her standing in the doorway, as she had when he arrived, but sad now, not hiding it, and all alone under the big trees, he loved her possibly more than he would ever love anything in his life. And his anger was just as strong. On the drive home he had to pull over just to breathe, to steady himself, to focus, so he would not drive off the shoulder into the trees.

⁕

Now, in another October downpour that gradually thinned to drizzle, under another afternoon sky as dark as dusk and roiled with low cloud and mist, he stood beside Storey and felt at a loss. There was no clear path. The strategy of running "back into the black," of moving into the wake of destruction and following behind, now seemed reckless. They were not as tactically nimble, for one. If they did stumble on a threat they could no longer sprint for cover, as they had in the village when they dove behind the bronze boat. Now they had the girl. She had been a champ so far, hushing finally when it counted, but she was five and could not reasonably be depended on not to scream when frightened. They needed to be as far away from the combatants as possible. Who, right now, seemed to be everybody. And everyone was trigger-happy. Shoot first, ask questions later, was everyone's MO.

Storey had just suggested going east again, but he wasn't sure. Neither was Jess. Right now no option seemed very appealing. "I don't know," Storey said again. He looked up at the barely brightening clouds. "Good, the rain's almost stopped."

Jess let his eyes travel up to the lightening sky, across to the ridge half obscured in mist, to the road at the crest. "Good. Be nice to really dry out." He pulled the hood of his rain jacket back, shook his head free. "I guess we should head east, and south. Seemed to be where those folks on the *Newsboy* were headed."

"Right."

"They said on the radio that the secessionists started up here in the big timber country of north-central Maine, didn't they? That's who they were punishing."

"I think so."

"So maybe it's better other places. Maybe the cities along the coast are safer. Maybe it's where the refugees end up."

"What refugees?" Storey said bitterly.

"Right. Yeah." Jess imagined the young woman in the lake holding a stone to her pregnant belly. "But maybe," he said, "it's where people like her parents are headed. Maybe we could find them."

"Sure. A lot of maybes."

"Hey!"

They both turned, looked down. Collie was standing beneath them. She had shed her rain jacket and stood in her lion suit. Her lips were set tight. Jess thought she looked determined, like when she was organizing her hand in Go Fish, putting the sevens with the sevens. She reached out and tugged on Storey's coat.

Storey immediately squatted down. His face was pained. He said, "I'm really sorry I hushed you so hard before. In the trees."

"It's okay," she said. She blew out, bit her lower lip, looked straight into Storey's eyes. Her right paw went to the edge of her hood, touched her mane. "Are you really a friend of Mom's?" she said.

Storey said, "Yes." No hesitation. "I want the best for your mom, and your dad. Just like you do. I already feel like they are somehow part of my family. Like you are."

His words struck home. Storey was a truth teller, and it would have been clear to anyone—any dog or horse, for that matter—that he meant every word. Her eyes welled.

"Um," she said. She worked her lips. The fingers of her hand pinched the hem of her mane. Storey reached and thumbed the first tears off her cheeks. "I know where Mom and Dad are," she murmured.

"You do?" Storey said, not hiding his surprise, but keeping his voice gentle.

"They said to wait two days and only tell one of our friends." She blinked and more tears spilled and Storey held her gaze, thumbed her other cheek.

"Okay," he said. "We are definitely your friends and we will take you there. Okay? Col?"

She nodded and pinched the edge of her hood and said, "It's in here. In here." And then she burst into tears and Storey put his arms around her and held her.

///////////////////////

After she quieted, Storey brought the hood back so she would not flinch from the blade, and he felt for the slight stiffness of paper. He found it and glanced up at Jess. He flipped open his clip knife and cut the threads of the hem. "Good," he hummed softly. "Good job, hold still, great." He worked in a finger, then two, and pinched out a torn scrap. It was lined, probably from a sheet of composition notebook. He smoothed and stretched it in his fingers. He handed it to Jess. Scrawled hastily across the three inches of damp and wrinkled stationery were two lines of numbers that Jess recognized. They were latitude and longitude.

Chapter Fourteen

"Good job," Storey said cheerfully. He brought her mane back over her head and palmed it and rubbed her hard through the hood. "You did good."

"I'll get the gazetteer," Jess said. Storey nodded. She stepped back, looked from one to the other. Her face had mostly cleared, like the afternoon, and she seemed relieved of a burden. Storey said, "You did really good, Collie. We're going to take you to your parents now."

She nodded mutely.

"And I'm going to sew the tear in your mane back up in a minute. Okay?"

She nodded.

"We're gonna look at a map."

Jess was already at his pack, which was on its back just inside the tarp. He dug around and pulled out the battered blue atlas of Maine topo maps and a pen, and stepped out into the now rain-less afternoon. He opened to the first double page, which was an overview of the whole state with the square subsection of each topo numbered. The key was gridded with lat-long lines, and it was easy to find which page held the coordinates on the paper. He squatted and flipped to page 33 and carefully tore it from its binding and laid it flat on the front of the book. A section on the coast. Half the page, the right side, was blue water and islands. Collie came behind him and leaned into his back to watch over his shoulder. He jotted the coordinates from the scrap into the upper left-hand corner of the page. Then he refolded the scrap and handed it to Storey.

"Right," Storey muttered. And wondered again how, when it mattered, Jess's essential nature kicked in: his mind sped up and his nerves steeled. Storey realized that Jess was thinking that he would take the folded map and Storey the torn paper, so that in case something happened to one, the other would have the precious coordinates.

"Take a picture of it, too," Jess said. "The map. Then turn off your phone. All the way off."

"Okay."

Now Jess studied the longitude lines that vertically gridded the map on his knee. They were divided into minutes. A degree of longitude was roughly sixty miles; a minute was a mile. The coordinates he had copied went out not only to seconds, but past a decimal to hundredths of a second. This map could get them to a town or cove, but with a GPS they could pinpoint a single house, or dock. Jess found at the top of the page the line that corresponded to the minute of longitude and ran his finger down it. It traveled over mostly trackless country, lakes, woods, tertiary roads. And it hit the coast at one spot, north of Portland. A small town. And now he ran his finger across the corresponding latitude line, and it, too, nearly crossed the black dot of the town. Grantham. He remembered hearing the name. He rocked back, closed his eyes.

"What?" Storey said.

"The town is Grantham."

"I can see that." He was now also behind Jess, looking down.

"I remember. I saw it in a photo at Collie's house. A photo of her dad with his own mother."

Collie's hands were gripping Jess's back, her head beside his. He twisted back a little, said, "Col, is that where your grandma lives?" And he felt her nod against his beard. "Ghee lives in Grantham," she said.

///////////////////////////

Well, it was south and east. What they had decided minutes ago would be the smartest direction. And Jess felt for the first time in what seemed like days the glimmer of a small win. He stood and stretched and turned. He caught sight of three of the bodies sprawled in the meadow on the far side of the burn pile and he quickly turned back and the glimmer died.

///////////////////////////

They slept all together in half-wet sleeping bags, crowded under the tarp. They slept in their damp clothes, and despite the intermittent sweeps of rain they all slept hard. At dawn there were fleets of dark flat-bottomed clouds skimming the ridges— moving fast, like raiding longboats—and no frost. In another half-hour the clouds had broken up and now, sailing, came the outliers, the sweeps, plying a dark-blue sea, an endless stream, and then the sun broke over the hills and fired the flotilla and lit the fog lying over the fields. Jess was peeing at the edge of the cinders and charred beams, which was all that was left of the sugarhouse. Timbers and the wreck of the long steel boiling pan, tipped and blackened. Whoever had boiled syrup here would never have imagined this end. But, then, any end always surprises us, doesn't it? he thought. No matter how much we think we are prepared, the end is always a shock.

He tipped up his face. The mobile clouds moved swiftly, and the sun, and the warmth of it, were intermittent. Still, it felt good. He could feel in his stiff bones the rising pressure. By noon, he bet, they would have more clear sky, and, tonight, stars.

Today they would head for the coast. It was over a hundred miles as the crow flies, much longer following the drainages, winding down the lakes and tributaries to the bigger rivers that flowed into the sea. They would backtrack, then head farther west, try to pick up Route 15, and follow it southeast down through East Corinth to Bangor. No. That would be very exposed. It would be a major corridor out of this country and patrolled, or fought over, by both sides. They couldn't walk it safely, not for a minute. So? There were old logging roads all through this region. Many disused, grown over, populated by tall grass and saplings of spruce and poplar. But passable, still. On foot, or on an ATV like the crazy old man's. They might find a track that headed generally east.

The problem was that, as in so much of the northern U.S. and Canada, the glaciers of the last ice age scoured the land north to south and back again as they retreated, and the valleys and lakes and rivers—and roads—mostly ran that way. Going west to east across the corduroy of ridges was tough. And so they could work their way south, as they had tried to do when this was all only a moose-hunting trip. And when the road was interrupted by a blown bridge and a substantial stream, they could wade across, or swim, or fashion a raft. Work south, get close to the coast, and edge over. Suss it out as they went and angle over to Grantham. Were the towns safe? After dropping off Collie, could they find a boat? A real lobster boat this time, and make their way down to Massachusetts, which was surely stable and solidly federal?

Daunting. That's what it was. The more Jess thought about it, the more he thought their odds were slim to zip. What was the point if it meant almost certain—

"You want coffee?"

He turned, almost ashamed of his thoughts. Storey was behind him, holding the girl's hand. He looked sullen and grim. Hungover. Collie's hood was down and her hair was disheveled, tangled, and sticking out in all directions, her own true mane. She blinked at Jess.

"Sure," Jess said. "I'll start a fire."

Storey gestured. "I got up a few times, kept it going. We still have coals, believe it or not. Probably some under all that mess, too." He lifted his chin to the burn. "Anyway, they didn't burn down the outhouse, so we're taking a trip."

"'Kay."

The two walked hand in hand to the slab-sided shed with the half-moon sawn out of the door. Jess headed down across the meadow through the sopping grass, and through the swift cloud shadows that swept over it. Something satisfying in brushing through the wet clumps of wild rose and milkweed, shaking off the sun-dazzled droplets, feeling them whisk against the legs of his rain suit, staying dry. Or only damp. He walked to the edge of the woods and broke off fistfuls of feathery dead twigs from the bottom limbs of a spruce, and gathered an armload of ground-strewn sticks and broken limbs, and came back. He knelt and blew on the dusted embers, which glowed to life, and he added the crumpled tinder and smaller sticks and built up the fire. He found the can of Folgers under the sailcloth of the wagon, and the saucepan, and he made a pot of cowboy coffee.

When they returned, he poured it strong and black into their stainless-steel mugs, and then he found a box of powdered milk and mixed it with purified brook water and gave Collie a full plastic cup. "I was gonna make pancakes," he said to her. "Sound good? With maple syrup?" She blinked and nodded and rubbed her nose with the heel of her hand. She had not said much since the raid. Was it a raid? No. It was a simple massacre. Why did they burn the sugarhouse, then? Not to hide any evidence of a war crime; they didn't even pull the bodies back into it before they fired it. Made no sense. He shook himself and drank the hot coffee, which tasted like crankcase oil.

So the only structures left untouched were: dock, riding ring and jumps, outhouse. There was a poetry in that, Jess thought as they walked past. They got to the end of the driveway and turned right, east, and backtracked up the road, climbing the good tarmac in stripes of running shadow. A warm morning. They were now a practiced team of draft animals, each pulling his wagon, and Collie curled to sleep again and jostled on her nest of blanket.

They rolled back down to the lake before midday and loaded into a rental skiff and started the outboard. They motored around the point of land, which to Jess was picturesque—a black rock outcrop crowned by a single gnarled cedar, could have been the coast of Japan, could have been four hundred years ago—any other day, he would have framed a photo with his cell phone— his cell phone . . .

"Hey," he said over the puttering engine, "just occurred to me that when we get to Grantham we can use the GPS on my phone to find the house or whatever. I've got the Gaia app and I know it gives coordinates down to fractions of a second."

Storey nodded without comment. Since the massacre he seemed to be on autopilot. He certainly wasn't saying much.

"I've got half a charge and the extra battery pack," Jess continued. Storey didn't respond. He turned his face into the breeze, shut his eyes.

They came around the point and angled into the dock where the *Newsboy* was tied. The cove was black and glassy, the only movement the swell from their wake and the scattered rings of fish rising like very slow drops of rain. Lake trout, probably. The *Newsboy* felt the waves and bumped gently against her bumpers, as if she'd been waiting. They tied up and transferred their stuff, including the carts. It took a few minutes. Storey heaved Collie over the rail and tossed in the lines.

"Are we going to find Juniper?" she said.

"Juniper?" Storey said. "Was she in the boat with you?"

"Juniper is a man, silly."

"Oh, right. Well, we might find him." Thinking, *If he was in the boat, the sonofabitch tried his hardest to kill me. We came in peace.*

Jess went to the helm, turned the key that still dangled, pressed the starter. She coughed twice and came to life with a diesel chortle, and he backed her out into the cove.

They hugged the shore. Jess steered in as close as he could; he didn't want to tear open the hull on a sleeper rock in some shallows. They had no sonar or chart. The tanks were over three-quarters full by the gauge, he could probably motor for days if he kept her slow. They slipped along at something like five knots, a slow jog. They weren't in any hurry. In a few hours they'd hit the southern end of the lake. The gazetteer showed the lakeside road they'd been on diving due south toward Four Corners. There was another long lake a couple of miles to the east, linked to the one they were on by a thread of blue. It ran farther south. Were the two connected? Was it navigable? Boating south on the lakes could spare them miles of walking. Then another lake to the south looked to be about ten miles long, maybe twelve. Little by little. There was no road skirting either shore, at least not on the map. Was that good or bad?

Jess had to put a hand on the frame of the starboard window; he felt vertiginous, and it was not just the steady rocking of the boat. The lake tipped and wheeled. He was hovering. Between water and sky, north and south, morning and evening. His friend seemed to be drifting, too, and as helpless as he felt.

Chapter Fifteen

Jess and Storey graduated from high school on a warm, overcast day in early June. They had to listen to an alum who had made a career out of being an eco-pirate. The speaker went on about smashing whaling ships on the high seas and our responsibility to other species. Preaching to the choir, really. But they leaned forward when she said that they had big speakers on their all-black attack ship, and that they blasted Wagner's "Ride of the Valkyries" at full volume as they bore down on the harpoon vessels, just like the choppers in *Apocalypse Now,* and it scared the crap out of the illegal whalers. One big tender was so terrified it sailed straight back to Japan. He and Storey sat up, a little nervously—they couldn't help themselves—when she said that if every other species on the planet had a vote we would all be kicked off the lifeboat. A ripple of laughter went through the seniors sitting stiffly outside in their folding chairs. She said that God would blow her whistle and say, "Everybody out of the pool!" They knew it was true. "I can tell by your response," she said approvingly, "that you are all biocentrists. Exactly what we need in the world. Not just to protect the ones without a voice, but to save ourselves. Congratulations." Pretty cool.

Then there was a big late lunch out on the newly mown field at the top of the hill, and then most of the class bade goodbye to their gathered relatives and said, "See you tomorrow morning!" and took off to the traditional keg party on the High Forty. The understanding was: Don't get alcohol poisoning and don't drive drunk and the school and the local parents will turn a blind eye.

The day student Jeremy Fine had not had a single sip when he rolled his Jeep on the way to the party. He was just in high spirits. His girlfriend, Alyssa, by all accounts adored him, they were going to colleges in northern Vermont, an hour apart, he had bought the twenty-year-old Wrangler he was driving with his own money, money he had earned working in a Brattleboro printmaking studio on the weekends, and he had a summer ahead of him with Alyssa, working on a trail crew in the White Mountains. He was a sweet, self-deprecating kid who could never keep his unruly curly hair in line, and seemed always baffled by his good fortune, both of which made everyone around him want to help him more. The two were climbing the rough road to the field and the party with a box full of chips and jalapeños and trying to tune in the Bellows Falls pop station when his front tire slipped to the wrong side of a wet rock and missed the edge and they tumbled down a steep eight-foot bank into the brook.

Jess was the one who found them. He was urging his Subaru, Sue, up the track with a keg in the front seat and eight students everywhere else, talking to her as to an old horse as the springs groaned and the engine lugged: "Old one, you sweet, you can do this, you can, you can!" When he encountered the same rock and steered carefully around it, he glanced down into the dreaded streambed and saw the white Jeep on its back, muddy wheels to the sky. It took all nine of them, in shin-deep water, to rock the car enough to pull out their classmates, who were already unresponsive. The coroner later reported that Jeremy had died probably instantly of head trauma, she of a broken neck.

The entire class followed the ambulance to the hospital in Brattleboro, a convoy thirty cars long mustered by local students and their parents. After the two were pronounced dead, Storey pulled Jess's arm and they walked out of the ER and down the hill to the river, and, silently, everyone followed. Storey had not spoken, and Jess had no idea where they were going. But Storey turned in at the Congregational church. The sign out front said, "Be Curious, Not Judgmental." They went up the steps. The door was open. They walked in. Not a soul was there, but candles burned in the dim chapel, and Storey slipped into a pew and Jess slid beside him. The whole class filed in and filled the benches silently, and not a word was spoken, but Jess felt the power of his classmates at his back. They sat for who knew how long. He could hear sobbing and an occasional cough, and the crick of a hassock as someone kneeled, and the groan of a breeze against the high, colored windows. That was it. They sat until night fell.

Jess thought later that it was the most powerful service for the dead he had ever been to. Not a single word. And for years afterward, for the rest of his life, he thought of Jeremy and Alyssa on some continuing parallel journey in which all their potential was not thwarted but they were twined and excited, as they were on that day, and would explore the possibilities of the world together, delighted and bemused by their own luck. He kept them there, just beyond arm's reach, as sort of spirit guides who could show him how lives could work—but, it seemed, never did.

Why didn't they? He thought this as he fought down the dizziness and nausea and steered the *Newsboy* off a stretch of marshgrass shallows. Why was everything, always, so fraught? The hammer had dropped so often in his life that when there was peace, when there was enough love, when he was cradled by it—the love of a friend, a wife, a dog—he knew that sometime around the height of his joy or contentment—right at the apex, when it seemed life might right itself like a ship in a cross sea, and turn, and sail smoothly—just then lightning would strike. A rogue wave would rise up and blot out the horizon.

Was it him? Or the nature of the beast? Born squalling, die retching, and in between tossed every which way like a chunk of broken Styrofoam. Wind and tide.

Why people seek God, of course. Why a church had been built for them to walk into on that June afternoon. Why candles burn. Why a cold stone floor echoes the footfalls and the sobs of the stricken. If Jeremy had been bewildered by the blessings in his life, by his uncooperative hair, by the love of a strong, joyful girl, then so are we all. And equally bewildered when it all falls apart.

It was falling apart now, big-time.

"You all right?" It was Storey behind him, hand on his arm.

"No. You?"

"Not really."

Jess edged the throttle forward with the heel of his right hand, to raise the volume of the motor so she wouldn't hear them, and to change the tempo. Maybe that would help. Maybe he was just feeling seasick. He raised his voice a little and said, "I can't see how we can make it to the coast without encountering either side. And we have no clue who is actually waiting there or if they'll be glad to see us."

"No."

"No meaning 'no,' or 'yes'?"

"I mean, yes, we don't know shit."

"Exactly."

"Well, we've gotta drop her," Storey said. "At Grandma's, at a safe house, wherever the location is. Maybe then we steal a boat and run." He put a hand beside the binnacle to steady himself. "South. None of it's very far. I helped my cousin Ted move his sloop once from Brunswick to Gloucester. We motored at, like, ten knots, and it took us one long day."

Jess didn't answer. He was thinking about the girl in her rowboat and the chopper. And *Clawdette* burning all over the water. "What about staying?" he said finally.

"Staying?"

"Wintering over. Somewhere up here. Waiting for it to cool down?"

"Cool down?"

"C'mon. We could raid whatever more we can get out of the boats, the houses in Beryl, maybe other villages, get a moose, hunker down. Then take her back. It's not gonna do her or her family any good if we all get shot up trying to get there."

"No."

"No?"

"No place is safe. The sugarhouse. Any town. One day they'll show up. Either side. And we'll be cooked. We need to drop her. Then get to a safe zone, wherever that is. Massachusetts, maybe. Then I can work north, home."

Home. That was Storey's true north, Jess thought. That's where Storey took his bearings. Where did *he*? Was home home anymore? No. Not, really. It was nothing more than a shell with a roof now.

Storey had said "I": "Then *I* can work north . . ." To Vermont. What about him, Jess? He, it seemed, was always the one left to fend for himself. "Okay," he said. "We'll tr— We'll go to the coast."

The sun was near its zenith, midday, and broke apart the clouds that ran against it. Still cool enough for a jacket, and the afternoons would bend colder and colder until, one day, a light rain would flurry into the first snow. Now they saw the headlands at the end of the lake. The forested shore dark with spruce curved eastward and dipped into coves backed by marsh grass. No town here ever, too rocky on the spurs and too marshy in the bottoms for the first settlers, Jess thought. In a shallow bay he saw a broken-down dock, silvered by weather and leaning over its own reflection, puzzling itself out at the end of days. The map had not shown a road, but if there was a dock, there would be a road. Some semblance.

Jess brought the *Newsboy* in slowly, inching her in the final feet, careful not to bump the pilings too hard lest the rickety dock fall over. He cut the engine and Storey jumped up onto the splintered decking and Collie pursed her lips and took one skeptical look at the landing and declared, "This is Nowheresville. And I'm hungry."

In the sudden cessation left by the motor they heard their wake wash against the posts and the whine of mosquitoes. They both stared at the girl. " 'Nowheresville'?" Jess said. He felt the laugh quaking his abdomen. "*Nowheresville?* Where'd you learn that?"

Collie shrugged. "Hungry," she repeated. The men exchanged glances. Neither had seen the other smile in a while, much less laugh. They were laughing now.

"Okay," Storey said, wiping a tear from his eye. "Let's make some Boston beans. 'Kay? Which are very best cold. Sound good?" She was still clearly suspicious but she nodded her lion head. "After lunch," Storey said, "we can check out this dump."

"Dump," she repeated, finally satisfied.

Well, Collie was right, pretty much. Back of the dock was an old road, grown in, that stuck to the highest ground it could find—

not much—and wound through marsh thick with mosquitoes. The first frost should have cut down the bugs, but the days had been warm, and the marsh held the heat. The water in the reeds was humped with beaver lodges and scattered with the gesturing skeletons of dead trees. The drowned tamarack were bleached, the biggest limbs broken. They weren't checking out Nowheresville, they were trying to get through it as fast as they could. Collie rode the wagon, and though they had tightened her hood and smeared her face with the last of their bug dope, the mosquitoes swarmed her head and bit and got into her mouth and eyes. At first she tried to bat them away, but her hands got bitten so badly that within half an hour they were swollen, too, and so she shoved them down into the side pockets of her lion suit and curled up and buried her face in the blanket and cried. Jess and Storey grimaced and walked, both leaning into the straps of their packs and rifles and tugging their loads. Where the ground was drier they pushed through shadowed spruce woods, and tall pines, and heard the insistent tuneless complaint of a nuthatch, one protesting note repeated and repeated, and Jess thought it a fitting accompaniment. *Wanh wanh wanh* . . . The bird was warm-blooded and probably as tortured by mosquitoes as they were. Why did it stay? Because this was its niche? Because natural selection had allotted it no other. One version of fate.

By mid-afternoon they had come to a fork in the track and taken the one bearing left, eastward. They were in hardwoods now, maple and beech, thank God. They got Collie out of her pajamas, and when they dropped to a stone-bedded brook they cooled her swollen face in the rushing current.

The men did, too. They took off their hot boots and sat on a smooth, rounded boulder and stuck their feet into the icy flow. Swift water and the pressure against their raw ankles and shins

and toes, and the cold—they closed their eyes and released.
From physical pain and uncertainty. For a moment there was
only the sound of water rushing against rocks and the blood
cooling in their feet and Collie climbing up into their laps as
they sat together, curling across both of them, heavy for someone so small, and saying, "Let's catch frogs," before she dropped
abruptly into sleep.

Chapter Sixteen

I have meant well, haven't I?

You took care of yourself.

Don't we all do that first?

No.

No.

Jess lay in a patch of sun on a rock ledge above the town. He had been glassing the lie of the buildings, the wooded hills cloaked in fall color, the slate strip of county road; also the harbor, the boats moored and docked. All intact. Actual living townspeople walked the streets. One dock was occupied by a long metal shed, "Matinicus Lobster Co." Matinicus was an island, wasn't it? One of the farthest out in Penobscot Bay, the famous one where lobstermen feuded and shot each other over territory for their traps. Now he lay back, face to the sun, which reddened his closed eyelids; he thought he could see there the fine branching of arteries like the map of some river system. He floated on his own fatigue, which somehow buoyed and rocked him.

He thought of the airline safety injunction to strap the oxygen mask on oneself first before helping others. More than once he had heard people use it, flippantly, to justify selfish behavior. *Strap the mask on first.* Go hunting with Storey two months a year, a mental-health prescription that he told Jan he needed so that he could stay centered and work the other ten. "Are we ever gonna go on vacation?" Jan had asked. "We used to talk about Spain."

He did not have to have the affair in Vermont. He did not have to make love to Storey's mother that first time; he might have closed his eyes, shut out the sight of her, called his parents to come get him. He did not have to shoot the little buck in the meadow when he was fifteen. He might have lowered the gun, whispered, "Graze on. Live on. We will both live out our lives."

Is that what people did on their deathbeds? Inventory their starkest failures? Was this granite overlook his last perch?

He wished he *was* in Spain. More than anything. With Jan. Sipping sangria at an outdoor table, on a cobbled street, above another harbor, maybe Barcelona. Anywhere but here and now.

Now he was going to walk down through the woods and straight into town. A living town. That was a shock; it made him queasy. How many weeks had they been out? Not many. He couldn't tally them. He would find the drop-off spot, surveil it, watch for anyone who looked like Collie's family. Maybe he would make discreet inquiries: *Is there an older Mrs. Beckett? Is it safe here? We are out-of-state visitors—hunters—caught in the cross fire. We have no dog in this fight. Can we get home to Vermont and Colorado? Is there a refugee center?*

Would he tell them where they'd been? What county? Where they seemed to take no prisoners? He didn't know. He didn't know anything. Would they believe him? Or would they look at the beard, the dirty clothes, the streaked campfire char on his thighs, and shoot him on sight? As some kind of spy or outlander.

He had studied the town for close to an hour. He had tugged the torn page of the Maine gazetteer from the inside pocket of his fleece jacket and unfolded it carefully and confirmed the numbers he had jotted in the upper-left corner. Confirmed again that the indicated lat-long lines touched the coast at one spot, the town of Grantham. And now he didn't need to turn on the iPhone to check his current position: he lifted the binocs and again scanned the street and found the flagpole flying the Stars and Stripes and read on the façade of the low brick building "U.S. Post Office, Grantham, ME 04031."

So this was the right town, good. He felt his heart thud in his chest, almost the way he felt back home when a bull elk stepped out of the aspen into a meadow and all he had to do was unsling the rifle and lift it slowly and brace the barrel against the fir tree against which he leaned. Good. But this wouldn't be that simple.

He moved the glasses now methodically from the north end of town, his left, down to the south end, his right, and from the moored boats in the harbor into the docks and across the clustered downtown. He followed the occasional pickup and the sand-colored convoys of armored Humvees and troop carriers that passed up and down the main street, which was the state highway. Groups of ten vehicles at most. Numbers, it seemed, for an occupation, not an invasion. Were the towns along the coast sympathetic to the federal government? Pro-union? The American flag still flying at the post office seemed to indicate that this one was. Towns like this were packed with folks From Away, second-homers, retirees, quality-of-lifers. They tended to vote much more liberal. Would the feds even need to occupy such a town? Would partisans and secessionist sympathizers sabotage and harry it? Would he be mistaken for one of them?

No telling. He would have to be careful. He would walk down. He would suss out the town and return to Storey and Collie and guide them in. If it wasn't safe, if he didn't return, they would know.

He had insisted. Somehow he owed Storey that much. The girl, too; he wasn't sure why.

Storey had said it out loud: "You don't owe me anything."

"Well."

"You don't. You—we were seventeen."

"I—"

Storey had cut him off. His face behind his two weeks of beard was haggard and his eyes were stony. "All you had to do was tell me. We were brothers. Why didn't you tell me?"

Jess could not hold his gaze. He looked away. "Like you said, we were seventeen."

"Yeah." The word not agreement, but judgment. Flat and hard. Jess flinched. *We were seventeen. And people are hardwired, cradle to grave pretty much the same. If I had some problem looking truth square in the eye . . .*

"Yes," Jess repeated. "I owed you that."

Collie's face was welted from bites she'd gotten four days before. Angry red swellings. Smudged with dirt and tracked faintly with tear salt. She had stared up at the two men, looking from one to the other, not understanding but feeling the import. Then Jess had touched her head, just that. And picked up his pack and the rifle and walked off the four-wheeler track and into the deep midday shadows of the trees.

Now he stood. He hefted the pack beside him and leaned it against the trunk of a black birch. He put his nose against the silk-smooth and peeling bark and inhaled the wintergreen scent. It smelled like sharp mint and cool water. He closed his eyes. *I have known this.* He opened his hand and placed his palm gently against the trunk, as he would the flank of a horse. Felt the warmth in it, almost as if it were an animal. *It's enough, isn't it? Almost enough.*

He opened his eyes and rubbed them with the same hand. The fragrance of the birch was on his fingers. He unslung the rifle and leaned it there, too, against the pack. And then he turned away from the tree and made out the deer trail that dropped off the bench and through the ferns, and he walked.

Chapter Seventeen

It was odd. Now that he was unburdened of the pack and rifle he had carried for the last three weeks, it was not only his body that seemed to float. His mind did, too. He followed the game trail as it contoured across the ridge through thick woods, and his feet felt nimble as they found their footing in the ferns, and over roots, and down the slick slabrock of a recent rain. He almost ran. He felt agile for the first time in weeks. It was not that he had left his grief and terror leaning against that tree, but that they did not bind him so heavily, and it was almost as if he could look down on himself moving through the woods as a hawk would, or an owl. And he slowed. He would not just stumble out onto the main street and get himself shot. That would be dumb.

He had seen from above that these woods descended right to the western edge of the village. Good. It was an older town, the buildings mostly brick, and he had scoped from his perch a café, a ship chandler, several restaurants, an antique store, a bookstore, an army-surplus outdoor store. Typical Maine coast. A few people were on the streets, going about, it seemed, their daily business; there were few vehicles on the road but the short convoys of sand-colored troop carriers and military trucks. He could tell by the lat-long lines on the map that his destination was somewhere on the southern side of the village.

The main drag ran one block inland from the water street which serviced the many docks and piers. And to his right, at the south end of town, the two streets ran together and continued along the edge of the harbor and past a large boat shed and an unfenced yard crammed with hauled-out fishing boats and small yachts on cradles. Also skiffs on trailers. A drydock. On the far side of the shed, there would be a set of tracks running into the water and a lift for smaller vessels.

In the yard—unlike the rest of the town, which seemed to be bustling—he had seen no soul, either because the place was empty, or because everyone was inside. His intuition told him that this would be a good place to land, both because it was somewhere near where he wanted to end up, and because he could hide easily among the parked boats. Also, the woods nearly touched the road there; all he had to do was cross the state highway. And if men were working, he might draw less attention if he walked from the large repair shed into the center of town, carrying, say, a lunchbox or thermos or travel coffee mug. Might. He knew he was fantasizing now, his reasoning too buoyant. In truth, he had no idea what he was walking into, or how, exactly, he would walk out of it, or if he would survive the next hour.

Still, he let himself run. He let himself free-fall down the steeper sections of trail, trusted feet to find their place. Where the game trails branched he hewed to the right, south, so as to bring himself closer to the yard, and he figured he was very close. And he almost did stumble out into the clearing, but pulled himself short and threw an arm around a rough-barked maple as if clutching a friend.

The clearing was a narrow overgrown field and the bright afternoon blazed over it and he blinked and tucked back into the trees. About three acres, an old hayfield maybe, or corn patch, now disused and grown over with mugwort and grass and a scattering of spruce saplings. Beyond it was the two-lane highway, and beyond that the rows of landlocked boats and the metal shed. Left of them, north, was a line of houses and docks along the water. Good. Any one of these might be the place. Jess might have exulted, except that a breeze huffed from the south and instead of sun-toasted conifers he inhaled the stench of death.

He gagged. He looked to his right and saw the blue tarp, and beneath it the paper sacks stacked like bricks. White dust spilled from tears in the bags and he knew it was lime. How had he missed it? The tarped pile presided over a trench that ran along the edge of the trees. Beside the stack, two spades had been stuck into the ground, nearly upright, like uncrossed markers.

The bodies, from what he could see, were fresh. From where he stood he could only glimpse a few yards of the ditch, and the cadavers were dusted over with lime and otherwise uncovered. They gestured in the abrupt and grotesque ways he had seen in war photographs, rigid and twisted, almost defiant. He winced his eyes shut. And then he forced himself to look again. There were men, young and old, and a woman, two women, three. And no children, thank God. He spun away from the scene and covered his mouth and nose with his forearm and made himself breathe.

Okay, okay, get your shit together. Breathe. Vomit if you have to. Steady. You got yourself down here; now do what you came to do. Right? Right. C'mon, straighten up.

I have no rifle. Nothing. I am defenseless.

You don't need a gun. You have your clip knife, don't you?

Yeah, what am I gonna do, slit some sentry's throat like in the movies?

You don't need a weapon. You came to reconnoiter; now reconnoiter as best you can.

Forget it.

No.

Jess's internal argument was interrupted by the sounds of engines. Around the bend, from the direction of town, came two pickups, not fast. They turned in at the shed. He lifted his binoculars and made out the sign at the entrance, "Grantham Boatworks, J. R. Brown." The trucks passed behind a steel longliner on a cradle and he lost them.

It was time to turn on his phone. He pried it out of the front pocket of his torn pants and held the On button and watched, gratified, as it came to life. The iconic apple, the one with the bite of knowledge taken out of it, except that now, to him, it looked like the mark of one who had bitten off more than he could chew. Ha! When the home screen lit he wondered again if he should change it, a photo of him and Jan and Bell in a meadow on Cottonwood Pass with the aspen in full autumn blaze behind them. As they would probably be blazing right now. Who had taken it? He couldn't remember—some passing mountain biker, maybe. Who must have snapped it as a light gust blew through, because he noticed again three yellow leaves above them, catching the light as they fell through bright-blue air. Why did he keep it? Because it was real. Nothing would obliterate it.

He tapped his password and turned on the Gaia app, which immediately displayed his location in two lines, latitude and longitude, out to hundredths of a second. He took two steps to his right, over a broken limb, and the last digits flipped. Good. No one on the road. He unfolded the torn map and checked the numbers at the top and moved fast into the field, watching his step and his palmed phone, too—the spinning numbers to the right of the decimal—and he realized before he got to the pavement of the highway that the location he wanted was inside the boatworks, inside, it looked like, the big metal shed.

****

"Where is he going?"

"To look for someone."

"Are you two mad?"

"Mad?"

"Are you mad at him?"

"No."

"Is he coming back? I want him to come back."

Storey's hesitation, which she catches. For a second her lips quiver. Too much loss, he thinks. And he reaches down for her quickly and lifts her to him. "He's coming back," he urges. "He's coming back soon."

She buries her face in his neck, and he feels the wetness.

"I promise," he says.

He can feel her wipe her cheeks back and forth against his neck, pull her face away.

"Is he your little brother?"

"No. Yes. Sort of."

"He's nice."

"Yes."

"He laughs more than you."

Storey leans his head away, looks at her. Her expression is defiant.

"It's true," he says.

She's relieved that he agrees. "Is he going to look for my dad?"

He hesitates again, covers it with a cough.

"Is he?"

He nods.

"Let's go."

"We can't."

"*He* went."

"He has to see if it's safe."

"He always goes first."

Storey doesn't say anything, but thinks, *That's true, too.*

"Your dad is named Silas, right?"

"Papa," she says.

"What do his friends call him?"

"Kernel." Kernel. She says it like "kernel of corn."

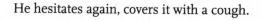

He didn't need it anymore. Jess stuffed the phone back into his pocket and ran. Across the empty road, which was humped with frost heaves and webbed with black tar where they'd filled the cracks. He leapt the ditch and brushed through the purple-stemmed asters and sweet clover and hit a section of toppled hurricane fence hidden by weeds. He stumbled, nearly fell, ran on. Closest to the shed was a row of three small inshore lobster boats, maybe thirty-footers. Paint faded, winchless, probably older iterations of the boatworks' own design. He ran for a gap between two of them and crouched. He was hidden from the road. Good. The grass in the yard was unmowed and thick, two feet high. He lay in it. He could hear voices. This part of the shed was not insulated. Fifteen feet farther down the wall was a door with a window, painted over. He belly-crawled to it and reached for the lever handle, but of course it didn't budge. Fuck it. He got to his feet again and stayed low. He would not be invisible from the highway, but hard to see behind the boats. He ran again. Along the metal wall of the shed, which was painted a faded yellow and streaked with rust. He ran toward the water, and when he got to the end of the wall he lay flat again and peered around the corner.

The bay side of the shed was all open, as he'd suspected. Rails ran down into the harbor between concrete barriers that extended into the water like two levees. Farther out, backlit sloops tugged at their moorings, and he counted five inshore lobster boats beyond them, angling in after a morning running traps; their snowy bow wakes caught the light. He twisted his head and looked inside. In a cradle, tucked back into the middle of the building, was a blue-water sailer, mastless, and stripped to the naked wood of its hull, which curved and gleamed in the light from the tall bays. Maybe sixty feet, with a long windowed deckhouse forward of the cockpit. Jess swallowed hard at the stark beauty of the vessel, which was clearly being given a new life. A voice raised. "Not a chance." It echoed in the drum of the vast space. He shifted his attention to the middle of the close wall, where four men in baseball caps stood in a small circle. They were close to the outside door he had tried. Jesus, he could have stumbled right into them. Three of the men were large; two were bearded and wore Carhartt coats; one had on frayed coveralls. The smallest man was broad-shouldered and wore a faded maroon hooded sweatshirt. He was facing away toward the back of the shed and it was he who was speaking. "Not a chance," he repeated. His voice held a frayed resonance, which carried in the cavernous shed. "We're moving now," he said.

Jess let his eyes adjust. The men were no more than fifty feet away. The biggest, in the coveralls, was facing the open bay doors. He seemed to be looking straight at Jess, but Jess had only half his face around the corner, and he knew that the bright harbor would backlight everything. The man said, "Your call, Colonel. We'll do it."

Jess felt his chest constrict. Partisans for sure. Secessionists who were not fucking around, who blew up dams. So what was he supposed to do now? The coordinates were definitely here. She was supposed to come here. Was he, Jess, supposed to turn her over to these militiamen? No. Maybe they could— He didn't finish the thought. Because the men bumped fists and broke and walked toward him and he saw that the one in the hooded sweatshirt wore thick black glasses that enlarged his eyes, and though he was not grinning now Jess saw him in an instant, in flickering overlay, holding a two-pound lake trout above his tiny, grinning daughter.

\\\\\\\\\\\\\\\\\\\\\\\\\

He ducked around the corner, lay flat in the grass, and heard the men walk out of the shed ten feet from where his head had been. Scuff of boots on the concrete apron, one saying, "He's safe enough; why the fuck would they come down here to look?"

One hacks a smoker's cough. "Go everywhere, don't they?" "Brown's been vetted at least three times. They think we're knitting socks. For the Marines." "Yuh, funny." "You know what to do." That was the one in the coveralls. Car doors slamming, one, two, three. He heard one truck start then the other, heard the tires crunch gravel, and they were gone. He heard a cough, pitched like Beckett's voice, and he knew that the colonel had stayed behind.

He could walk right in. Right now. Say, "Your daughter had the coordinates sewn into her lion suit. She is safe, I promise. We can bring her down." But he doesn't. Why not? Because the man's voice was tuned like a preacher's. Not deep, but it would tunnel through a crowd, carry the way the sound of water carries through trees. His absolute authority over the much bigger men. He was dangerous, very. Jess intuited that his ruthlessness would be as natural as the irresistible resonance of his voice. And that it would be better if they showed up with Collie in tow, unharmed and an ally.

Chapter Eighteen

Jess lay in the tall grass beside the boatworks. For a minute he just breathed. He inhaled the sun on the painted steel of the wall, and harbor water—the seaweed and barnacles of probably low tide—and spar varnish or epoxy from inside the shed. These guys were planning something big and violent and imminent. Military convoys passed the place all the time. Bad timing to introduce a little girl. Better to find Grandma, wasn't it? Yes. That should be easy, she should be right up the street.

How did he look? He dug out his phone and flipped the camera to selfie and brought it over his face. He started. Was that *him?* Two weeks of dark beard, flecked with gray and bits of probably oatmeal. His eyes nested in pockets of shadow, red-rimmed, and stared back at him with surprise and a shy temerity: *What the fuck did you think we would look like, after what we have seen?* They were recessed and haunted, and years older. Firewood char streaked the side of his nose. Well. He rubbed at the smirch and combed the debris out of his beard and pressed off the phone. He didn't look too much different from the men in the shed. It would have to do. He stood. No one on the road. He took off his jacket and shook it hard and patted off grass seeds and dirt. He swiped at his pant legs and dusted off his butt. At the road end of the building was a stack of wire lobster traps. Good. He picked up two, one in each hand, and instead of shoving them back through the hurricane fence he walked across the yard and straight out the drive under the big boatworks sign, and when he hit the paved road he took a deep breath and straightened tall and turned right toward the first line of buildings and the main street.

///////////////////////

He hadn't walked fifty yards when he heard the first engines. He heard them coming behind him loud and he felt the reflex to swerve into the weeds but made himself stick to the white line of the shoulder. He lived here, he was a proud lobsterman, why should he move over?

The first Humvee passed within two feet and did not slow. He raised a chin in greeting, but the helmeted soldier riding shotgun barely glanced. Two more Humvees and an armored truck followed, grinding gears in a downshift that pitched the engine higher. They left him in a wind-wake laden with diesel exhaust.

His heart hammered. He gained the narrow sidewalk by the first buildings on the harbor side—Cape cottage on its own dock and a sign over the door: "Debbie Beveridge Gallery, Original Watercolors"; then "Casco Bay Ship Chandler," a brick storefront with a model of a clipper ship in the window. That's when the second convoy passed. Two open jeeps, two tarped troop trucks. It, too, was heading into town, or through it, and the first jeep slowed, and an officer in a patrol cap with a captain's single silver bar twisted back and surveyed him. Jess could see the automatic pistol on the man's hip, and he lifted a lobster trap in salute, and the lieutenant waved the driver on.

Jess let out a long breath. *Summary and extrajudicial,* he thought. Someone, maybe these guys, were executing people. He didn't know who the people in the trench were, or who put them there, but he didn't want to join them. He focused on the sidewalk a few feet ahead. He had places to go, he was deep in thought. He passed a few people—an older couple in cheap tracksuits, a boy carrying a soccer ball, two young lobstermen in white rubber high boots, folded down. No tourists. The fishermen smelled like diesel and bait and must have just come off the morning trap run, and Jess made sure not to meet their eyes, but he noticed a hitch in their banter as they met and passed him. He also noticed that their tone was not light, but grim, and he heard no laughter. He kept his pace, neither slower nor faster, and he marveled at the discipline it took. He only scanned the store signs hanging from their quaint hooks with fast glances. Did he stand out? Would a lobsterman carry old traps down the street? Maybe—probably not. But these were not normal times, right? He was starting to scare himself and trying to decide if he should ditch the traps when he hustled across a ramped drive leading down to the Matinicus Lobster Company dock. *Slow down, slow down, don't panic now* . . . And he attained the next row of shops and tried not to hurry along them when he looked up and saw the sign "Grantham Gifts," three stores up. His heart hammered. It was on the corner, and the intersecting street ran up the hill on its left. It was three blocks long. Could it be this easy?

At the top of the street he could see a white clapboard church with a steeple and then the woods of the ridge. Collie and Storey were just up there at the top of it. They could descend to this wall of trees and come right down this street, do it in the dark. A nearly novel sensation warmed him: elation. Grandma would take Collie. She would be safe at last. He made himself not accelerate. A boxy and battered Dodge pickup rumbled down the main street toward him, and he set one trap on the sidewalk and found himself waving, and the driver, whose face was rimed with white stubble, waved back. And went on.

Jess picked up the trap. The store was fifty feet away. It was then, in his excitement, that he forgot to not look in the shopwindows, and he realized that all the businesses were dark and closed. One even had a "Will Return" paper clock in the glass door with the hands pointing to noon—or midnight—and a big black question mark scrawled at the bottom. He felt his pulse race again. *It's okay, it's okay.* He would knock at Grandma's door, ring the bell; it was a two-story brick building with curtains in the windows upstairs; she probably lived there. He was thinking about what he would say first when he got to the door and saw that the big window he remembered from the photograph was now boarded up with plywood and on the wood was spray-painted a large red "X."

Flush of panic. He hoisted the lobster traps. There is no war movie in which broken plate glass and a big red "X" in an occupied town means anything good. He spun toward the climbing side street. And noticed two women on the next block. They were on the opposite side of the street, thirty yards away; they wore business slacks and black nylon jackets; their heads were together, and they were staring at him and talking fast. One lifted a cell phone.

He shrugged. Not sure why. Still gripping the lobster pots, he crossed the street toward the climbing hill and the church—and

the woods—and sauntered. He tried. Tried to seem casual. But
once he had entered the side street and lost them from view—
for a moment—he threw the traps into the bed of a parked
pickup and ran. As fast as he could in his boots. When he hit
the corner of the first block he twisted to look back; they were
not in the street yet. He turned right and doglegged. Down a
block and then up the next climbing street to a cul-de-sac and a
wall of beeches and pines.

Chapter Nineteen

Late afternoon. The shed in shadow, the shadow of the ridge halfway into the slate-blue harbor. Cold. Clear sky, and tonight would freeze hard. Smell of wood smoke drifting from the village. On another evening he would have been enchanted.

He had run up the slope so fast he could taste blood in his mouth and he had dry-heaved as he topped out on the wooded ridge. Would they have marked him as so suspicious? Would they bother to send a patrol? Who knew, they might. The women, who were some kind of officials, were clearly alarmed. He could not unsee the mass grave. He told Storey with no explanation that they had to move, right now.

They left their packs but slung the rifles. He guided them back down, angling south, right, away from the town center, but as far from the trench as he could. So, when they got to the narrow field and the road, they had to cut back across the meadow as they ran. Storey carried Collie clutched to his chest and made sure she couldn't see the bodies. They moved fast without the packs.

They did hear engines and dove. Into a tall thicket of mugwort and grass, Storey tumbling with her as best he could, taking the hit on his opposite shoulder, all three watching through weeds, hearts pounding, as five sand-colored military vehicles passed, heading into town. Flatbed trucks and Humvees with mounted machine guns. When they rose cautiously again and crouched, Jess saw that Storey's face was cut and bleeding. No time. No time to ask. They ran.

Brown's big boatshed was right across the road. They crossed the two lanes of undulating pavement, skirted the toppled hurricane fence, ducked behind the row of old lobster boats eight feet from the shed wall. "Hold on," Jess whispered. He bellied forward as he had before, peered around the corner. Twilight in the hangar, no light on. There wouldn't be, would there? He hesitated. Then stood, took two steps through the open bay so that he was standing just inside the dark warehouse, and shouted: *"Beckett! Silas Beckett!"*

It echoed flat off the metal walls and died somewhere up in the girdered trusses of the roof.

"I've got your daughter, Collie! She's safe, well fed. She's wearing her lion suit and she loves her dog, Crystal, and oatmeal with milk and honey!"

Nothing. The words lapped against the steel drum of the building like the ripples of tossed stones.

"I came to bring her back. Just that. I have no dog in this fight. I was here moose-hunting. I am from Colorado. I just want to get Collie back home."

He caught movement up and to his right. Gleam of light in one window of the cradled sailboat. He could see now that all the windows of the yacht's deckhouse had been blacked out, covered and taped as if for staining the wood. But the light swam out of the hatch, flashlight or spot, and then he was blinded. It was on his face. He winced, blinked, raised both hands. Looked down, saw the red dot skittering on his chest.

"You're alone?" Not a shout, even. The voice so clear and commanding it traveled the distance without effort.

Jess made an instant decision, no need to put Storey at risk. "Yes!" he shouted.

"Let me see her."

Jess half turned toward the open bay. He called, "Collie, c'mere."

And now she ran from the corner like a pony out of the gate and Jess knew Storey had uncovered her mouth and released her. "Papa! Papa!" she was yelling, running past Jess, her tail swinging and her mane brushed out from the top of her hood; she ran straight to the middle of an expanse of open concrete and she couldn't see in the sudden shadow and she stopped dead. She raised her paws. "Papa?" she yelled. Jess could hear the panic. And he watched the beam of the Maglite swing to her and saw her cringe away. "Papa? Papa, where are you?"

The light snapped off. Silence. Jess held his breath. He could hear metal crick in the roof and water lap on the ramp below. Finally:

"Col?"

"Papa!" The shout a cry now, more desperate than relief. "Where are you? Papa, where are you?"

"Col! Col!" The man's voice cracked. "Col, I can't come out now." The emotion reined in. The man's timbred words echoed from the drydocked yacht, from back in the dark and above.

"Papa! Come out! Come out!" Her cry rose into the girders. Jess was riveted to the floor. She ran. Straight to the boat, straight across the open floor, into the shadows, and Jess saw her trip over the wheeled tank of a compressor. She hit hard and flew onto concrete and he jumped. He ran to her, fuck the red dot, and he picked her up, and she was sobbing so hard she could not breathe. He picked her up and covered her and squeezed and held her and the gasp of her without breath was louder than his own exhortations, "I got you, Collie. I got you, honey, I got you . . ." Until her arms reached up and found his neck and she squirmed herself higher and gripped him until her face was tight in his beard and she cried and he soothed and soothed her.

When she had finally quieted he said, "Here, let's stand." He slid her down gently to the floor and held her hand. She shook it free and took two steps and put one paw straight into the shad- ows. "Papa? Papa! Where *are* you? Papa, please."

"I can't, honey. I love you, Col. I love you so, so . . . More . . ." Silence. Then his preacher's voice again, utterly command- ing. That was it: it harnessed something greater than he, the speaker. Jess heard a hard resolve.

"Take her."

"What?"

"Take her. Wherever you are going."

"What?"

"If she stays here she will die."

"I . . . what about the grandma, your mother?"

"How did you—?" Voice cold and hard. Then silence. The red dot crawled on his chest again. He felt it, looked down. His heart hammered. Collie was frozen, unable to digest the words. She looked wildly from the boat in the shadows to Jess.

"Her photo was in your house! Grantham Gifts. Looked like you, two of you together."

"Okay." Red dot relented. But Collie was running again. She was running in her suit and screaming, *"Papa! Papa!"* and Jess didn't think but bolted after her and she hit an extension cord and fell again. She howled and slid and he scooped her up into his arms and she did not struggle but screamed into his chest until she had no voice.

///////////////////////////

No more Maglite. Dusk moved on the harbor. Almost dark inside the cavernous shed. The man called, "Listen to me. They will shoot you on sight. There's a Boston Whaler on the dock below. Keys under the coffee cup in the holder. As soon as full dark, take it. There are extra fuel cans forward. South along the shoreline, stay within a quarter-mile of the coast. Four hundred yards, no more. Closer if you can. Run without lights, half throttle. They are short on patrols and the radar will not pick you up. You'll have to cross the mouth of the Fore at Portland Harbor. Gun it, you should be okay. You can make it to Portsmouth in six hours. When you pass the point and first see the lights of the town pier, cut inland and tie up at the docks with the brick shed and the green security lights. Understood?"

"What about the grandmo—"

Hesitation. "Detained. Deceased. Cuz of . . . It's on me."

"And your wi—her—?"

"Same."

Silence.

"I'm sorry," Jess croaked.

"When I jotted the coordinates I thought it'd be different. By tomorrow I'll probably be . . ."

He didn't finish.

"Why don't *you* take the Whaler? We could all . . ." Jess let his voice trail off. He knew why. Beckett's soldiers depended on him in the next actions. And he had ignited such a hell the feds would hound him to the ends of the earth. The man knew there was no way out, not anymore.

She had crumbled in his arms, what it felt like. Like he was trying to hold her together, the whimpers less about grief or terror now and more about limbs, heart, lungs, struggling to stay intact. Jess squeezed her to his chest as she shuddered.

"I'll try," Beckett lied. "Leave your coordinates, where you live, under the cup. Where the keys were. I have a man at the dock."

"Okay," Jess said. He turned away.

"Hey!" The call was abrupt, decisive. Jess turned back.

"I want to say goodbye. To her."

"Okay." Jess was confused.

"So many people depend . . . If I come out, is your man gonna shoot me?"

"My man?"

"What do you take me for?"

He knew. Beckett knew Storey was back somewhere with rifle leveled. He knew his daughter—that unless someone else had been holding her back she would have run out at the first sound of his voice. Again the sense that the colonel was very smart and very dangerous.

"I want to say—I want to hold my daughter. Once. Your word." It was a command.

"My word, of course," Jess stammered. "I brought her all this way." Lame, he knew. It could still be a setup. But he believed what he was saying and he thought Beckett would hear it.

He did. The Maglite flashed in his face again, and then he could see it moving to the side of the dark hulk of boat, and stutter as the man came down a ladder fast. It stayed on his chest and got brighter as the man came on, and then it flicked off and he heard, "Okay," and Jess blinked and Beckett was there, ten feet off, compact, thick glasses, sweatshirt hood down, lit dimly by the arc lights of a dock to the north. He was aiming a handgun level with both hands, aiming at Jess's head, close enough to kill him and miss his daughter. Was she passed out? Face buried in his chest? No. She might have smelled her father. Or heard the soft, "Col? *Col?* It's Papa." She squirmed and stiffened and slid from his grasp. In an instant she was grabbing at her father's leg. Beckett must have been overcome, because the gun was gone, shoved somewhere into his work pants, and he was kneeling and his arms were around her. Her paws clutched at his head, knocked his cap to the concrete, and she was bawling and bawling and crying "Papa" over and over.

Beckett could not convince her. He forgot about Jess, about Jess's buddy outside with a rifle, about his own army, his command. He must have. Because he knelt on the cold floor of the shed and held his daughter. And she clutched him, pawed at his hair, his face, tried to crawl into his sheltering chest. Jess could hear him trying to utter words, to quell his own quiet crying, to comfort her, but he could not. He could only sob with relief, with fresh sorrow. This man who had already lost his wife and mother. He gasped, summoned himself, held her face in both hands, enough away that she could look at him while he spoke.

"Col, Col, listen to me. Listen, okay?" She could not listen. He kissed her cheeks again and again, thumbed her tears, and she tried to crawl close again but he held her inches away. "Listen, baby. I will come find you. If I can. Not today, but later. I promise. Know why?"

She would not know. Refused. But he repeated it again and again until she squeaked, "Why?"

"Because I love you more than anything on earth. You know that?"

Jess could not see her face but he saw her head tilt.

"And you're the strongest little lion, right? And I have to go to work now, and you will go with these nice men where it is safe. These are good men, and, honey, you will be safe, and you will grow up—"

He stopped himself. He pushed her gently outward. Her fingers were tangled in his hair. She would not let go. "You go now, honey. You go with him, and I will find you."

Jess stepped forward and swept her up and she went limp. Completely. As if she had lost all fight. Her lion hood was crumpled down and her hair was wet. The man looked up and Jess saw the nod. Jess turned. He carried her against his chest and walked toward the open bay door.

"One day," the man called. Jess turned back. "One day . . ." Silence. He heard the water lapping at the ramp. Jess waited. In the middle of the dark shed. "One day, please try to tell her . . ."

"I will," Jess said. He thought of the man and the girl grinning, each holding up a fish, the one huge, the other tiny. How they beamed. He thought of Collie's mother behind the camera, probably the happiest, proudest woman on earth.

Jess turned. Through the bay door the harbor was all shadow now, and the sea and sky merged in a slate-dark blue with no horizon.

Acknowledgments

This book would not have been written without the keen insights and thoughtfulness of my first readers: Kim Yan, Lisa Jones, Donna Gershten, and Helen Thorpe. Your generosity and love have sustained the work, and given this novel wings. Thank you.

Sascha Steinway lent his expertise, as did Adam Duerk, Win Duerk, Bobby Reedy, Mike Reedy, Jim Le Fevre, Isaac Savitz, Tiara Sharma, Justin Ward, and Geordie Heller. Thanks to doctors Melissa Gillespie and Mitchell Gershten for always being on call.

A special thanks goes to the brilliant Myriam Anderson, whose graciousness and wisdom have meant so much, and to the transcendent translator Céline Leroy.

David Halpern was with me on this novel from the first pages to the last. He has been the most steadfast and insightful friend and mentor. Jenny Jackson shepherded the novel through with brilliance and great care. She has been an inspiration and a champion, always. To you both: I am grateful for your minds, your humor, and your hearts.

It is an honor and a privilege to know you all.

A NOTE ABOUT THE AUTHOR

Peter Heller is the best-selling author of *The Last Ranger*, *The Guide*, *The River*, *Celine*, *The Painter*, and *The Dog Stars*, which has been published in twenty-six languages. Heller is also the author of four nonfiction books, including *Kook: What Surfing Taught Me About Love, Life, and Catching the Perfect Wave*, which was awarded the National Outdoor Book Award. He holds an M.F.A. from the Iowa Writers' Workshop in poetry and fiction and lives in Denver, Colorado.

A NOTE ON THE TYPE

This book was set in Scala, a typeface designed by the Dutch designer Martin Majoor (b. 1960) in 1988 and released by the FontFont foundry in 1990. While designed as a fully modern family of fonts containing both a serif and a sans serif alphabet, Scala retains many refinements normally associated with traditional fonts.

Typeset by Scribe,
Philadelphia, Pennsylvania

Printed and bound by Berryville Graphics,
Berryville, Virginia

Designed by Soonyoung Kwon